Kaleidoscope

Kaleidoscope

Diane Eklund-Āboliņš

Published by AoE Publishing 2021

First published in Australia in
2021
by
AoE Publishing
Sydney, Australia

ISBN: 978-0-9873473-9-8

Cover design Abolina Art

In loving memory of Signe

Introduction

It was my grandmother's funeral, and I remember standing on the neatly raked gravel pathway outside the squat white-stone chapel. The service was over, and I believe that I could have been thinking about my grandmother while watching people offering each other words of comfort and sympathy, when someone came up behind me and placed a hand on my shoulder. It was an unexpected greeting, followed a split second later by a single word: 'Sorry.'

I spun around, unable to connect the voice to anyone I knew. In the nanosecond it took for me to face the person, I found myself wondering whether it was someone who needed to erase the possible indiscretion of touching me on the shoulder, communicate feelings about my loss or simply say sorry. For everything.

My vision, up until that moment filled with a jumble of individuals, most of them dressed in black or different combinations of neutral colours, rippled softly before refocusing itself on the person standing in front of me.

'Sorry,' he repeated (it was obvious now that the voice belonged to a man). 'I do hope I didn't startle you. I'm Joshua. Your cousin,' he added as I looked at him, most probably with an expression of slight bewilderment on my face.

With the speed of a yet-to-be-discovered internet search, I pushed my mind back across a couple of decades and brought up a black-and-white image of myself, aged about ten, sitting on someone's worn, possibly red-brick, doorstep with a small boy not much older than five.

Joshua.

'Of course,' I said, hesitating a moment before giving him a quick kiss on his cheek. 'It's been a long time.' While I was trying to appear as though he was somewhere near the top of my Christmas-card list, in spite of our not having met for years, my mind was attempting to find and process a vast array of events and happenings, a few of them real, most of them imagined.

There was a flicker of a smile as he said, 'To be perfectly honest, I really can't remember when we last met.' He paused for a moment, looking at me. He was trying, no doubt, to equate the real me standing next to him with some rather illusive memory that possibly had the name *Charlene* attached to it. 'It must be at least twenty years,' he said at last.

I caught sight of my Aunt Margaret, my mother's older sister, out of the corner of my eye. She was nodding imperceptibly in my direction while speaking with a man I did not know. Of course, it had to have been Margaret who had pointed me out to Joshua; how else would he have known who I was?

'You're right,' I said as fragments of information slotted in around the two children sitting on the step. 'It would have been 1955, and we had made the trip all the way to Tasmania to visit you.' I laughed, 'Well, not just *you,* but your whole family.' Then I remembered that he was an only child, so the word *whole* seemed awkwardly out of place.

With the image beginning to come to life in a pale wash of colour, I reminded myself that Joshua's grandfather, Thomas, was my grandmother's youngest brother. Our 'cousinship', though still firm, suddenly became somewhat removed, even if only slightly. I was trying to work out why we would have taken such a trip in the first place when, for us, the word *trip* usually described a day at the beach or a picnic in the bush somewhere west of Sydney.

As if he were able to tune into what I was thinking, Joshua said, 'It could have been my father's thirtieth. Not that I remember much about it, but I have heard that it was quite a family gathering. Almost everyone was there.'

I noted his black curls, long, thick and seductively messy, and the robust sturdiness that seemed to be part of the male O'Connor DNA. I was average height, neither tall nor short, and I found myself looking up at him in a comfortable, relaxed way.

'You're probably right,' I said. The colours in the image were becoming brighter, and I was starting to discern a number of scattered shapes and lines. Some of them were slowly breaking out of the shadows to take the form of faces and figures, while layered on top of the diffuse images were imaginary sounds and even smells. I understood that my senses were working overtime to bring this small snippet of memory to life.

Nevertheless, there was an unreal, cryptic aspect to the whole experience, and having ascertained our relationship I decided it was time to move on to something else. Something that was unrelated to red-brick steps and black-and-white photos; something that was definitely part of the 'now'.

'It was kind of you to come today,' I said, immediately regretting the banality of the words. Their predictability, together with a false sense of ownership, or even superiority concerning the day's event, made me secretly cringe. Before he could answer, I continued, 'It's not as though you live around the corner... '

Joshua smiled. 'Well, almost. I moved to the mainland some years back. I'm living in Parramatta at the moment, it's close to where I work. And as for being kind, I'm not sure I agree. I liked your grandmother, but I can hardly say I knew her that well. Perhaps I should have made an effort to catch up with her more since moving to Sydney.' He paused, obviously thinking about things that were now irretrievably locked into the past. 'But, for whatever it's worth, I'm here now.'

I nodded, fully understanding what he was trying to say. 'She was definitely an interesting person. In many ways, though, she was a mystery. On the surface, she appeared completely open and friendly, while underneath it all… '

'… there was a person you would have liked to have known better, but it was a person you could not actually reach. No one could reach.' Joshua finished the sentence for me and then waited for my response.

'Yes, I think you're right. I would have liked to have known more about her, what it was that made her the person she was, what she really thought about things. Now, unfortunately, it is too late.'

His hands were playing with the Order of Service, on the front of which was a photo of my grandmother taken when she was not much older than Joshua was now. Underneath, in Celtic script, there was just one word: *Bridget*.

'My grandfather is much the same,' he said, after a short pause. 'Perhaps it is a generational thing?'

I had not thought of that possibility. I hurriedly did a mental survey of all my great-aunts and great-uncles, both living and dead, wondering if Joshua was right. It was not easy: in the same way that I had never really known my grandmother, I had to accept that neither did I know her siblings.

For the second time in a matter of minutes, I felt a need to change the conversation. Smiling at him, I asked, 'So, what are you doing up here in Sydney?'

'I'm an electrician. I was apprenticed to a company in Hobart, but after a year they offered me the chance to continue my apprenticeship at their sister company in Clyde, just outside Parramatta.' He shrugged and then continued, 'My apprenticeship finished several years ago, but I'm still with the same company.' He paused, the Order of Service now firmly clasped in one hand. 'And what about you? What do you do?'

Even though I could direct the question to others without hesitation, it always threw me a little when people tossed the same question back at me. What *did* I do? Most people would expect me to say that I looked after a husband, chased after small children, cooked, cleaned and did other domestic chores. I suppose that the domestic part was more or less unavoidable, but none of those answers defined me in the least.

I answered, 'I'm an astronomer.' I could see that it was not at all what he had been expecting. For many men, and even some women, sorting people into specific boxes was still extremely important. There were unfortunately many who felt that I had taken an unacceptable step over some kind of invisible gender line.

'That's amazing,' he said, looking at me just a little more closely. 'I've never met a real live astronomer before. Perhaps you can tell me who I'm going to meet and whether or not we will live happily ever after... '

His comment caught me somewhat by surprise, and I was unable to stifle a smile. 'I think you may be mixing up pseudoscience with genuine scientific discipline,' I suggested, the smile still firmly in place. 'I can tell you a lot about the universe but nothing at all about your love life.' I was used to the error, but it never failed to astonish me.

'It's been lovely catching up,' I said, knowing that I really needed to talk to my brother who was beckoning to me from the grassed area beyond the chapel. I pulled a notebook from my bag, ripped out a page and scribbled my address. 'This is my address if you ever feel like getting in touch.'

He took the small piece of lined paper and put it into his coat pocket. 'I may take you up on that,' he said with a quick parting kiss.

As it turned out, Joshua did not get in touch with me — at least not then — nor did I try to find out anything more about him. I suppose, to use a clichéd expression, I could say that life got in the way. There were so many other things, and people, that simply squeezed him out of my memory until March 2015, when completely unexpected, I received a letter.

Dear Charlene,

You may not remember me after all this time. After all, you didn't remember me when we met so many years ago — I believe it was at your grandmother's funeral. Life has a way of making its own plans, and beating its own path, and sometimes it is difficult to keep up.

I hope that your life has been successful and happy and that you have discovered many new stars and galaxies (I still shudder when I think of my faux pas all those years ago). My life has certainly been successful, though I have not discovered anything of note, earthbound or celestial. I actually met that person I had been wrongly hoping you might be able to find for me, and we had three beautiful girls. They're all married now, with families of their own. My wife (Pattie) and I live in Raymond Terrace outside Newcastle. Water views and not too much hustle and bustle. There's no family left in Tasmania: my mother passed on more than thirty years ago, shortly before we moved Dad to a retirement village in Newcastle. He was only there a couple of years before he also died.

When we moved Dad from Hobart we had to go through everything in the family home. We were confronted with years and years of clutter, but among the few things we kept there was a small cardboard box of letters. Although I came very close to getting rid of them, Pattie said they could be important to someone, so we kept them. The box has sat on a shelf in my garage all these years, gathering dust, I suppose you could say.

Recently, I cleaned out the garage and found the box, and I pulled out some of the letters, all of them addressed to my grandfather. They're pretty old, some of them were written at least one hundred years ago, and they're definitely not in any special order. Most of them are from your grandmother, but there are also cards and a few letters from his other siblings. It made me wonder what this present generation will be leaving behind. Mobile phones?

Anyway, as I was picking my way through the letters I suddenly thought of you, and I wondered whether you might like to have them. I can't see any point in keeping them, but they do have a connection with your grandmother, and they may help you understand her a little better.

As I had imagined, getting in touch with you after forty years was not at all easy. I had not expected that you would still have been at the same address as you were in the seventies, and of course you weren't. And I wasn't even sure of your surname. In the end it was Aunt

Margaret's daughter Tracey who came up with most of the missing information, and I managed to find your contact details.

I could have phoned, but I suppose, in spite of all the now not-so-new technology, I am still somewhat old-fashioned.

If you would like the letters, let me know, and as you said all those years ago, we really should keep in touch.

Your cousin

Joshua

I tried to cast my mind back to my grandmother's funeral. From what I could remember it had been a warm, sunny day in November. The jacarandas had been blatantly in flower, painting the streets with a lilac-blue haze, and there had been a smell of early summer in the air. I remembered Joshua's gorgeous black curls and decided that they probably looked very different now. I regretted that we had not kept in touch, but then I thought of all the things that I had packed into the last forty years. Time had never been a commodity I had in surplus.

I pulled out my mobile phone and called the number that Joshua had added to the bottom of his letter. He sounded delighted to hear from me and even more delighted when I said that I would be very grateful for the letters. We chatted for about twenty minutes, about family and the last four decades. When we ended the conversation I thought, yet again, that it was sad that we had not kept in touch. After all, we had the same great-grandparents.

A week later, the letters arrived. As Joshua had said, there were not only letters but also a few cards. There were even a couple of fairly tatty-looking notebooks and some loose papers. Everything was, as Joshua had already warned me, extremely old and fragile. I spent a morning carefully unfolding the pages and laying them flat on the table, before placing them in plastic sleeves, ordering them after date. The few letters without dates I placed together in a pile of their own. When all the letters had been given a new home in one of the many now unemployed folders that had been relegated to a shelf in my spare room, I made myself some strong black coffee and began to read.

The letters both saddened and fascinated me, and I found that I needed to share them with someone who knew at least some of the people they mentioned. My mother was dead. Aunt Margaret was dead. In fact all those people who could have filled some of the gaps were dead. I phoned my cousin Tracey, with whom I shared the same grandmother, and as I read out excerpts from the letters, we mixed our own memories with the unfinished stories in the letters, inventing possible endings and adding a running commentary on who and how and when and even why.

Later, I dreamt about the letters, and my imagination, now without a Tracey to add some glimmer of balance, tended to run riot. I could clearly see lines connecting the hows and the whys, and where there were gaps I drew my own lines. People who had been dead for half a century, and longer, came to life, offering suggestions, explaining why they had done what they had done and why they had not done what they had not done.

After a couple of days, the excitement of the letters waned a little as I forced myself to accept the reality that the letters, though many, focused on relatively small, scattered periods in the lives of these people. Also, because most of the letters had been written by my grandmother, I was only looking at one side of an idea or an experience. My initial response, impacted by the erroneous belief that the letters would give me an unblemished and accurate picture of my grandmother and her siblings, at least some of them, had been naïve. There was so much that I would have liked to have known about the family, but there were too many strands that simply disappeared around corners or became so tangled up with other strands that nothing made sense any longer. Most of the strands were twined together with all the usual questions: why, who, when and how?

Although I would have liked it to be otherwise, I had to admit that a life cannot be confined to a few letters. I thought back over my own life and tried to picture parts of it ending up in letters on a shelf in someone's garage. The resulting picture could never be complete. Life was far too complicated. There were too many levels, and I thought again of all those strands, tangled up with each other and often running in what seemed like opposite directions.

I phoned Joshua and tried to explain to him that there was ever so much more beyond the letters, a whole universe that I would never be able to access and even less understand. At the same time, I acknowledged that the letters had certainly given me a very small glimpse of the person who had been my grandmother.

Joshua said that he appreciated what I was saying, but he then added that such small glimpses can still have an important part to play. Although they can never give a complete picture of anyone's life, he argued that they can give perspectives: a bit like a kaleidoscope where it is only possible to see one pattern at a time, knowing that there are hundreds, if not thousands, of others hidden away.

Over the next few months, we spoke several times and wondered why we had not kept in touch. When he suggested that the universe may have listed our need to connect as low priority, I nodded my head, although he could not see me, and I decided that there are lots of things that the universe considers low priority until, suddenly, they are not.

Bridget's story was not low priority, at least not to me, but the many gaps and unexplained situations made the story itself seem insignificant. The omissions and breaks could not simply be ignored without some kind of clarification: they may have been unclear, but they were an important part of the whole. Like with a child's colouring book, colour needed to be added, while retaining the outline, in order to bring the whole page to life.

I doubted that anyone could know Bridget's story completely: different people knew unrelated parts of the story, pieces that were sometimes patched together to form new, often contrasting, stories. Bridget's letters were simply a very small part of the psychedelic pattern that we call life: a pattern that included not only Bridget but also everyone around her, and everyone around them. It was very obvious to me now that no one can really know anyone else's story. All we can ever have are the bits and pieces that create their own patterns, in the same way as Joshua's kaleidoscope.

Bridget's story, like any story, is not just one story but a collection of many stories spread across the countless levels and layers of life, each created from the perspective of the infinite number of people who in some way interacted with her, however briefly.

Kaleidoscope

Chapter One

Every story has to have a beginning, and every beginning is dependent on earlier beginnings, all of which can be traced back through the millennia to a point when there was no time. It may have been during that fraction of a second when nothing expanded into something, or perhaps at a point a little later when the something had evolved into a planet covered with land and water, or at a point even later when a slimy water creature discovered that it had legs and took its first hesitant steps on dry land, that the first link in the infinitely long chain of events leading to Bridget Mary Kathleen O'Connor making the decisions she made was forged.

Bridget O'Connor, the fourth of seven children, was born on a winter's day in Orange, New South Wales, in the year 1890. That winter day could be said to be Bridget's beginning, the beginning of her story, but stories do not just begin, nor do they just end. They *are* and they continue *being*, even after the person at their centre is no longer present. The story about Bridget could not just burst into life on a winter's day in 1890; it began decades, perhaps centuries earlier. Perhaps it even began with that tetrapod discovering a completely new element and a new way of living.

Chapter Two

Bridget could not understand how she dared do what she had done. It was as though someone else, someone she had never met and did not know, had pushed their way into her body and, after taking command of her mind, made the decision for her. She had been like a conch, sleeping innocently at the bottom of the sea, or more possibly like a sleepwalker, completely oblivious to what she was actually doing and to all the consequences. Though she was trying her best not to think about what had happened and could no longer be changed, her thoughts involuntarily rolled back over the past few hours, and her stomach clenched, filling her with an overwhelming, draining anxiety. She was uncomfortably aware of being both hot and freezing cold at the same time, something which she normally would have thought was impossible. Images, unclear and confused, danced at the front of her mind like the tiny unordered spots of light heralding a migraine.

For a fleeting moment, while she struggled unsuccessfully to ignore the images and what they were trying to tell her, it occurred to her that there was a very small chance she had not done anything at all, and that what she believed had happened was nothing more than a distressing, alien thought thrown up from some dark, negative part of her mind. As she mentally embraced the unlikely idea of her innocence, a rush of relief surged through her body and almost managed to drown her uneasiness. But the relief was short-lived. The idea, fragile and transient, faded, and then disappeared, before she had time to claim it as her own.

While watching the horrifying images parading past her mind, and while considering the part she most probably played in creating them, she could do nothing more than acknowledge the trepidation that was building up within her. She needed confirmation that she was still in a world that was real, not imagined, and that this real world was inhabited by real, ordinary people. She ran a hand over the smooth, polished wood of the unfamiliar hard wooden seat, conscious of its warm brownish redness. Both experiences, the physical and the mental, brought her another very brief moment of bliss quite disassociated from her spiralling unease. Her other hand was supporting the child sitting on her knee, his head cradled by her arm. He made a sound, somewhere between a sigh and a cry, but he did not wake, and Bridget wondered about the dream that could have initiated such a cry. He had been there when it happened, and it was not so strange if he, like her, was now being plagued by nightmares. She hugged him to her, wanting to be able to undo the last twelve hours, wanting to erase all frightening memories from her child's mind.

But, as far as she knew, it was not possible to undo or change things that had already happened. The past was like a painting behind glass: it could not be tampered with, and the fact that the past could never be changed was now a major part of her concern and her fear. Her eyes and ears told her that she was sitting on a train and that everything around her was real: she was not simply imagining things. She was not in some nightmare from which she would soon wake up. It was becoming increasingly evident that what she feared might have happened did actually happen.

She attempted to force her mind to concentrate on other things, and she focused on the sounds of the train: the chattering of the iron wheels along the track, the erratic hissing of the steam and the occasional long, drawn-out sound of the whistle. The repetitious, almost soothing, sounds wrapped around her. Safe in some kind of auditory cocoon, she tried to assure herself that she had done the right thing and that it was the only possible thing she could have done. She tried to convince herself that she had nothing to worry about.

Vestiges of smoke from the engine wafted into the small compartment, having found their way in through the sliver of open window. She considered closing the window completely, but she desperately needed the air even if it was spiced with soot. She did not particularly like the smoke that stuck in her nose and throat, while leaving small grey and black flecks on her face and clothing, but she did not mind the smell. Everything — the smoke, the soot and even the smell — confirmed that she had drawn a line under one life and was now poised on the threshold of another. The life before her had no discernible shape, and there was no indication as to whether it would be positive or negative, although everything so far was pointing to the latter of these two possibilities.

She was twenty-six, average build and height, with attractive green-grey eyes in a pleasant, almost-round face. A mass of thick dark curly hair was partially hidden under a narrow-brimmed straw hat. Her ankle-length grey skirt — she had been far too stressed to have given any thought to her other, better skirt — had already seen several summers, and she did not have to look at her brown boots to know that they had not been new for many years. In spite of the late February heat, her white blouse was buttoned up to her neck, each small round pearl button having once been carefully sewn in place by her own two hands, hands that were now covered by the short cream-coloured gloves she had almost forgotten in her haste to leave. She had stopped at the door, knowing that something, something else, was wrong, and she had then turned back to the room, her child on her hip, the shabby leather bag thrown over a shoulder, and picked up the gloves from the table. The worn woollen jacket, which she had earlier wrapped around the small boy, was now lying on the seat next to her.

In the small compartment where she was sitting, there was a young man directly opposite her and, next to him, an older woman. She had thrown indirect glances at the young man a few times, possibly being drawn to the presence of a certain pensiveness and even an unease that somewhat paralleled her own, and she guessed that he was probably no more than eighteen or nineteen. When she first noticed the boy after boarding the train in Gilgandra, she assumed that he and the woman were travelling together: mother and son? Grandmother and grandson? Aunt and nephew? But she now understood that they were strangers to each other, like she was to both of them. Every so often the boy's gaze moved erratically between things beyond the window and the people with him in the compartment, though it was obvious to Bridget that he was not particularly interested in his surroundings and that his thoughts were centred on something else.

Without warning, and on the spur of some random moment, he looked directly at Bridget and said, 'I'm on my way to Dubbo.' The words sounded hesitant, and they tumbled over each other as they tried to find their right place in the sentence. Then, most possibly remembering that everyone on the train was travelling to Dubbo, or somewhere in between, he added, 'I'll be enlisting. In Dubbo. They gave me a free ticket.' His thin adolescent face, beneath a shock of unruly light-brown hair, was flushed with tempered excitement and obvious apprehension. Having wrapped his intention in words, it was more than likely that he was suddenly forced to face the reality of what was about to happen. Yet, as he confronted that reality as a bystander, looking from the outside in, instead of from the inside out, some of his pressing anxiety and uneasiness seemed to disperse.

Bridget nodded and tried not to think too much about the many distressing futures that could be waiting for the boy. She would have liked to have offered him a few words of encouragement, some kind of support, but the right words were beyond her grasp. As her thoughts revolved around the idea of him enlisting and everything that such an action encompassed, she decided that there was a possibility that he did not need, or even want, her reassurance and that he was completely concentrated on the adventure in front of him. Perhaps he was thinking about the ship and the journey by sea, or perhaps he was captivated by the excitement of going to a place that was not Australia or even New South Wales. Nevertheless, she had a feeling that there was possibly a tiny shred of fear wrapped around all those thoughts and images, a fear that occasionally must conjure up other images, of killing and being killed, a fear that was squashed between the excitement and the anticipation of daring to take such a step.

As she tried to imagine what the boy might be thinking, and as she let her mind scroll through some of the futures that could be waiting for him, she involuntarily remembered what she had done. The recollection caught her unawares, and she mentally took several steps backwards. She knew that she had absolutely no idea what shape her future might take, in the same way that the boy could not know anything about his future.

When Britain declared war on Germany all those months ago, Australia, as part of the Empire, found herself automatically part of the declaration. Although this piece of political and legal reality did not cause an uprising, most people accepting it without thinking, it did manage to provoke a number of questions concerning what was meant by loyalty and patriotism, and the basic concepts of right and wrong. The majority of people were convinced that by helping Britain in the War Australia would be able to show that she was grown up and that she should be taken seriously. A minority questioned the ethics of Australia taking part in a conflict on the other side of the world.

Since the War broke out, Bridget had heard many patriotic speeches, all of them nothing more than a call to war, a war with which she did not agree. Her disagreement had very little to do with politics: she simply hated the idea of young men killing each other. Not everyone agreed with her when she attempted to point out that the young German or Turk or Hungarian must also have people who loved him and people whom he loved. Or perhaps, she thought, it was not so much a question of agreeing or disagreeing: it was more about not wanting to see the enemy as an ordinary human being. It was easier if he could be depicted as an abstract entity, faceless and without emotions.

She refused to change her mind, arguing that a man might wear another uniform and speak another language, but he was basically no different to any of the O'Connors or the drinkers in the pub. She found it difficult to understand how it was possible to hate a person one had never met and did not know. Did this person also believe that he hated the English and the French and the Australians, simply because he had been told that he must hate them and because he was following orders? As far as Bridget was concerned the whole concept of war was insane.

Nearly always the argument ended up pitting right against wrong. What was right and what was wrong? What was right about giving those wearing one particular uniform a rifle and ordering them to kill others wearing a different uniform? Was it right to kill people simply because someone with more status and power claimed that it was the right thing to do?

Killing was a difficult word, she thought as she recalled her overall dislike of the War. She had already seen that men did not have to be killed outright to die: they could be destroyed gradually, physically or mentally, piece by piece. The dying could go on for a long while; it could be a slow stripping away, like peeling an onion. In the end, though, the result was always the same: death, however it came, or however long it took, was still death.

She smiled at the boy, trying to reassure him that he was doing what was right, what was patriotic. Her reassurance was in spite of her own feelings, of which he could not possibly know anything. In another part of her mind, she was fumbling for some good reason why she should try to convince him that killing and being killed were morally correct. The two parts of her mind, the part that needed to reassure him and the other part that hated killing, had decided on a truce, and he, unaware of her fumbling and her indecision, acknowledged the smile with a fleeting, shy smile of his own.

The black-clad elderly woman sitting next to the boy asked him if he would be so kind as to get her a glass of water, and he rose obligingly and lifted down the water bottle and glass from the holder on the outer wall of the compartment. Bridget watched the water being poured from the bottle into the glass and speculated as to whether or not it was possible to reshape life and start all over again.

Chapter Three

She was travelling from Gilgandra in the north-west of New South Wales to Sydney. At Dubbo, the young boy helped her off the train with her bag and the child, Joseph. She thanked him and wished him well before he walked towards the station exit. Part of her wanted to run after him, take him by the shoulders and ask him if he had truly thought through what he was about to do. She wanted to ask him if he had looked beyond all the talk of obligation and duty and sacrifice to what *he* wanted to do, to what he intuitively, truthfully, felt was right.

But it was more than possible that he was not thinking of obligation or sacrifice. Focused on the excitement he believed was ahead of him, he most probably felt that what he was about to do was the right thing for him. She tried to look at his decision from what she imagined was his point of view while trying, for a moment, to forget her own ideas about war and killing. She decided that this must be what he felt he wanted to do. No one was pushing him. Or were they?

The adventure that he was anticipating would have its roots in the many patriotic slogans he had been hearing and reading. His head was doubtlessly filled with images telling him that his country needed him, telling him that the Empire needed him. Images that were also seducing him with a promise of new places and new experiences.

While she thought about the boy and what it was that was prompting him to enlist, another part of her wondered about right and wrong and how easy it was for the two words to change places as in some stately, well-choreographed, dance. Thinking of her own situation, she knew just how easily these two opposites could change places. She did not feel that she had the right to pass any kind of judgement on others.

She forcibly moved her thoughts away from herself and the boy and considered the shocking, unbelievable news about her cousin, and all the others who were with him, that had been filtering through from a place called Pozières. At the same time, she reminded herself that it was months since she had heard anything from Daniel. Her second-youngest brother arrived in Egypt the previous May, and in the last letter she received from him, sometime in June, he wrote that he was waiting to be moved further north. He described the sandhills that surreptitiously changed shape with the wind, the ungainly camels, the peculiar language he did not understand, the heat that was somehow different to the Australian heat and the long days of waiting. She had tried to read between the lines, and she was almost able to experience a little of his boredom and frustration: he never liked standing still, doing nothing. Though *doing nothing* was probably wrong: there would have been hours of training and routine military exercises; he would not have been standing around *doing nothing*. While revising the image in her head, she had wondered if the enforced interlude in an unfamiliar environment might have given him the space to think. To re-think.

She had also asked herself, many times, whether or not her husband, James, ever had second thoughts after he had signed up. She had often wondered whether he had analysed, recalculated and re-thought. He had been adamant that going to war was the right thing to do, but had he fully understood what his signature on an enlistment form meant? Had he considered what it could lead to? Was he fully aware that he could be injured, or even killed, or was his acceptance of such consequences the essence of what he was prepared to offer for the Empire?

Her thoughts remained focused on James, wondering if he had actually understood what he was doing, his hand poised over the 'sign here' line at the bottom of the enlistment form. Did he, during those few seconds, follow the thoughts of loyalty and duty just a little bit further and reflect on those who could be unwittingly caught up in his sacrifice, those who would later have to care for what was left of him, those who would be left to mourn him?

Was she grieving for him? Or was she simply mourning what had once been and was no more? The throbbing bruises and angry welts on her arms, carefully hidden beneath her sleeves, reminded her that lingering feelings of sadness had to be pushed aside. Tears would not change what had happened; there was no longer anything, or anyone, to mourn.

She stopped her thoughts abruptly: she did not want war and its consequences to be about herself. She only wanted to concentrate on the James from before and what it was that had motivated him. James was not at all unique: others had done, and were still doing, the same as he had done. Whether they had been motivated by the promise of new experiences or adventure, or whether it was a feeling of duty, or an obscure sense of loyalty to Australia or the Empire, or both, they had been enlisting in their thousands.

He had often spoken to her about obligation while she had felt that wrapping the reality of killing others in a thin veil of patriotism was both cruel and deceitful. In her opinion, love of one's country was something that could easily be exploited: a positive response to the War was possible only when people clung to the perverted idea of nationalism put forward by those wanting the War. She was not certain that such sentiments could be anything but warped.

Had he ever given thought to the moral implications of killing another human being: a human being like himself, with emotions like himself, with a family like himself? She tried to bring all her scattered thoughts together, asking herself if there was any point in all the killing. It was this question that kept her awake night after night. No matter how she twisted and turned it, she had been unable to find an answer.

Her family was being slowly pulled apart: no one had heard anything from Daniel O'Connor since early last July, when Martin received the news that Daniel and his battalion were finally being moved to France. Bridget dared not put her thoughts into words for she was no longer certain that he was still alive. In December, her parents were officially notified that their son was missing in action, and it was only then that it became apparent that Daniel, like his cousin, had also been at Pozières.

She tried not to let her thoughts dwell on the possibility that he could already be dead, hoping that if she did not permit such thoughts to settle in her head he would remain safe. The word *missing* did not have to annihilate hope. As far as she knew, *missing* simply implied that a person could not be found, because he was not where he was expected to be. This did not necessarily mean that the person was dead. *Reported missing* had to mean that there were people out there looking for him. They knew where they had to look; eventually they would have to find him.

While she tried not to think about what might, or might not, have happened to Daniel, she sent God a silent thank you that her youngest brother, Thomas, had been rejected by the enlistment board because of his bad eyesight. She was well aware that the rejection may well have saved his life.

For a moment she contemplated on the word *saved*, thinking how it meant different things to different people.

An image of the young boy from the train pushed away some of her other thoughts, and she wondered briefly if she should have pleaded with him to return home. She would have liked him to forget about the War and the idea that he had to be, or wanted to be, involved; however, should he back away at this stage, she feared that people would never let him forget what he did not do, or what he should have done. Returning home without having done what he set out to do, he would become a magnet for everyone's uncertainties and fears, all of which would be piled upon him. Was he a pacifist? Was he a coward? Was he unpatriotic? Unlike the scapegoat in Leviticus, he would not be chased out into the desert and forgotten. Instead, he would remain where he was, bent low by the burden of collective imagined national pride, indignation and even guilt. Bridget was all too aware that there were many different kinds of fear and that the fear of war, with its black-and-white images of unrivalled horror, was only one of them. Another fear was the fear of being on one's own when daring to take a different path. She felt strangely sorry for the boy, because she knew that even if, at this late stage, he should question why he was actually enlisting and whether the attraction of new places and adventure was sufficient reason to kill and be killed, he would most probably come to the conclusion that he had no other choice.

Like Daniel.

The large wooden indicator, affixed to one end of the station building, showed Bridget that she had more than an hour to wait for her connecting train to Sydney. She hesitated for a moment and then opened the door to the waiting room, ushering Joseph to a seat near the window. There were several other people in the large room: an elderly man reading the newspaper, a couple of women deep in conversation, a young girl with a baby in a pram, three men in uniform. She observed the three men, wondering whether they were new recruits or whether they had been on leave and were now on their way back to Sydney.

She ran her fingers through Joseph's tousled hair, ostensibly in an effort to bring some order to it but in reality to savour the feel and the smell of him. She breathed in deeply, wanting his untainted innocence to wrap around her like a blanket, shutting out all the worry and horror of the last few hours. He squirmed a little and shook his head. Reluctantly, she withdrew her hand, brushing it lightly against the side of his face while appreciating the smooth softness of his skin.

He had slept for most of the trip from Gilgandra, and Bridget guessed that he would now be trying to equate the images around him with remembered images from Gilgandra and even Molong. Had it been possible, she would have removed anything that could, in any way, cause him worry, and she would have left him with only positive, happy images and memories: the smiles of those who loved him, the rhythmic sound of windmills, wide expanses of purple wildflowers.

Aware of how good and bad memories were often intertwined and how coils of concern could pull together tightly, not wanting to let go, she repeated what she had already told him several times: 'We're visiting Aunt Sarah, but she lives so very far away.' As she continued speaking, telling her son how happy Aunt Sarah was going to be to see him and how she was probably already sitting at her window, hoping to get a glimpse of them walking down the street towards her house, Bridget opened her bag and pulled out a small parcel wrapped in a white cloth. The child's attention immediately moved from everything around him, including his mother's talk about his aunt, to the familiar hunk of soda bread and the couple of pieces of cold meat now lying on Bridget's knee.

Bridget broke off a large piece of the bread and handed it to her son with one of the pieces of meat. She then re-wrapped the bread and meat and returned the package to her bag. Before closing the bag, she took out a tin mug, looked around for a few seconds and, telling Joseph to remain where he was, walked to the other side of the room. On a small unadorned table that had been pushed into a corner, she had seen a couple of decanters full of water and several glasses. Not needing a glass, she carefully filled the mug, thinking, somewhat distractedly, of the elderly woman and the bottle of water on the first train.

Back on the seat with Joseph, she took a mouthful of the water that was neither cold nor warm, delighting in the sensation of the liquid moving through her body, before handing the mug to her son.

Since they had entered the waiting room several more people had arrived, and Bridget was well aware that everyone in the room would be travelling on the Sydney train. She watched them uninterestedly for some minutes before her attention returned to her own situation.

Although she did not want to dwell on the present and the immediate past, she was suddenly confronted by the uncomfortable thought that she may not have done the right thing by running away. The thought, coming at her from different angles, upset her, and for the first time since she slammed the door behind her in the murky middle point of the night, she let herself acknowledge a hard, cold twinge of doubt. Her stomach clamped and remained like a heavy stone somewhere inside her.

Should she have waited? Should she have remained where she was? Should she have gone for help? Could she possibly have explained how it had happened? Would they have listened? Could she have talked about things she had never dared talk about before? Her mind was racing: was it possible that they might have actually listened, and if they had listened, would they then have chosen to believe her? She was not sure. In all likelihood some of them would have believed, but that did not necessarily mean that they would have excused her action. The more she thought about it, the more she understood why she did not stay: the risk was too great. The stone in her stomach crumbled, and she felt a little stronger in her resolve. She mentally fractured all her doubts into small pieces, leaving ample dark space for other thoughts and other anxieties.

That the police would eventually be involved and that they would then wonder as to her whereabouts was, for whatever reason, an idea that had not occurred to her before: she had been too centred on getting as far away from the house as possible. When the police discovered that she was not with her parents, they would naturally assume that something had happened to her as well. After all, a dreadful crime had been committed, and she and the boy were nowhere to be seen. It was not inconceivable that the police, and others, might believe that they had both been killed and their bodies dumped somewhere.

She stopped her thoughts in their track, suddenly aware of just how naïve she had become. The images of search parties and newspaper headlines quickly broke up and then dissolved completely as she acknowledged the fact that everyone would know for certain that she was somehow responsible. There would be no need to drag the Castlereagh river or call in the native trackers. Now, when she was able to consider things more lucidly, she could see that she should have stayed where she was, in spite of her fears. She had always been impetuous: it was becoming very obvious that she had not thought things through properly; in fact, she had not thought at all. The part of her brain that was acting in her defence insisted that there had not been time to think or plan, but the prosecution side countered that had she stayed she could have at least tried to defend herself, and perhaps someone would have listened.

Or, perhaps not.

Even if she had been able to look at everything in a calmer, more balanced, manner and had remained in Gilgandra, hoping to be able to defend herself, there was no guarantee that people would have wanted to understand her explanation: she was, after all, a woman in a world that belonged to men and was run by men. Her explanation would have been filtered through men's experiences and men's understanding, and it would have been found both unlikely and wanting. Some of the women who accepted this unbalanced state of affairs, because they knew they had no choice, because they had been told they had no choice, would stand behind their men and urge them on. For a brief moment, they would feel powerful and important.

She shook her head, trying to push all the images and thoughts beyond herself and as far as possible past the railway station and the surrounding countryside.

Despite her attempt to cast out all negative images and thoughts, the pressure in her chest remained, and she took several deep breaths, hoping to be able to banish at least part of the enormous cloud that was weighing her down and troubling her. She would have liked to have been able to move into some parallel universe without the horrors of the last twenty-four hours: if she tried hard enough, then perhaps it could actually happen.

While she was fixating her energies on emptying her head or pushing through some invisible barrier to that other universe, she was unable to let go of the probability that those looking for her and Joseph would eventually assume that they had fled to her parents in Molong or her brother's family closer to Cudal. She hoped that it would take a while before someone stumbled on the idea that they could have travelled all the way to Sydney. The thought that no one really knew where they were was a comfort on one level while, on another level, it was opening a Pandora's box of problems that she had not even considered: what would her parents think when they heard what had happened?

She felt the beginning of a dull headache, and she became preoccupied with the idea of a cup of hot sweet tea. Attached to the waiting room there was a refreshment room where tea and sandwiches were being served, and a tempting image of the dark brown beverage expanded to fill the entire space between her and the canteen. She sighed and shook her head. There was little she could do about it: she had no idea how much money she would need or how long what she had would last. The future was not only clouded, it was also firmly studded with question marks.

Later, on the Sydney train, with Joseph ensconced in the corner of the seat next to the window, she looked out at the apparently endless stretches of brittle, brown grass beyond the window, grass which at times seemed to lose its brown-beige colour beneath the searing whiteness of the afternoon sun. In places she could still see sheep, sometimes huddled under lone blue-grey trees, and she knew that during the heat of the day there would have been crows lazily circling, filling the air with their hoarse, shrill cries, alert to the lamb that had strayed too far from the flock or the animal that could no longer keep up with the others.

None of this was new to Bridget. It had always been a fundamental part of her life.

When Patrick O'Connor was feeling sentimental, which was more often than not, he would sometimes talk to his daughter about soft round hills covered with thick, emerald-green grass, slipping down to seas of the same colour. Even as Bridget listened, she knew that he, like her, had never seen such things: he had spent almost all his life in central New South Wales. His father, Micheál, had grown up with the hills and the astonishingly green grass. As far as she knew there was no large expanse of water, just a couple of small streams fighting their way across the green hills towards the river further south.

She understood her father's need to hold on to images from the past, even if they were borrowed images. The idea of green hills was a handed-down concept, a virtual picture that could be pulled out and looked at, like the small, cheap trinkets in her mother's jewellery box. It was a mental image that tied the present firmly to the past, creating a feeling of continuity. When Patrick took out that particular picture and described it for her, she knew that it was foreign and unreal, but in spite of her having no connection with the reality that was the basis for her father's vision, she liked the idea of continuity. Neither she nor her father could reconcile the rolling green hills of Ireland with the reality surrounding them in Australia, but they were both keenly aware of the impact of the one upon the other.

Chapter Four

Bridget's uncle Timothy, dead for the past twelve years, had never mentioned rolling green grass or emerald waters. Instead, he had talked incessantly about the darkness and the hunger. He had often spoken of the rain and the sleet and the mud; woven through all his memories of the past there had been constant mention of the never-ending cold. He described the small village of Ballinure with its church, cemetery and crossroads, and how, tucked away between the hills, there were ruins from some other time. Both Bridget's grandparents had died before she was born, and it was Timothy and, to a much lesser extent, her uncle John who had filled her mind with Irish stories, leprechauns and superstitions. Timothy was not even ten when they left Ireland, and there were many things of which he was unaware: it was not until much later that he had fully understood why they had had to leave.

He did remember that he had lived in a one-room grey-stone cottage, a clone of all the other dwellings scattered across the fields, with his younger brother, John, the baby, Grace, and his parents, Micheál and Catherine. Also living in the cottage were his grandmother and his aunt Nora. His grandfather and his aunt Eileen had died within weeks of each other in the second year of the famine, two events that for the then six-year old Timothy were hazy and out of focus. He had one memory of his grandfather sitting at the roughly hewn table, smoking his pipe, and then there was a deep gap, and on the other side of the immeasurable space, people were sad-faced and weeping and his grandfather was nowhere to be seen.

In his teens, Timothy became aware that two of his uncles, Liam and Brian, uncles he could by then no longer remember, had left Tipperary in 1846 and moved to Liverpool. His third uncle, Brendan, was to have moved with them, but weeks before the boat sailed he attempted to stop a runaway horse and cart, was pulled under the wheels and died three days later. For some months after hearing about Brendan, Timothy had nightmares where he was Brendan trying to grab on to a frightened horse's trailing reins. In his dream he could see terror in the eyes of the horse, he could smell its fear, and he could hear the terrifying noise of the loaded cart as it hurtled along behind the out-of-control horse. His dream-hand grasped the reins, but even as he imagined that he could feel the leather between his fingers, he knew what was going to happen. The stones on the road were loose, he lost his balance, and he was swept back beneath the horse and under the cart. At some point in the darkness that followed, Timothy would invariably wake up, not sure at first if he was still alive.

With his grandfather, Liam, Brian, Eileen and Brendan no longer part of the family picture, his grandmother and aunt Nora automatically became two extra responsibilities for his father; something Timothy was too young at the time to fully appreciate.

When Bridget was still a child and was asking questions about what it was like 'before' — before they left Ireland, before they came to Australia — Timothy would tell her about the cold. He would also tell her about the darkness that pervaded the small cottage. 'The door was low, not that it was a problem for me,' he used to say with a smile, 'and inside it was gloom and shadows. Always.' He spoke of a bed in the far corner of the cottage where his grandmother sat, speaking endlessly with God, at times accusing Him, at times beseeching Him. Timothy, young as he then was, remembered her telling God she was prepared to understand why He may have needed to take Eileen, who was, after all, so sickly, but her husband and Brendan were both strong men. Surely they were not supposed to die so soon? Her husband should have been there to lead his family through the chaos and the blackness and into better times.

When she was really angry, she would sometimes add that perhaps it was true, as many were saying, that even God was dead.

Timothy rarely spoke of his mother; when he did, his somewhat meagre description of her as a thin, quietly spoken, devout woman left the young Bridget wanting to add more features to a picture that was sketchy and lacking. No matter how she tried, she found it difficult to create a satisfactory portrait of her grandmother from what her uncle had told her, and her image of Catherine could easily have remained somewhat blurred and grey.

Thanks to her father's memories of his mother, Bridget was eventually able to put together a more rounded and accurate likeness. Patrick's recollection had touches of warmth and colour, perhaps because he remembered her against an Australian background, the only background he had ever known. With the two images, her father's and her uncle's, Bridget had a better picture of who her grandmother really was, but when she attempted mentally to place Patrick's Catherine in Ireland, the colours quickly disappeared and were replaced by Timothy's greys and shadows.

Blending descriptions from her father and her uncle, she understood that her grandmother was short and slightly built with thick black hair pulled back severely into a bun. Although her expression was usually stern, there was, if she was to believe her father, always a glint of humour behind the green eyes. In contrast to her very vocal husband, she was reserved, and she did not speak a lot. Putting together everything she knew about her grandmother, it was obvious to Bridget that Catherine O'Connor had been a determined woman and that it was this determination that held her together and kept her going, even when everything was against her.

Bridget felt that there were distinct similarities between her mother, Mary, and Catherine: both women were strong-minded, but there was a quietness and a gentleness behind the determination. She wondered whether or not most O'Connor women — O'Connor by either birth or marriage — came from a similar mould, and whether people looking at her would also see her as resolute, yet docile. She was not sure.

Catherine had managed to keep things together, in spite of children dying and family foundering around her. Bridget was not sure that *she* was capable of holding anything together, not even herself. She would have liked to have been able to push away the shadows and reach out to this person who had been confronted by so much tragedy and hopelessness. Surely such a person, the grandmother she never knew, would have understood why she had done what she did, and she might even have been able to tell her what she should be doing now.

She wondered if Catherine had also needed someone to understand her, and if Micheál had been that person or if he had been too occupied with the paramount question of survival. Did he occasionally put his arms around her and profess some kind of love or affection? Nothing that Timothy, or her father, had told Bridget contained the answers to such questions.

The thoughts about her grandmother gradually mutated into other connected and unconnected images, and she found herself trying to remember what Timothy had told her about the O'Connor cottage. From what she could recall him saying, there was a low wall of stones dividing the main part of the room from the part where animals lived, though it was unlikely that there were any animals living there from the time Timothy was old enough to remember. Before the famine there would most probably have been hens, and there could also have been a cow. What had been most vivid in Timothy's memory were the ugly, skinny cats that occasionally slunk into the cottage, looking for shelter.

Timothy believed that before the Hunger they had eaten potatoes three times a day, but even then, even while their stomachs were full and before the potato had turned against them, there was already a heavy cloud of eviction looming above the small stone cottages. Timothy was not aware of what was happening at the time, but later his father told him how everyone was waiting for the storm that was certain to break as landlords began looking for excuses to evict cottiers and those with smallholdings. They were hoping to be able to free up land for more profitable forms of agriculture, and in many ways, the Hunger simply gave them the excuse that they needed.

Bridget looked out of the train window at the bone-dry grass while her mind insisted on wandering backwards over the past twenty-four hours. As it randomly pulled out images and sensations she was trying to forget, she wrapped her arm around Joseph, hoping to be able to anchor herself to something that was perfect and undefiled. The unwanted images teetered for a moment, not sure whether to remain or whether to withdraw, and finally chose to fade into the background.

She took a deep breath, sensing the weakening of the images while enjoying the reality of her son next to her. She noticed that he had fallen asleep, and she thought how wonderful it would be to be able to slip into a place of complete unconsciousness, a place where there were no images, no feelings of guilt, no panic.

Was there someone with whom she could share these images and feelings of guilt? Her eyes glanced at the colourless grass and grey-green trees beyond the window while she mentally listed the people who might understand. The list was unusually short. She had not really spoken to anyone about James: she had written to Sarah and intimated that things were not particularly easy, but she had never gone into detail. She had never explained how difficult things actually were.

Bridget imagined that her mother, Mary, would both understand and not understand. Kind but pragmatic, she would tell her daughter that life is not supposed to be easy. She would hold her hand between both of hers, promising to pray to God that He would help her accept all those things she could not change.

She sighed, thinking that if anyone would be able to help her it would have to be Sarah. Then, with her arm around her son and her thoughts focused on the support and understanding her sister would give her, she very soon drifted into an exhausted sleep.

Like most dreams, her dream was strange: she believed that she was walking down a country road, but it was not any country road that she knew. There was a hazy figure in front of her, and for some reason she was certain that it was her grandmother. How she could be so certain that the person in her dream was someone she had never met, a person who was nothing more than a collection of memories passed down by others, she did not know. Still, without reflecting on all the whys and wherefores, she intuitively knew who it was.

The road appeared to follow the gentle rise and fall of the landscape, a landscape that changed shape, occasionally folding in on itself, often becoming uneven and obscure at the edges, sometimes turning fragile and cloud-like or else disappearing altogether. There was something about the landscape and the vague images that made her believe that it could have been a winter afternoon, the light seeming to hang halfway between day and night. There was sleet or snow rushing against both the figure and herself, obscuring most of the already sketchy landscape. She believed that her grandmother had a shawl pulled tightly around her shoulders, and somewhere inside her dream-mind was the question as to why either of them would be walking along the road in such weather.

It was at this point that the dream began to fade as Bridget became more awake. Finding herself now partly conscious and able to steer thoughts in certain directions, she attempted to create an answer to her question as to why Catherine was walking along the road. Could she have been helping a neighbour, a woman in childbirth, a family mourning a loved one? Perhaps she had been laying out the body of a child, an old person or a friend, someone who had succumbed to hunger? Or perhaps she had been to the church to light a candle, to ask God for His help?

Was her grandmother thinking of the body now washed and dressed, or was she thinking of God or of the unwelcoming cottage and the hungry children waiting for her at the end of the road?

Then, without warning, the dream and her thoughts suddenly convulsed and disappeared. Had the train jolted or was there some other reason why she should be almost awake when, seconds ago, she was drifting between a baffling dream and an odd sense of reality? She looked around her, still dazed from the sleep that had now disowned her; nothing seemed completely real, yet nothing seemed beyond the bounds of possibility.

She wondered how long she had been asleep, and tried to remember what it was she had been thinking about or dreaming. Gradually, she remembered that there had been something about her mother and Sarah, but then she recalled images of her grandmother and snow and Ireland. Wondering why she should have been thinking or dreaming about her grandmother, she frowned a little, gently removing her arm from around Joseph and covering him with her jacket.

The dream, or as much as she could remember of it, intrigued her. Why would she have been dreaming about someone she did not know but would probably have liked to have known? Was the dream trying to tell her something, or was it simply a product of all her worry and anxiety? Was she imagining Catherine into being so that she would have someone who might understand her and take care of her? Did it have something to do with her moving from one terrifying certainty to another similarly terrifying uncertainty? While she definitely needed someone who could understand her, she suspected that uncertainty was the ultimate trigger. Uncertainty could be seen as a cloud hanging above the earth, randomly sending down lightning strikes on unsuspecting people. For a few seconds, she concentrated on an image of being attacked by lightning, feeling that it certainly described her situation and that it could well have also described her grandparents' situation. Now that the thought about Ireland and her grandparents was in her head, she found it impossible to get past it, and half-asleep, or half-awake, she let her thoughts return to what Timothy had told her, all that time ago.

While remembering the Great Hunger, Timothy spoke to his then twelve-year-old niece about the road-and-drainage projects that were hurriedly put in place to provide work for those who were destitute. Timothy told her that the wages were paltry: the English Treasury did not particularly like parting with money to prop up the poor in Ireland, and very soon the works were halted in favour of soup kitchens, which were cheaper to run. A year later even the soup kitchens disappeared, and the poor were told to fend for themselves. Timothy clearly remembered his father's anger: he had no work, there was no food and the alarming prospect of eviction was already hanging over him. When Micheál managed to find a day's work, digging trenches or, more often than not, graves, he would thank God. He would also thank Him when he was selected for a few hours of building or dismantling stone walls or making packing cases for the food neither he nor his family were permitted to eat. His success at finding work, though, was sporadic: there were always many others who desperately wanted the same couple of hours of work, the same pitiful remuneration and the same uncertain promise of food, no matter how basic or scant.

As a child attempting to process her uncle's words, Bridget's head was filled with images of her grandfather pleading with anyone and everyone to give him work. As an adult, she was aware that Micheál being without work meant that the burden would have fallen on Catherine to somehow keep the family fed without food, and to provide comfort and hope when she was quite sure that they would all soon be resting in the graveyard. Her husband might well have lamented and even cursed the situation, but it was she who would have had to keep everything afloat.

Bridget was almost sure that in the same way as she had no idea a week ago, a month ago, a year ago that she would, in the late summer of 1917, be on a train heading for Sydney, Catherine would have had no idea that she and her family would eventually have to leave Ireland. The only difference was the thing that drove them both. In Catherine's case it was the hunger; in her case—

She stopped her chain of thought and looked beyond the window where the flat plains stretched to the horizon. The afternoon shadows were already beginning to paint the landscape with their own strange patterns, creating clumps of trees where there were none and obliterating the realities that were already there.

By 1847 the Hunger had already spent several years gnawing its way across the country, like a mediaeval plague of rats, leaving skeletal forms and overfull graveyards in its wake. It had moved across the country, causing towns and villages to disintegrate as the people fled aimlessly or simply lay down and died, too weak and emaciated to do anything else. It clung ferociously to empty, shrunken stomachs, filling them with pain when there was nothing else with which to fill them.

Bridget was certain that she did not want to dwell on images of hunger and dying, but just for a moment she would have liked to be able to feel the cold, wet snow from her dream. It was so warm in the carriage, and the idea of submerging herself in cold snow was as attractive as it was impossible. In spite of all her wanting, she knew that it was not going to happen: there was a very wide gap between reality and fantasy. Putting the snow to one side, she returned to her belief that Catherine could have seen only one possible end to the catastrophe: everyone would eventually die.

From what she had been told, so many had already died, and Bridget reasoned that from her grandmother's perspective there could be no reason why those who were still living would be spared. When there was no food, the outcome was more or less conclusive. Although death was a way of escaping the futility of the situation, Catherine would not have wanted to see her husband and children die; nor would she have wanted to see her children become orphans, needing to fend for themselves. Perhaps she prayed that the children would die first, if there was absolutely no chance of anyone in the family being saved. Bridget could picture such a request sitting at the very bottom of Catherine's list of entreaties to God. A request that would never actually need to be processed; a request that would hopefully never become a reality. The majority of her grandmother's entreaties were, no doubt, prayers to God to save her family. She could imagine her grandmother making a deal with God, promising Him extra prayers, novenas and masses.

Bridget's thoughts wandered again. She was in such a heightened state of disquiet and anxiety that she found it difficult to fix her thoughts on one thing for any length of time: the shadows beyond the train window, Gilgandra, the boy on the first train, Joseph, Sarah, her grandmother. She wondered what kind of deal *she* should be doing with God, and whether or not He would even want to listen to her.

For a brief moment she remembered what Timothy told her about it always being cold, then her thoughts darted off in a slightly different direction and returned to the fractured images from her dream: the imaginary path and the sleet. Whether or not Catherine was the figure in her dream, Bridget felt that it was beyond question that her grandmother would have been worried about the lack of food and the very real possibilities of both eviction and death. She was not as certain that her grandmother was worried that something dreadful and unforeseen might have happened to God, though if God was still in His Heaven, it would have been logical for Catherine to expect that He would have been trying to help in some way. Bridget had no way of knowing how Catherine thought and worried: she suspected that she was attempting to create a state of mind for Catherine that was, in many ways, a reflection of her own concerns and distress.

She wondered a little about her own relationship with God, and whether or not He could have done more to have prevented what had happened in the house on the outskirts of Gilgandra. Surely, looking down from the safety of Heaven, He must have been aware of her situation. She thought back over the past months and came to the conclusion that her problem had not been a divine priority. After weighing all the evidence, both for and against, she concluded that He would have felt that He already had enough on His hands. Just wondering whether or not He should involve Himself in the woeful mess humankind, His own creation, had made of both itself and the world in which it lived would definitely have been sufficient to occupy all His time.

More than anything, Bridget wanted to be able to slide into a completely inert state. While she longed to be able to wipe her mind clean of all thoughts, both negative and positive, she pondered for a moment as to whether she had ever experienced such a state, quite empty of all ideas, impressions, images, and decided that she had not. Although she was exhausted, she was unable to fall asleep, her mind constantly sorting through the things she had done and the things she probably should have done but had not done.

She looked at Joseph, asleep next to her, his head resting against her arm, one hand holding the edge of the jacket. She envied him his cocoon of innocence. Had it been possible, she would have liked to have crept into the cocoon with him, his soft, warm body next to hers, all thoughts and troubling mental images locked outside, beyond the invisible barricade.

Soon they would arrive in Sydney, and finally she would be able to share her worries with Sarah. In the meantime, unable to sleep and unable to still the anxiety within her, she let her thoughts wander unhindered, and without wanting or not wanting she was very soon back in her uncle's Ireland.

It was in the autumn of 1845 when the potato crop failed the first time. From what Timothy had told her, Bridget imagined that the Hunger was no more than a vague shadow on the horizon during those first weeks, but very soon it grew to embrace everything and to become the only reality.

Even Patrick, her father, knew about the Hunger. It was, after all, the reason why their world had been turned upside down and why he had been born on Guernsey and not in Tipperary. It was a story that had been handed down and embellished. It was not necessary to have been part of it to eventually own it, but as Bridget looked past the glass of the window and well beyond the fields to the horizon, she wondered if she had ever really owned any part of the story.

When her father was in his story-telling mood, he would describe the yellow- and orange-tinged leaves, which had already begun to fall from the trees; the days of incessant rain, which caused water to pool around the stone walls of cottages and outhouses; and the fields turning to mud that sucked at boots while giving off a heavy, musty smell. He had never seen the leaves or the rain or the mud, but they were part of the story he had heard from his father, and over time the story became his, and the lines between what was experienced and what was not experienced became blurred until, eventually, they disappeared altogether.

His voice would take on a hushed, almost theatrical, quality as he explained how his father had anxiously checked the potato crop every day, the cold rain relentlessly smacking against his face and his hands. While walking slowly along the lines of raised beds, Micheál had not been thinking about either the rain or the cold: Patrick was quite certain that he had been completely preoccupied with the multitude of black-blotched leaves that he was picking off the already withered plants. He had wanted to ignore what the leaves were telling him. He had wanted to believe that there was nothing wrong with the plants and that there would still be a crop even though all the signs were telling him something else. Every day he prayed that the harvest still hidden beneath the soil might be saved, but his prayers went unheard, and the hope that he had nurtured revealed itself to be nothing more than an unreliable expectation born in hopelessness: all across Tipperary the potato crops had failed.

They called it a canker, a fungus, a pestilence. It started on the leaves and then burrowed into the soil and turned the potatoes to black mush. Without potatoes no one knew how they would survive the winter. They sorted through nettles and berries for the few that had not frozen, and after cutting away the blackened bits from potatoes that had not yet become completely putrid, they ate the rest. When desperation led them to eat the blighted potatoes, they became ill. They were constantly hungry: they had already forgotten what it felt like to have a full and satisfied stomach.

At this point Patrick would often pause and relight his pipe or, more often than not, take a mouthful of ale, looking around the room at the same time, gauging the impact of his story. Meanwhile, the nine- or ten- or eleven-year-old Bridget, watching her mother spread half-soft lumps of dripping over uneven slices of grey bread, would wonder at what point it was possible to talk about being constantly hungry. She would ask herself if black tea with bread and dripping qualified, and then she would repent of such thoughts, silently asking her grandfather and even God to forgive her.

And while Bridget was trying to come to terms with such insensitive and heedless musings, she would possibly hear her father repeating in an almost inaudible, measured voice that everyone was starving and frozen, or something similar and just as dramatic. Then, waking out of her reverie, she would probably hear him continue: 'Against all expectations,' he might say, or 'It was quare unbelievable,' or he might skip the introduction, launching immediately back into his story. 'Spring finally came,' he would announce, his eyes quickly scanning the room, 'and everyone looked around them in surprise, and they gave thanks to the God Almighty that they were still alive.'

Bridget remembered how her father would then say that everyone believed that the worst was now behind them, and they set about planting new potatoes.

ℭhapter Five

ridget's thoughts were momentarily distracted as the train pulled to a stop, and above the hissing and screeching of the brakes she could feel the enormous strength of the train running like a taut wire through her carriage before suddenly letting go. A rush of smoke and steam surged past her window, then disappeared, revealing the familiar shape of the railway station. She did not need to read the sign to know that they were in Orange. Looking out at the station building, she experienced a tsunami of emotions: fear, sadness, anxiety, even homesickness. While her more logical self argued that it was unlikely that anyone would be looking for her — nothing could possibly have been discovered as yet — her less logical self worried that the police, relying on some sixth sense, could already be at the station, waiting for her to alight. The thought that they might know she was on the train expanded inside her, and she flattened herself against the back of the seat, hoping to become one with the inanimate object, hoping to disappear.

She should have thought through things better. She should have been more prepared. It was becoming clear that she had not been thinking coherently; she doubted that she had been thinking at all.

People were getting off the train; others were waiting to board. A young porter in a blue uniform was helping the exiting passengers collect their luggage while his workmate was lifting new cases and boxes into the luggage compartment at the back of the train. Despite her illogical fears, there were no police anywhere on the platform. She breathed deeply several times and tried to relax, concentrating her thoughts on removing at least part of her burgeoning anxiety.

The porter who had been assisting the exiting passengers was now helping an elderly woman into Bridget's carriage. Bridget noted the smile on the woman's face, and assumed that she was thanking the young boy, his hand still on her arm. That was what she needed: a friendly, supportive 'someone' who could hold her hand and tell her that everything was going to be all right. A 'someone' who could allay her fears, tell her that she was doing the right thing, hold her tightly just for a moment, comfort Joseph.

The train had started again, slowly at first. She had a fleeting glimpse of the blue-clad porter standing on the platform, and then the platform disappeared and the train, and everyone on board, was sucked into the encroaching evening.

Although all she wanted was to be able to sink into oblivion, her mind refused to stop processing unnerving images and worrying ideas. It wavered between the present, filled with too many unknowns, and the immediate past, which was what she was actually trying to forget. Unable to achieve the state of nothingness she desired, she let her thoughts wander back to her father and, beyond him, to Ireland.

In her head, she could hear her father in the kitchen, talking about how the next crop had also been infected. She could hear him saying that when the second crop failed there was absolutely no one who believed that the devastation was confined to Tipperary. By the second year of the blight, everyone knew that it was the same across the entire country and that thousands were already dead or dying.

It was rumoured that other countries across Europe also had the fungus, but none of these countries had a whole population forced on to minute holdings where the only thing that grew was the potato, the very thing that was affected by the infestation. Micheál had heard it said that the fungus or canker had been brought across the Irish Sea purposely by the English, some even used the word *genocide*, while a few churchmen and others claimed with dubious authority that God was punishing them for their sinful ways. Micheál had not been so sure about the English, or even God for that matter, but he chose to side with those who claimed that the anti-Catholic policy in Ireland, where English landlords owned most of the land, was to blame. Whether responsibility lay with the English, the sins of the Irish, politics or even the whim of some supreme being, no one was able to ignore the gruesome reality of the dead.

Although Patrick had been spared the harsh realities of the 1840s, he had no problem sharing his very vocal opinion of the English with anyone who wanted to listen, or even with those who had no option but to listen. He agreed with his father that the anti-Catholic policy would not have helped. In fact, with the English landlords exporting all Irish grain and food to England, there could be only one possible outcome for the Irish people. Bridget wondered if, on some hidden level of herself, part of her antagonism towards England's war was somehow connected to events more than half a century ago.

She wanted the train to move faster: the sooner she could reach Sydney and be collected into the arms of her sister, the better. There was so much that she needed to tell

Sarah, and her body ached as she anticipated seeing her again, feeling her next to her, hearing her voice. In her mind, she dwelt upon the image of her sister opening her door, and she treasured the deep and wordless understanding that would immediately pass between them. Bridget was quite sure that once Sarah knew what had happened in Gilgandra, everything would fall into place and all her anxieties would instantly dissolve.

Though Bridget was relieved that Joseph was still asleep, she did not expect to get any more sleep herself: there were too many thoughts swarming around in her head. She seemed to have no control over the pictures that inundated her mind, pushing themselves forwards before being overtaken by other, even more perturbing, thoughts and images. She wanted to concentrate on Sarah, but the mental pictures of her sister kept disappearing behind all the unwelcome images from Gilgandra. Her speculations about Ireland were definitely sketchy; like the images of Sarah, they also kept being pushed to one side, but they gave her something on which she could fix her attention, and she held on to them as a person being swept downstream towards a steep and thundering waterfall will hold on to any kind of branch, no matter how flimsy.

Keeping Ireland in the forefront of her mind, she recalled bits of an odd dream where she had been following someone, possibly her grandmother, down a road. She believed it could have been snowing, or perhaps it had been raining. She was no longer quite sure: the dream had already dissolved into a collection of hazy images and feelings. Was Catherine on her way home, and if so where had she been? Bridget tried her best to resurrect the dream, but it was elusive, and the images taunted her by scurrying away as soon as they seemed to be within her grasp.

With the small pieces of the dream that still remained, Bridget attempted to patch together a story about the woman walking along the road. She knew that her story probably had little to do with the dream she had dreamt, but she needed to make some sense of the images, and she had nothing better to do. Indeed, the activity kept her from thinking of things she did not want to think about.

The story that was unfolding in her mind was running parallel to the small fragments she could remember from the dream. At its centre was Catherine, walking along the road towards her home with the wind behind the sleet and the snow becoming fiercer and stronger. Growing up outside Orange, snow and sleet were not foreign to Bridget, but she doubted that her experience could ever be quite like Catherine's. In her mind, she imagined the mixture of rain and snow as rows of wet, white sheets stretched across the landscape. Sometimes they slapped against the small, insignificant woman on the road;

sometimes they wrapped tightly around her; sometimes they beat her harshly from all sides. Occasionally, there were unexpected breaks in the sodden veils of snow, and Bridget decided that Catherine would then have been able to make out the familiar grey shapes of small hills and perhaps an uneven line of naked elms. Beyond the trees that Bridget had imagined into being, was the place Catherine knew as home.

While part of Bridget's mind was focused on her grandmother fighting her way home through the miserable cold and wet, doubtlessly feeling despondent and even helpless, another part of her mind was attempting to bridge the gap between the grandmother of her imagination and the terror and foreboding now confronting Bridget herself. Bridget could have no way of knowing whether or not Catherine felt that no one was listening, not even God, and whether or not she ever came close to believing that death was the only alternative. But the thought of giving up completely refused to go away and expanded until she found herself wondering if, in her case, it might be better and easier for all concerned if she were dead. She shook her head and pushed away the thought. By concentrating on her grandmother, she had foolishly been hoping that she would be able to forget the uncertainty that was taking shape in front of her.

But now that the word *dead* was fixed in her mind, more images from nineteenth-century Ireland pushed their way into her awareness: bodies left in church grounds in the hope that someone would take pity on them and lay them to rest; bodies hurriedly buried in shallow, badly dug graves; bodies left among the half-living until, eventually, all were dead and the shelter itself collapsed. Bridget thought that *dead* was a hard word. It did not compromise.

Her thoughts swung around briefly to Daniel and even to the young boy on the train who was about to enlist. She did not want to think of them together with the word *dead*, but the word had come to stay, and she was unable to move away from it. She closed her eyes and breathed in and out deeply several times, trying to ignore the panic that was rapidly building up around her, like a high unscalable wall.

When she reopened her eyes seconds later, some of the images from Ireland of more than fifty years ago had splintered, forming even more images, and she remembered being told that the second winter was even worse than the first. By then there were no potatoes, not even ones that were partially edible, and there were no longer any animals left to kill, not even dogs. The soup kitchens had all been closed, and people were now supposed to get by without help. There were food handouts, but few knew how to cook the strange, unpalatable Indian meal that had been shipped from the other side of the ocean.

Bridget's emotions were running precariously close to the surface, and a random image or thought, even something as unconnected and normal as the soft, rhythmic sound of Joseph's breathing or the shadowy patterns beyond the window, could easily cause them to spill over. The upsetting images of starving, miserable people troubled her much more than she had expected. She wanted to believe that all those wretched people had eventually been saved, but she decided that their survival, if at all possible, would have been dependent on there being something for them to cling to, something that might have offered them some small glimmer of hope. Thinking of the unfortunate people all needing to be saved, her thoughts regrouped around her own situation: Sarah was *her* shred of hope. Sarah was the rock to which she needed to cling, the calm in the middle of the storm, the light that would assure her that everything would be better in the future and, more importantly, that there would *be* a future.

The *something* that people clung to was most probably God, but Bridget could see how some people might have found it difficult to continue believing in God when everything around them was descending into chaos.

Nevertheless, she hoped that her grandmother continued believing. She wanted to imagine that God remained that very small sliver of optimism to which she continued clinging, in spite of all the distress and misery.

Bridget's grandmother had been only one of so many grey, emaciated people; like all of them, she would have found herself anticipating certain death or possible expatriation. Bridget doubted that her own situation could in any way be compared with her grandmother's, but she began to wonder if she was being pulled into a reality that, on some level, was just as impossible and just as frightening.

Her mind lingered on the grey people and the grey landscape. Grey was a melancholy colour, a non-colour, and she tried adding some colour to the pictures milling around in her mind, but there were no colours to be found.

While she mentally hunted around for colours, the ouroboros symbol filled her mind, pushing to one side the gloomy images of starving people. She had heard that it was a symbol for eternity, but now she could only see it as a symbol of eternal suffering: the cottages abandoned by the dead, or by those who had fled the country, meant increased rents for those who remained behind, and increased rents eventually meant eviction. Eviction was simply another word for the workhouse, and the workhouse was almost certain death. Bridget reflected on the fact that she kept coming back to that same word.

She felt that she was simply exchanging one set of anxieties for another, and she tried unsuccessfully to rid herself of all the pale, miserable images associated with her grandmother's Ireland. Was there a reason why her mind kept churning through images from the past? Was there a message for her somewhere among all the heartache and tragedy? Or was it simply her anxious state of mind singling out events that had most likely been responsible for her being where she was now, perhaps even responsible for her doing what she did?

Shaking her head slightly, she left her questions unanswered and returned to the picture she had created of Catherine walking home. Somewhere behind the figure of the small woman wrapped in the grey shawl, Bridget could discern other images: a stone church, a graveyard, a body dressed in its best and surrounded by candles.

The wind had finally dropped, and the sleet was no longer as intense. Her grandmother had reached the end of the elms, and ahead of her, surrounded by black fields flecked with the white and wetness of the sleet, was her cottage. At first Bridget imagined that there was a faint line of smoke coming from the chimney, but then she supposed that without food there would have been no need for fire. At this point she halted the images rushing through her head, and, deciding that a fire would at least give a little warmth, she reinstated the smoke coming from the chimney. At the same time she wondered who would have lit the fire: was it Micheál? Was it Micheál's mother with the help of the children? Was someone stirring the watery gruel in the pot above the fire, or was the pot empty, and everyone was waiting for Catherine to return home and feed them? Bridget guessed that everyone was waiting.

Many landowners had been waiting as well. Bridget remembered Timothy telling her how many of them had secretly thanked the famine for clearing the land. Once the survivors had been shipped elsewhere, cottages and stone walls were knocked down, and what had once been a chequerboard of small grey dwellings and tiny fields became large agricultural estates that were more profitable and easier to run.

As a child, Bridget puzzled over a very hazy image of men with big sticks chasing people towards the water. She had never seen a proper boat, though she had once seen a painting of a ship in full sail, and she imagined that it would be wonderful to be able to travel on something so beautiful. As an adult, she understood that sadness and anger would have overshadowed the wonder, and she doubted that the people were at all awed by the vessel that was to take them so far away from their beloved homeland.

Although the O'Connors were not among the people being piled on to ships, Bridget guessed that Micheál would have been angry at everything happening around him. Catherine, on the other hand, would have said very little, accepting the frightening situation with a grim kind of resignation.

Watching the evictions and understanding that people were being scattered across the globe, Bridget's grandparents would most likely have feared that the same would happen to them, if they did not die beforehand. They would not have wanted to leave their farm, small though it was: Ballinure and Tipperary was all they had ever known.

Outside it was already dark, and Bridget was now unable to see anything beyond the window. The darkness had come quickly: the sky turned red and orange, and only minutes later, when she once again looked out of the window, it was dark. The shadows had been eaten up by the darkness, and all she could see was her own reflection in the glass. She automatically lifted her hand and attempted to bring some order to her unruly hair. She was exhausted and hungry, but overriding both of these basic states was a heavy cloud of uneasiness. Compared with the uneasiness, hunger and exhaustion seemed paltry concerns.

Given that her own future was an immense cloud of terror and uncertainty, Bridget understood how the idea of having to move beyond Ireland would have been extremely daunting for her grandparents. While trying to keep focused on other things, Catherine was no doubt hoping that the prospect of either death or emigration would fade and, more importantly, disappear. In the same way that her grandmother prayed that the blight would end, that there would soon be plenty to eat and that there would not be any reason to move anywhere, Bridget was praying that the past could be miraculously changed and that the future she was fearing would simply disintegrate.

In both cases, her grandmother's and her own, Death was on sitting on the other side of the scales, and Death was not interested in prayers, compromise or secret deals. It would not have taken long for Catherine to have seen that they had no choice: the decision was not theirs to make. For a while, she might have tried to keep Micheál positive by telling him that things would soon change, that the next crop would be clean, that life would soon revert to normal. But deep down she would have known that no one can pit themselves against Death.

63

For a moment Bridget wondered if it was the thought of Death that had influenced all her decision-making during the past twenty-four hours. She did not want to die, but her actions and their consequences seemed to be propelling her in a direction that could have no happy ending. Death was obviously heavier in the scales, and there was nothing she could do about it. She could try to convince herself that she could run away from the consequences, but there could only ever be one outcome.

She paused in her train of thought, reflecting for a moment on the next life. She had been told that it was better than the one she was already living, but as far as she could see, there was no logic behind the belief: it was simply a theory, a conjecture, something that one believed without question. Were she to begin pulling apart the threads that were part of the belief, she suspected that she would find too many question marks, and she did not want to have to confront more uncertainties. Not now, when she was being harassed by doubts coming at her from all angles, and when she had no idea what the life she was actually living might hold for her.

Regardless of the presence or absence of logic, she wanted to believe that death was simply a gateway to something sublime. Words like *paradise*, *eternal bliss* and even *heaven* ran through her mind, filling it with images of soft, white clouds and celestial beings. Closing her mind to all the questions, she concentrated on what she had been promised: everlasting happiness was the reward for an earthly life of hardship, humility and obedience. Then she thought about the word *hardship* and everything connected to it. Had she forfeited her share of the heavenly happiness and bliss? Would she end up in the terrifying, never-ending fires that were hell?

The thought of what she had done once again pushed its way to the centre of her mind, and she regretted having let herself move off on a tangent of punishment and hellfire. She knew that she needed to remove as many negative thoughts and images as possible, if she were ever to return to something that equated with normal. Thinking about raging flames and devils holding pitchforks was not going to help her find the equilibrium she so desperately needed and desired.

While attempting to force her thoughts on to another path, part of her mind refused to let go of the terrifying idea of what might be before her. Surely God would be understanding? Surely He knew that life was not always easy, that it went up and down and swept around in unexpected curves and circles? It was never straightforward. People themselves were not always straightforward. Life was unpredictable: things happened and no one need be at fault. She revised her last thought, wondering whether she might actually be wrong and whether there must always be someone who was at fault.

Her thoughts were turning up too many worrying digressions. Was someone to blame for the tragedy in Ireland? Was there some connection between her grandparents' starvation and her present anxiety? She doubted that her situation could be compared with the persistent hunger, the suffering and the thousands of people dying without reason. Or could it? She was not sure: both situations eventually led to the same negative outcome.

Did her grandmother ever feel like giving up completely, reasoning that death for herself and her family would at least open the gateway to a better life? Or did she continue trusting in God, hoping that the worst would soon be behind them and that life in Tipperary and, indeed, the rest of Ireland would soon return to normal?

Letting her thoughts wind around the concepts of hope and despair, she decided that the will to live, the desire to hold on to life, however miserable that life might be, was possibly stronger than blind acceptance of a better life somewhere beyond all the suffering and pain. She knew that she wanted live. She did not want to die. It did not matter what the next life might be like, this was the only life she knew, and she wanted to hold on to it.

Echoes from the past, present anxieties and confused images of Catherine, Micheál and the rest of the family finally began to recede as Bridget slowly slipped into an exhausted sleep. As she was falling from consciousness to another state where there were no images, no dreams, nothing, she decided that God's hands had been tied regarding the man-made calamity that had spread out over Ireland more than fifty years ago. She also decided that His hands had been tied concerning everything that had recently happened in Gilgandra. It need not have been a case of His lacking the time or inclination to intervene: it might simply have been that it was something well and truly beyond His area of jurisdiction.

She was still thinking about God and the extent of His powers while wondering whether things might have been different for her grandparents, and everyone else in Ireland, had O'Connell's campaign to repeal the union between England and Ireland actually succeeded. Then, as she as she was losing her grip on consciousness, she decided that had O'Connell succeeded, had there been no famine and had the O'Connors not needed to leave Ireland, her father would never have met her mother, she would not have been born and she would not now be sitting on a train, rushing towards an uncertain and frightening future.

Chapter Six

Without actually able to put her feelings and thoughts into so many words, Bridget regarded herself as a kind of pivot, something like the hinge at the centre of a see-saw. Being the middle child, with three siblings above her and another three below, she had always felt that it was only natural that she should have a different, individual perspective on things. As far as she was concerned, she was not exactly the same as her siblings.

Whether she was correct in this assumption was difficult to say: in spite of the limited opportunities that defined women, she liked to think of herself as independent. She could be restless at times, occasionally even defiant, but she was not rebellious. At times she had a yearning to go beyond accepted barriers, though having such a yearning was one thing, acting on it was another thing altogether. Most of the time her desire for better and more varied prospects for women remained carefully concealed just below the surface of what she, and everyone around her, would have considered normal behaviour. The fact that the desire existed at all was, perhaps, why she saw herself as somewhat separate and different.

Her father, Patrick Francis O'Connor, began life on the small island of Guernsey, and only a week later found himself on a ship heading for the ends of the earth. With him were his parents, Micheál and Catherine, and his siblings, Timothy, John and five-year-old Gertrude. The O'Connors, after six years on Guernsey, had decided to abandon the northern hemisphere, leaving behind them on Guernsey, Mary, who had died at birth in 1852, and in the small graveyard at Ballinure, their first daughter, Grace.

Depending on which uncle's version Bridget chose to believe, the voyage took anywhere between three months and forever. As a child, Bridget had listened with fascination to elaborate descriptions of the endless expanses of water that could change colour from black to bright blue to emerald green, and how, at times, this water could rise up above the sides of the ship and threaten to join with the sky, and how the ship would then be thrown hither and thither. In her mind's eye, she pictured the creek behind their home and the small branches being swept away by the flooded waters after heavy rain.

The uncles also talked of the strange noises made by the ship's timbers, rigging and sails, noises that sometimes sounded like songs sung in a language that only the ship knew. Young Bridget decided that a ship that sang was something very special indeed, and she imagined sad songs, filled with longing and even regret, but also carefree, happy songs, overflowing with promises of a new, exciting life. However, from what she understood, it was not often that any of the O'Connors actually saw the ocean or the billowing sails or heard the songs the ship was singing: most of the time, they were confined to the bowels of the ship with at least another hundred souls, many of whom were terrified, sick or just plain miserable. Bridget gathered that conditions below decks must have been disastrous, and it was possible that Catherine, with a newborn to care for, would have wondered many times about the wisdom in journeying to a place that was so far away. Even before arriving in Sydney, it is likely that she was convinced that they should have either remained on Guernsey or returned to Tipperary.

When they finally arrived in Sydney in early January 1855, the sun was glaring down upon them from a cloudless blue sky. The sun and the unmarred skies had followed the ship all the way up the east coast of

Australia, boasting about summer in the southern hemisphere. The burning heat had forced everyone, even those who had been free to walk around the ship, below decks, while it made the hold, if possible, more suffocating than usual, accentuating not only the lack of space and comfort but also the assortment of smells accumulated during the long and arduous months at sea.

Sydney itself was also unbelievably hot, and layered through the heat were swarms of irritating insects, many with wings and some with high-pitched voices that either complained or threatened or did a bit of both. Furthermore, a frustrating humidity caused sticky rivulets of perspiration to gather under clothing and on arms and faces, attracting many of the insects, and causing discomfort while sapping both energy and patience. Many newcomers, used to the gentle, soothing caresses of a northern summer, were unable to cope with such brutality. Some sought shade from trees ill-equipped to give them what they wanted; others remained in the shadowy darkness of their dwellings, helpless against the sun's penetrating heat.

The majority, unable to seek such dubious relief, continued with the work and activities expected of them, their focus on the respite that might, or might not, come with an evening wind change.

In the early years of the new century, and only shortly before his death, Timothy could still remember his mother's restrained, but unmistakable, lamentations on arrival at Port Jackson. After the couple of days needed for health checks, the completion of certificates of arrival and, finally, the long-awaited permission to disembark, they were eventually able to step off the ship. Catherine, however, had already made up her mind that Sydney actually was, as she had feared, the middle of nowhere, and had it been possible she would have gladly suffered an immediate return journey, if it could have reunited her with her beloved Ireland or, at the very least, Guernsey.

The O'Connors did not remain in Sydney for more than a couple of months, even though Catherine's preconceived conviction that the town was primitive and backward had been proven to be quite erroneous. As with all big towns and cities, there were streets inhabited by the wealthy and streets filled with those who had nothing. The streets for the affluent and those who believed themselves to be important, with imposing sandstone buildings, the newly established university and the many handsome carriages, gave the town a sense of stability and purpose, far from what the family had experienced on either Guernsey or in

Ireland. Nevertheless, Catherine held on to the image she had created in her head: the image of Europeans relegated to living in huts and lean-tos beyond the confines and the morals of modern society, while bartering for life's necessities and fighting to make ends meet. The impressive buildings may have managed to hide from others some of the things that Catherine feared, but for Catherine the things that could not always be seen were the only things that existed.

It was much later that Timothy understood that his mother's aversion to Sydney had very little to do with the place itself and was prompted by her deep-seated feelings of homesickness and the terrifying understanding that there could never ever be a way back.

Micheál's fondness for Ireland and Tipperary was also very strong, but he could not allow it to erase the fact that he owed something to God for the chance he had been given. After having narrowly avoided the graveyard in Ballinure, any life after the famine was a gift that could only be taken with a large amount of gratitude and humility. He could understand Catherine's frustration with the sticky, oven-like heat that forced its way inside clothing and which also filled dwelling places with a suffocating breath from hell, heat that never relented, not even at night, and which, together with dust and small black flies, made everyone's life a misery. He could even understand that she missed the green of Tipperary, the cold mists of autumn and the explosion of summer scents when the woodbine, the elderberry and the chamomile were in flower. Most of all he knew that she missed being able to visit either of her daughters' graves, and being able to reassure both children that they were loved and still not forgotten. Micheál understood all of this, but there was no way his wife's longing and homesickness could compete with the alternative: a hastily dug hole in the ground in a cold churchyard.

Gold had recently been discovered west of Sydney and once Micheál O'Connor heard about the precious metal that was evidently there for the taking — some accounts told of nuggets strewn about randomly on the ground — and he understood that all of this was happening in a place not so far from where he was living, he was unable to let go of the image. As far as he was concerned, it was an image studded with possibilities.

He was sceptical about the nuggets lying on the ground, waiting to be picked up, and after the years of stone-breaking on Guernsey, he was not sure that he wanted to start digging for gold, even if there was a slight chance of a large reward. But with so many people moving to the goldfields, he was certain that there had to be some other opportunity for him there, if only he could work out what it was.

Then, only a few weeks after arriving in Sydney, he crossed paths with a Rory O'Rourke, originally from Cork, who had already discovered the nature of that other opportunity. Rory, late twenties, single, with two missing teeth, a nose that had been broken sometime in the past and a full black beard, had migrated five years earlier. Then, after stints in Sydney as stable boy, stonecutter, tree feller and dock worker, he moved out west for a couple of years. As he said to Micheál, gold diggers got thirsty and they needed pubs, and pubs were flourishing businesses in the central west. Micheál decided that Rory probably had the answer he was looking for, and agreed to enter into a partnership with him. Within a week, the O'Connors and Rory were on their way to Orange.

Chapter Seven

There had been no time to contact Sarah. When Bridget was pushing things into her bag in the dark hours of the night, she had not been thinking of Sarah. She had no proper plan. She had not been thinking of anyone or any place in particular: her one and only thought had been to leave, to get as far away as possible. It was not until the house was well behind her, and she was walking towards the town, the moon shining a pale, wavering path across the paddocks, that she suddenly thought of the train station and the train and, finally, Sydney. Sarah would be able to help her: she would know what to do.

Forethought had not been part of the equation, but by the time the train climbed the mountains and began to draw closer to Sydney, Bridget had calmed down considerably, and her thoughts dared to delve into some of the events of the past couple of days. She picked through the many images, discarding some of them at once as though they were hot coals from the fire; others she retained for a brief moment, attempting to look at them from other, different, perspectives. Carefully. She had already been forced to acknowledge that she had possibly acted too hastily, and now her thoughts returned reluctantly to that idea.

If things had been different, if there had been time, she would have written to her sister, and she would have tried to explain. But, if things had been different, there would have been no need for her to have acted as she did, and there would not have been anything to explain. Trying for a moment to force herself into an unlikely space where the motivating events were different and where time was not a factor, she was aware just how ridiculous she was being and, in an effort to rid herself of all thoughts and images, she wrapped her arm tightly around the sleeping child next to her, breathing in his innocence and the reality of his presence.

There was far too much rushing around in her head: everything seemed to be colliding or, at the very least, falling down and breaking up. In an impossible situation, like the one she was now trying to escape, she was certain that Sarah would know what to do. The thought that she might be able to share her anxiety and fear with someone who would understand her brought tears of self-pity and relief to her eyes. She was almost beginning to believe that everything would work out all right after all.

She had never been to Sydney before, and she was overwhelmed by the size of Central Station. From where she was standing, the building itself seemed enormous. Like her grandmother before her she was intimidated, not so much by being confronted with the ends of the earth as by coming face to face with physical realities she never before knew existed.

Having stepped down from the train, she remained on the platform, looking first upwards and then in all directions, absorbing the images: the physicality of the building, the trains approaching and leaving the many platforms, the scattered groups of people and the station workers with their blue uniforms and their sense of importance. As well as all the images, there were the sounds: sounds of whistles and steam and the trains themselves, station staff calling loudly to each other, passengers talking, luggage being moved and the noise of shoes and boots reverberating against hard surfaces. Everywhere there was the strong smell of smoke and asphalt and people.

She noticed the grey and white pigeons flying in long graceful arcs beneath the dome or foraging along the platforms, avoiding people's feet. Occasionally there was a brown pigeon, the same as the others, yet different. She could not help but think of herself as a brown pigeon in relation to all the people around her: she was the same, yet different.

Her thoughts refused to leave the birds, and she thought that this was their home; this was how they lived. They did not have to worry about what happened yesterday or the day before yesterday. They were not concerned with what might happen tomorrow. She added a footnote to her earlier thought about herself and the brown pigeon, deciding that she might be the brown pigeon in relation to everyone around her, but she was not like the pigeons: she was extremely concerned about what was likely to happen tomorrow and, indeed, any time after tomorrow.

Her thoughts having finally moved from the pigeons to herself, she considered the fact that it was now more than twenty-four hours since she slammed the door behind her. Time had not been an important detail during those hours: it had simply existed in the background, silently noting and recording her anguish and decision-making.

Thinking about the events that had led to her being in Sydney, she lifted Joseph on to her hip and adjusted the bag hanging from her shoulder. Slowly she walked towards the Grand Concourse and station exit, where she was relieved to see that there was a world beyond the maze of platforms and railway lines.

It was still very early in the morning, but the sky already had a look of unabashed brightness that usually predicted a hot summer's day. She was stiff and tired after sitting up all night, and although Joseph had slept soundly for most of the journey he now clung to her, looking lost and unhappy. Bridget knew that he was also hungry, and she was hoping that it was not far to Sarah's place. She pulled her fingers through her son's hair, attempting to bring a little order to his straw-coloured curls, and told him that soon they would be at Aunt Sarah's. He had never met Sarah and would have no idea who she was, but for Bridget his knowing or not knowing was of very little importance.

While thinking about Joseph and the impossibility of his knowing anything about his aunt, it occurred to her, for the first time since she had hurriedly decided to travel to Sydney, that Sarah might not be able to take them in. Even worse, she might not *want* to take them in. Though, on second thought, Bridget felt that Sarah not wanting them to stay was implausible. She knew that Sarah was on her own, her husband, Oswald, having sailed some weeks back. She made an effort to shift her thinking to a more positive place, and tried to focus on the slight chance that her timing, given Oswald's recent departure, might not be that awkward after all.

She had committed Sarah's address to memory: *Wells Street, Redfern,* and asked one of the station workers for directions. He touched his cap and told her to turn right into Eddy Avenue and then right again at Elizabeth Street.

Bridget noted how the confusion from within the station managed to spill over beyond the building itself. Beyond the station, she could already see the many carriages and trams and people in Central Square. She was only used to Gilgandra and Molong, and even Orange, where streets had a beginning and an end and things did not run together in an impossible mess. She began to wonder how she would be able to navigate her way though all the likely obstacles between her and Wells Street.

The man was possibly aware of what Bridget could be thinking, because he suggested that she take the tram.

'It's not so far, ma'am,' he said, 'and it won't cost more than a penny. Take yerself across to Elizabeth Street, there'll be someone there who can set you a'right.' He smiled briefly, the smile of someone in uniform handing out instructions.

Bridget heaved Joseph higher up on her hip, thanked the man and began to walk towards Eddy Avenue. She tried to remember if Sarah had ever mentioned either Eddy Avenue or Elizabeth Street, but her mind had moved into an area where only basic, urgent matters were of any importance, and whether or not she had heard the names of particular streets was definitely not classed as urgent. As the man had indicated, Elizabeth Street was close by, and it did not take her long to find the tram stop.

Morning was becoming slightly more pronounced by the time she alighted from the tram a few stops further south, and if she had not been so exhausted and apprehensive, she might have enjoyed being part of the city waking up. While she was aware of life beginning to stir around her, she was unable to completely remove her attention from what had already happened and could not be changed. In spite of her attempt to remain calm and positive, a certain uneasiness about her sister's possible reaction, something she had not previously considered, was beginning to expand exponentially.

The house was similar to most of the other terrace houses along the street: two or three storeys, narrow, red or grey brick, occasionally stucco-covered, all standing wall to wall with their neighbours. Most of them had a run-down, tired appearance; a few had a fence of sorts, cutting them off from the street, defining a boundary between public and private; and many had balconies on the top storeys, protected by iron lacework. Several of the fences were broken and not all of the iron lacework was intact. Some of the houses had curtains at the windows; others had no curtains and from those there was often litter spilling out of doorways, creating an unwanted connection between the house and the dusty street.

The house where Sarah lived was only two storeys, and it had no fence drawing a line between the communal and the individual. Nevertheless, Bridget was relieved to see that it seemed to be well-tended and clean.

She hesitated for a moment in front of the heavy front door, to the left of which there was an excessively curtained window. When she cautiously tried the doorknob, she noticed that the door was not locked, so, after a few moments of further indecision, she opened it and walked in.

She found herself in an unlit hallway. Halfway along the hall a solid, dark timber staircase rose up into the darkness above, clinging to the right wall of the building, while the passageway continued past the stairs into the darkness beyond. Peering past the stairs she could almost make out what she imagined was the back of the building. On her immediate left she noted a door that probably belonged to the room with the heavily curtained window.

There were indefinite, stale cooking smells that had affixed themselves to both the darkness and the walls, and she could hear noises that could only belong to people in the building, but she could not see anyone. She wondered vaguely just how many people lived in the house: Sarah had never written to her about such things, but she decided, given the circumstances, it was hardly important.

Bridget put Joseph down on the floor with a small inner sigh of relief and spent a couple of minutes trying to work out how she was going to find her sister's flat. Then she remembered that Sarah had written that they lived on the top floor. Taking a deep breath, she gripped Joseph's hand firmly with one hand and, her bag still hanging from her shoulder, slowly ascended the staircase.

The steps were wide, and in the centre was a carpet runner held in place with a metal rod at the back of each step. Bridget noted that the carpet had once been dark blue with a red and green pattern, but the colours had faded, and in places the carpet was now almost threadbare. An unessential thought about worn carpet being dangerous ran through her head.

But, she thought, lots of things could be dangerous, even fatal: her growing misgivings about the decisions she had made, and about what she intended to do, were multiplying by the second, and she was very close to turning around and leaving the house. She seriously wished that she had thought things through more carefully, but she had come this far, she desperately needed her sister, she had nowhere else to go, and, as far as she could see, she clearly had no possibility of turning back.

Chapter Eight

Bridget had always felt especially close to both Sarah and Thomas. Her eldest sibling, Martin Boyd O'Connor, seven years older, had been followed by four girls: Anne, Sarah, Bridget and Catherine. In 1895, Daniel was born and two years later, Thomas.

Although the siblings were in many ways different from each other — Martin was reserved, Daniel talkative, Anne overbearing, Catherine shy — and although they most probably did not always understand or agree with each other, there was still something that tied them together. Should any of them be faced with opposition from some external quarter, they would usually display a united front even if they were not always completely certain about what it was they were defending.

Martin did not approve of Bridget calling the War 'England's War'. As far as he was concerned, the War belonged to Australia just as much as England, and as an Australian he felt that he had an obligation to defend his country. Things were different in Australia, he said. Even if people claimed to be Irish or English, Catholic or Protestant, they were basically Australian, and the War was a chance for them to show that they were unified. Had he been at all able, he considered that it would have been his patriotic duty to fight the Germans, not for the King of England but for the country that had given his family a chance for a new life.

That Australia had been automatically included in Britain's war declaration with Germany did not seem to worry Martin, though it was this automatic inclusion that made Bridget refer to the War as 'England's War'. Bridget argued no matter how unified or disunited they might be politically and religiously, if they wanted to call themselves Australians, they should have the freedom, as citizens of a separate country, to make their own decisions about something as serious as going to war.

Daniel did not deny that Bridget had a point, and he agreed that Australia should have been given a chance to state her own position regarding the War, but he tended to lean more towards Martin's idea that involvement in the War was a way of showing thanks for everything the country had given them. He completely backed his brother's suggestion that by accepting such responsibility the country showed unity, adding that it displayed a certain maturity as well. Nevertheless, even though he could accept most of Martin's argument, and although he agreed that they were all Australians now, he felt that he could not just throw off his Irishness as if it were a garment to be discarded. His Irish-Catholic background was part of him in the same way as the name O'Connor was part of him. Thomas nodded his head and smiled, but chose not to commit himself one way or the other.

Putting Thomas' apparent hesitation to one side, the discussions were usually long and oftentimes heated, with no real chance of anyone convincing anyone else to change their mind. It was simply a matter of everyone needing to be able to articulate thoughts that seemed so obvious to themselves even if they were unacceptable to others. For Bridget it was not about convincing anyone: she simply hated the idea of men killing and getting killed. She had the whole British Empire, Martin and even Daniel against her, but she was quite certain that she was right. She liked to remind her brothers that war was completely unethical, and quite apart from the ethics, she believed that it was written somewhere in the Bible, 'Thou shalt not kill'.

Martin may well have sided with those who felt that Australia should be playing an active part in the War, and it was obvious that he saw it as his duty as an Australian to enlist, but to his great disappointment he knew that any recruitment officer would have rejected his application without giving it a second look. Although his farm and his ever-expanding family could have excused his not joining up, had his feelings about the War been similar to Bridget's, he was not looking for excuses: he wanted to be part of the war effort. To his great frustration this was not to be: a nasty fall from a horse a couple of years earlier had made him less than suitable for military duty. The fall, which could have killed him, had left him with a leg broken in several places. The leg finally healed, but the breaks knitted badly, and although he was eventually able to walk again, he did so with an obvious limp. It was the limp that came to identify him: people might not have always known his name, but they all knew the man who limped. With such an impediment, he knew that it was useless for him to even consider enlisting, not when men in perfect physical condition but with bad teeth were being knocked back. It made him feel inadequate and inferior, and somehow lacking as a man. When he was arguing with his siblings, he often suspected that he had no right to defend something that could never be part of his reality.

Then came the Easter Rising in April 1916, and after that many things changed. New perspectives came into play, and many began to question with whom and what one's loyalties lay. Discussions between the O'Connors allowed for more accommodating words like *perhaps* and *possibly*. Those who had wanted to keep things separate began to get an inkling that being Australian did not, could not, obliterate the fact that one was also Irish. The idea of automatic inclusion in Britain's affairs no longer seemed quite so indisputable: not everyone necessarily supported Britain emotionally even if they supported Australia. As the discussion moved from loyalty to questions of equality, the O'Connors had to admit that their Irishness had stamped them as second-class citizens long before 1916.

While the events of the Rising hovered in the back of her mind, Bridget thought of Martin, his untidy moustache, his receding hairline and his limp. She thought of the timber cottage and the few acres of land he owned outside Molong. She thought of his wife, a pale, red-haired Irish girl from Limerick, and all their children, her nephews and nieces. Thinking of his very strict moral compass and his clear-cut interpretation of right and wrong, she had to admit that everything — ethics, morals, life itself — was most probably dependent on individual insights and judgements. Everyone was right, at the same time as they were very likely all wrong. She was aware that, depending on the perspective, even she was wrong at the same time as she was right. It all depended on who was doing the viewing and who was making a judgement.

She admired Martin's sense of patriotism, even if she felt it was misguided. Thinking about patriotism and all it implied, she decided that James had felt much the same as Martin as regards the ethics of war. She had to admit to herself that James and her brother shared many similar compasses and almost identical ways of interpreting good and evil. They had never had much to do with each other, and now they never would.

From Martin and James her thoughts moved to Daniel, and she wondered, as she had wondered so many times over the last few months, where he was and whether or not he was still alive.

Chapter Nine

There were two flights of stairs; where they met, on the half landing, Bridget noticed a door to another flat. She could hear muted voices and sounds from behind the door, but feeling confident that her sister lived on the top floor, she continued up the second flight of stairs.

At the top of the stairs there was a landing and to her right there was a door. She closed her eyes for a moment and then knocked several times. After a period of time that seemed interminable but which in reality was probably no more than seconds, the door opened, and Sarah was standing there, a look of amazement slowly spreading across her face. For one short instant, solidified in time like a still image, her hand holding on to the door, her body poised somewhere between action and inaction, Sarah said nothing.

Then the instant passed, and she moved towards her sister. 'Bridget! Is it you? Is it *really* you? It can't possibly be you. Or is it?' She was obviously overwhelmed, flustered, confused. She said: 'But, how did you know? How *could* you have known? So quickly.' She stretched out her hand and took Bridget by the arm. Then, seeing Joseph, she let go of her sister's arm and bent down and lifted the child up, carrying him inside. As she closed the door behind the three of them, she said, 'I would never have… '

Bridget did not know what to say. She had done what she set out to do: she had reached Sydney and now she was standing in her sister's flat. Everything from the past couple of days descended upon her in a rush. She was totally exhausted, and the flat, the building, everything, was suddenly so grey and horrible and depressing. She wished that she were somewhere else. Anywhere at all, but not standing in her sister's kitchen filled with the morning's half-light filtered through a grimy window.

Now that she was where she thought she had wanted to be, she was quite sure that she had made the wrong decision. As the awareness sank in, she felt like a balloon that had been forcibly emptied of its air. All at once she was certain that she should have stayed where she was, or she should have gone to her parents in Molong. Coming to Sydney had only complicated everything and made it all ever so much worse.

She looked at her sister and was taken aback by her appearance: had she been ill? Was it Oswald? Had something happened about which she knew nothing? She thought again of Oswald, and remembered that he left Australia in November or December. She stopped her thoughts from running in such a direction: she did not want to think the unthinkable.

Sarah set Joseph down on the floor, kissing him as she did so. Bridget was aware that she should say something to remove an obvious misunderstanding: what was it that she was supposed to have known? But she had no idea where to begin. All she really wanted to do was to explain why she and Joseph were on her sister's doorstep. All she wanted was for her sister to understand and then tell her what she should do.

The present, with its many obvious question marks and its feeling of nameless, unexpressed disaster, was making her wish that she was somewhere else. Anywhere at all. She knew that she was being selfish, but she did not want to have to involve herself in someone else's problems. Not even her sister's. Not just then. She wished that all difficult and unexplainable things could simply disappear, and that life could be uninteresting and normal again. Then she wondered if her life had been anything like 'normal' these past few months. She took a deep breath: she doubted that this was the time to talk about why she *really* was in Sydney.

As Sarah turned to face her, Bridget noticed that she hesitated for a moment. Was she, like Bridget herself, unsure of what to do or say next? Was she being pulled between a need to have someone who knew and a need for no one to know anything? In that short moment while no one moved, and the scene took on the appearance of a painting hanging on someone's sitting-room wall, Bridget became slightly more aware of the space. She registered the walls covered with a brown floral-patterned wallpaper and the short sofa against the far wall. There was a bright, multicoloured rug spread over the sofa, at one end of which there was a large, rectangular box with its lid partly open. She ran her eyes quickly around the room, noting the table in the centre, the bureau to the right of the door and the one window looking over what was possibly the back courtyard.

On the wall opposite the window, she glimpsed part of a second room through a door that was slightly ajar, and from the light leaking through the doorway, and from what she had seen of the outside of the house, she knew that there would be doors opening on to the balcony with the iron lacework.

In the few moments it took for Bridget to absorb her surroundings, it occurred to her that Sarah might have been sleeping. Although she was aware of a feeling of discomfort at having disturbed her sister so early in the morning, and a feeling of anxiety that was rooted to some unexplained upset or trouble into which she had inadvertently stepped, she was at the same time strangely, almost ludicrously, comforted by the fact that the living room looked reasonably well cared for, with cloths on both the table and the bureau, and several pictures on the wall. Small, easily forgotten, unessential things, she thought. Unessential, especially at the moment.

Bridget broke the spell of the painting and sat down on one of the chairs near the table. She was watching her sister remove Joseph's shoes, but her mind was elsewhere. She was desperately disappointed. She had spent hours willing herself into her sister's arms, hoping for her advice, her understanding and her love. Now, when she was finally in Sydney, in her sister's flat, she could see that nothing of what she had hoped for was likely to happen: Sarah obviously had problems of her own, she was not in a position to offer love or understanding. Bridget tried to banish the thought that she really wanted to be somewhere else.

While Sarah opened a tin above the stove, lifting out a couple of dripping biscuits for Joseph, Bridget reprimanded herself mentally. It was not Sarah's fault that things were the way they were: Sarah had not asked her to come to Sydney. She knew nothing about James and nothing at all about her sister's expectations.

Bridget was still trying to come to terms with her disappointment as Sarah gently placed the small boy, the two biscuits clenched in one hand, on the coloured rug on the sofa. Then picking up the box and pushing the lid firmly back into place, she disappeared with it into the other room.

Moments later, when Sarah returned to the kitchen and sat down, Bridget, wanting to obliterate the unnecessary space that had for some reason pushed in between them, stood up. Awkwardly, she moved closer to her sister, bent down and silently embraced her, holding her tightly, willing all known and unknown problems to some place far away. Finally she said, 'What has happened, Sarah? You must tell me. Is it Oswald, or is it something else?'

The anxieties that had plagued Bridget for hours had been unceremoniously pushed into some dark corner, like old clothes that no one wanted to wear any more. She knew that they were still there, but her focus had been forced elsewhere. Turning her back on the dark corner, she tried to forget the relief and the comfort for which she had been hoping.

Sarah, slightly shorter than her sister with the same thick black hair tamed into two untidy plaits hanging over her shoulders, moved uneasily out of Bridget's embrace and attempted to smile. As the almost-smile turned into a sigh, she looked over towards the window and shrugged, and Bridget thought about the plaits that would normally have been twisted skilfully around Sarah's head. She closed her eyes for a moment, desperately hoping that when she opened them again her fun-loving, beautiful sister would have returned. It was becoming very clear to her that she was not the only one for whom the world was threatening to break up into small pieces.

Chapter Ten

Patrick Francis O'Connor stood behind the bar in the almost empty pub in Molong. Everything he had ever known had been caught and stored between walls that constitute pubs: in Molong, Cudal, Bathurst, Orange, Dubbo.

He grew up in pubs, the first being in Bathurst, where Micheál discovered that Rory was right about 'the opportunity' out west and the hundreds of miners and would-be miners needing the occasional and the more-than-occasional drink. Then, after a couple of years, Rory tired of pubs and moved north, chasing some other dream, and Micheál moved his family to Lambing Flat. The anti-Chinese problem, constantly overflowing into riots, finally gave him no choice but to move again, and the family settled in Orange and then Dubbo and finally Cudal, where, in the 1880s, first Catherine and then Micheál breathed their last.

His large hands moved restlessly along the ale-stained counter, pushing a grey-tinged cloth over some wet spots he had missed earlier. He traced his fingers around the distinctive grain patterns in the wood, and then picked up a couple of stray glasses. He was constantly on the lookout for something to do. The shadowy interior of the pub offered welcome relief from the intense, white heat outside, but the relief came with a heavy feeling of late-afternoon, grey ennui, which seeped in through the not-perfectly-clean windows, sidling past the few rays of sunshine that had dared to push their way into the semi-darkness. As Patrick let his gaze move slowly over the plain wooden stools just beyond the counter and then across the rough timber floorboards all the way to the heavy, wide door, he could not help but be aware of the inertia that seemed to cling to everything in the room. He raised his eyes to the walls, the lower half covered with vertical timber panels, the upper half painted white like the ceiling above him. Several imposing, almost-black beams obliterated parts of the ceiling, which was supported on similar posts affixed to the walls. The pub's skeleton, he would sometimes say, thinking briefly of people inside whales.

But on this particular day, he was not thinking of skeletons or whales. Wrapped in a cloud of weariness, his thoughts were still dissecting the letter Mary had received from Sarah, telling her about Oswald. Somewhere on the edge of his thoughts, he was also thinking about Bridget.

He thought and worried about all his children, but not at all in the same way as Mary did. If he should ever have been asked to analyse the way he related to anyone in his family, he would most likely have contended that men were usually more pragmatic and less emotional than women. If at times he seemed detached from what was going on around him, his perceived indifference was superficial only: he regarded himself as an emotional man who occasionally had difficulties managing and directing his feelings. Without being able to put his feelings into words, some small part of him was thankful that Mary was there to hold the family together.

Relationships and everything else that was mixed up with the words *love* and *affection* was women's business, he thought as he gave the counter a final wipe before dropping the cloth on to the shelf underneath. Women were constructed differently, and they were able to handle such things. Was it emotional connectedness or was it simply an awareness? He stopped at the word *awareness* and pondered it for a few seconds before returning to Sarah and Bridget.

From Bridget his thoughts were only a hair's breadth away from James, and he thought of Gilgandra and wondered whether James was off droving again or whether he was now working closer to home. It was months since he last saw either James or Bridget. His thoughts were drawn back to the word *awareness*, and he wondered why. What was it about James that irritated him? Was it the fact that James was an outsider, an Englishman *and* a Protestant? Or was it simply that he did not understand him?

He tried to remember if he had always felt like this about James, or whether it was a feeling that had grown over the last couple of years. The more he thought, the more he believed that the James who went off to war in 1914 was not the same James who came back in 1915. For a few moments he pondered the idea, deciding that it was more than likely the latter James who was the cause of his annoyance.

His eyes moved aimlessly around the pub, but came to a stop when they fell upon the several small paintings on the far wall. Although he could not pick out the details from where he was standing, he knew the paintings off by heart: they were paintings of home.

It was Fergus who painted them. He came into the pub a couple of years back, on his way from nowhere to anywhere. He had been in Victoria and then on the road for several months with nothing to show for it. Patrick took pity on him and hired him as a general handyman, even though he really had no need for anyone extra. Fergus, thin as a black snake, with a head of orange hair, lived in the small room behind the storeroom out the back. It was not much bigger than the canvas bed and the straight-backed chair it housed, but in return for Patrick's generosity, Fergus painted the four paintings that were now hanging on the wall in the pub. Green hills and small white stone cottages and even smaller white black-faced sheep. 'A real artist, he was,' Patrick would say to anyone who wanted to listen, 'and he lived here, in this very pub.'

That was at least two years ago, and Fergus had long since moved on towards Queensland, or that was where he had said he was headed. Patrick had not heard anything from him, but then again, he had never really expected to. As he looked across at the paintings, he wondered where Fergus was now.

Although he wanted to think of the paintings as depictions of home, he knew that home was nothing like the paintings. Home was a place where green was always sandwiched between dry and dusty and was completely dependent on the rains that often did not arrive. He believed that the sheep could be more or less the same, although he was not completely sure. He had never lived in Ireland; he had never seen the green hills or the white stone cottages.

He knew that he had been born on Guernsey on one of the first days of October 1854, and he also knew that when he was only a few days old he left the small Channel island with his parents and three siblings, never to return. However, any memory he pretended to have of Guernsey, or even Ireland, had to be a memory filtered through the memories of others. As the years passed, these memories had been subtly changed, added to and embroidered.

His father had often told him how the steamer bringing them from Waterford had docked at Saint Peter Port harbour on an October morning in 1848. Micheál said it had been half-dark and cold, and that there had been a strong wet wind blowing. In spite of the weather, he had scrambled up on to the deck to take a first look at their new home. Ten-year-old, and fifteen-year-old and even twenty-year-old Patrick never really questioned whether it had been raining or not on that morning so long ago. At all stages of his life he was simply fascinated by the picture that had stuck in his imagination: his father pressed up against the deckhouse, looking out across the black water at something completely new and foreign.

On a couple of occasions, Micheál talked to his son about the grey stone buildings, clustered close together, clinging to the harbour, looking out across the water. He explained how the land, following the curve of the harbour, rose very slightly behind the tightly packed buildings before reaching up to the plateau which formed the centre of the island. Beyond the harbour, in both directions, the coastline became more rugged with steep cliffs falling down from the plateau above.

When the O'Connors arrived on Guernsey in the autumn of 1848, the few trees around the harbour were already autumn-yellow, although in the half-light of early morning Micheál was unable to pick out any colours and, as he later told Patrick, his first impression of Saint Peter Port Harbour was grey and black. It was fairly clear to Patrick, even the young ten-year-old Patrick, that his father longed for Ireland and Tipperary, but Patrick himself had never known any other place than the Central West where he had grown up, so any emotions connected to the concept of longing or nostalgia for another place or country were not part of who he was.

If it was Micheál who told his youngest son about his first impressions of Guernsey as they entered Saint Peter Port, it was Patrick's older brother Timothy who talked about the chain of unreal days that stretched out between Ballinure and Guernsey.

Timothy was still a child when the family left Ireland, and his memories were later pit-holed with black spaces where there were no images and no memories. What he did remember was that his little sister Grace died in the spring of forty-eight, and, in spite of so many people already having died, many of whom he no longer remembered, he had not forgotten how his mother had slid into a frightening kind of melancholy where her normal resilience was replaced by a confusing passivity.

Years later, in an unusual burst of openness and sentimentality, Catherine confided in her eldest son that she fell into a deep, dark hole after Grace's death. For a long time she feared she would not be able to find her way up again, if a way up even existed: she had, after all, as a very last resort, asked God to take her family and not leave any of them to face further misery. But when her daughter died, she feared that she had been too hasty. Somehow the deep hole seemed an appropriate punishment for her loss of faith. Afterwards, she awaited the almost certain loss of the remainder of her family. After several weeks, unable to pull herself out of the hole and unable to thank God for having listened to her, she added an afterthought. She humbly explained that she had changed her mind, and she hoped that God would forgive her and have mercy on her poor wretched soul. She did not expect anything for herself, but could He possibly save the lives of her two remaining children and her husband?

When Timothy recounted this to Patrick, several years after their mother's death, he went on to say that both Catherine and Micheál would no doubt have despaired of things ever righting themselves again. Both their families had visibly disintegrated, with many names added to the list of the dead or to the long list of those who had already left the country. Catherine's only surviving sister had fled to Liverpool, and two of her brothers had left for America with their families. Catherine told her son how both his uncles had pleaded with her and Micheál to join them, but that was when Grace was still alive, and she was holding on to the stubborn belief that things were going to improve. More than anything she did not want to have to leave Ireland.

Standing in the bar and letting the many things that Timothy had told him float in and out of his conscious mind in no particular order, Patrick attempted to put himself in the place of his parents. It did not really work as he was unable to conjure up the suffocating closeness of death and despair, but from what he knew of his parents, he doubted that Catherine would have had much say in whether they should have moved or whether they should have stayed where they were. Thinking about it just a little longer, he felt that no matter what his mother wanted to do it was highly likely that by the time Grace died she would have had to admit that staying in Ireland was no longer possible.

While Patrick was thinking about paintings and Ireland and Guernsey, he let his gaze wander haphazardly around the room until it stopped for a moment on the two men at the far end of the bar. Although sitting near each other they were not together: one of them, a large man wearing a grubby singlet and dungarees, had finished drinking and was reading a newspaper that had been lying on the counter; the other, possibly a travelling salesman, had both hands around his glass of ale, still savouring some minute remnant of coolness.

There was no one else in the pub. Patrick turned around, leaning back against the counter while he looked at himself in the oval mirror hanging above the long shelf with glasses stacked in neat rows. A round, ruddy face looked back at him. With skin marked by many hot, Australian summers and far too much ale, his face was only one of the things telling him that he was already over sixty and that his life was all but over. He was not particularly tall, but he was solidly built. He raised his hands to his face, and noted that they were covered with welts and rough skin: working hands. His eyes were blue — not that he could see the colour in the dim light, but he knew, without needing to see — and his thick eyebrows and hair were already grey. He picked up a couple of glasses from the shelf and, turning around, placed them on the counter, thinking of all the years behind him and the very few in front of him.

He had been told that 1848 was rushing towards midsummer when what was already devastating became, if possible, even more devastating. His train of thought broke off as he thought about the word *midsummer*. Midsummer as he knew it was white-hot with cloudless blue skies and dry grass that muttered short staccato words when anyone walked on it. He found it difficult to imagine his parents' midsummer, the one with the green canopies, the coloured carpets and the smells of strange flowers like hawthorn and elder.

In early June of that dreadful year, in the middle of all this unimaginable colour and vitality, Micheál heard that he and the family were to be evicted. This was the end of everything: there was nowhere to run to, nowhere to take refuge. There was not much else to do but wait for the inevitable.

Then, when the fragile house of cards that had been Micheál and Catherine's reality for several years suddenly collapsed, and the world was unable to look any bleaker, God finally decided to listen to them.

Three more men came into the pub and the man who had been reading the newspaper left. Patrick served drinks, listened to some snippets of gossip, collected empty glasses and once again wiped down the counter. His thoughts veered away from his parents and Ireland and back to the letter that was now lying on the kitchen table.

That the letter about Oswald should have pushed his thoughts in the direction of Bridget and James, and even further back, was not so strange: Patrick had been around long enough to know that thoughts, and the patterns they form, were usually without rhyme or reason. Although he wanted to concentrate on what he had been told about Oswald, and the fact that his daughter Sarah was both distressed and worried, his thoughts, having settled briefly on Bridget, now moved on to James. James Jackson was the thought that he did not want to think, and yet it was the only thought that filled his mind.

He nodded to one of the three men who, having emptied his glass and pulled on his hat, lifted his hand in something that resembled a wave before walking towards the door, pushing it open and disappearing. The heat from outside began to rush in through the opening and then suddenly stopped as the door swung shut.

Patrick had to admit that he found James' tendency to keep to himself, listening without saying very much, unnerving. He quickly put aside a thought connecting such feelings of unease with James' cultural and religious background, and pushed everything backwards to his earlier suspicion that James had changed since he returned from 'over there'. He remembered hearing that he had been wounded: was it somewhere in the Middle East? He had been told that he could have died, but Bridget had mentioned a while back that James was much better and that he was working again. Patrick sighed, trying to summon up positive images of his son-in-law, trying to avoid the thought that there was something about the tall, fair-haired man with the ice-blue eyes that never failed to irk him.

He tried unsuccessfully to focus his thoughts on something else: James Jackson was really not his concern; people were as they were. Although Patrick did not want to accept that his dislike and irritation were possibly triggered by James' English background, he was unable to come up with any other reason. For a moment he watched a fly darting backwards and forwards in the half darkness. He flicked at it half-heartedly with the cloth, which he had retrieved from under the counter.

The word *awareness* crept back into his head: was it possible to be aware without understanding what it was that one was aware of? He might be aware of James Jackson's differences but that did not help him understand him. The fly landed on the counter a little to Patrick's right, and Patrick flicked at it again. This time he was successful, and he brushed the small carcass on to the floor.

Pouring refills for the men and a drink for himself, he tried to force his thoughts back to Oswald, but the thoughts would not stay tidily where he wanted them to stay. Even though he needed to be thinking about other things, he found himself back in 1914. He remembered how insistent James was, even then, about the need to go to war and support the Empire. While he thought about James and his conviction that it was right for Australia to be part of the War, Patrick reflected on the fact that he himself would never have considered enlisting, even if he had been younger and fitter. While trying to understand why Daniel eventually enlisted and both Martin and Thomas felt it was the right thing to do, he found it difficult to equate the concepts of patriotism, war and past injustices when England was part of all three concepts.

While he was thinking of his sons, he remembered hearing that James' mother was German. Or perhaps it was it his grandmother who was German? It was not something that James had ever talked about, at least, not to him. Anti-German sentiment had escalated since the War started, and it made sense to Patrick that James had decided to forget his ancestry and not mention Anna or Hertha or whatever her name was. For a moment, thinking of the surge in anti-German feeling and the Australians with German heritage now having to register as aliens, Patrick felt a small twinge of solidarity with

James. The Irish had never had to register, but in many ways they were still considered to be aliens or, at the very least, second-class citizens. Since the Rising, many outspoken people with an Irish background had been interned alongside the Germans, the government having understood that internment was a good way of controlling anyone who disagreed with its commitment to the War.

With the spectre of an internment camp looming over James, Patrick could have understood had his son-in-law decided to avoid the enlistment office altogether. After all, enlistment was not yet compulsory, and questions about his background could easily have branded him an enemy alien. Had Patrick been in James' shoes, he decided that he would have gone about life as usual, hoping that people might assume that he had tried to enlist but had been rejected, like so many other men. A word dropped here and another there. Patrick could not imagine that it would have been difficult: people were extremely adept at creating their own small realities based on an image or hearsay.

But that was not what happened. James managed to hide the foreign mother or grandmother well out of sight and presented himself to the recruitment office as a loyal subject of the Empire. Like Daniel, he had seen it as his duty, and Patrick remembered how Bridget had written home, her anguish and her anxiety filling all the spaces between the words and the lines. In her letter, she wrote that she could understand that James might have feelings of patriotism, but she could not understand his willingness to support his country by killing others and possibly being killed himself.

Patrick had never given the killing business much thought: if there was a war then it was be expected that people would get killed. Unlike his daughter, he divided wars into two distinct groups, honourable and not-so-honourable. Thinking of the Rising, he was quite certain that honourable wars, where people fought for justice, could be defended. He was not so certain that a fight for justice was the rationale of the present war. He was not an educated man, and there was much about which he knew absolutely nothing, but he feared that the world would be a very different place after the War ended, no matter who won.

One of the men at the counter had been talking to him, asking him a question. The three men were now looking at him, waiting for an answer. He waved his hand, drawing an abstract shape in the air. He begged their pardon and said he had been elsewhere, that he had not been listening, that he had a lot on his mind. His mind that insisted on coming back to James Jackson.

Chapter Eleven

He might have been thinking about James Jackson and the War, but part of his mind was still filled with Mary and the letter, and somewhere way out on the edges he was remembering what he had been told about God deciding to help his parents just when everything was on the point of collapsing.

His father had recounted, many times, how he had been pushed hard against the wall, looking Death in the face when, for no obvious earthly reason, a neighbour of his, Cormac O'Sullivan, stepped into his life. Cormac, no doubt sent by God, told him that he had heard that they were looking for quarrymen and stone breakers on Guernsey. Micheál admitted that he had stared at Cormac blankly: he had never before heard of a place called Guernsey.

The move from Ballinure to Guernsey was such a momentous occasion for the O'Connors that it gradually adopted the same significance as the birth of Christ, with Micheál referring to things being either 'before the move' or 'after the move'. For Patrick and his siblings Gertrude, Mary and Margaret, all of whom came 'after the move' and were blissfully ignorant of the situation that had instigated the relocation from Ireland, 'after the move' became synonymous with life as they knew it, and 'before the move' was packed together with animated descriptions of the years of the Hunger, the general plight of the Irish and the Irish/English question, which were all somehow woven together with pictures of green hills and the little people.

According to family legend, Cormac had a flat cart and an old horse, and he shifted anything from anywhere to anywhere else. Some of the time he transported peat from the bogs; other times he carried feed or furniture or people or animals. Anything at all. Anywhere at all. He and his horse were a familiar sight on the roads around Tipperary. 'Here comes O'Sullivan,' people would call out, catching sight of the chestnut horse with the strange white markings on its forehead. And, as the cart disappeared around the next bend in the road, there would always be someone who would at least be thinking, 'There goes O'Sullivan'.

With both parents dead long before the Famine, and his many siblings either dead or scattered across the face of the earth, Cormac had been forced to accept the fact that he was the only surviving member of the O'Sullivan family left in Ireland. He had never had any desire to follow in the footsteps of his siblings; he was unmarried; he was completely and utterly on his own. He was also somewhat slow-witted and naïve; even a vague awareness of his almost hopeless situation could easily have caused him to spiral downwards had it not been for a friend who was about to leave for Canada with his family.

Sometimes, either intentionally or unintentionally, a decision made by one individual can have a pronounced effect on another, and it was this that happened to Cormac. Aware that life was heavily weighted against O'Sullivan, the friend, a villager who had grown up with one of Cormac's brothers, left him his horse, insisting that Cormac take good care of her.

The horse, no longer young, came with a long list of aches and pains, a somewhat ambivalent attitude towards everyone with whom she came in contact, and a simple cart, but she gave Cormac all he needed to avoid that downward spiral. Two misfits, the horse and Cormac, found each other immediately. Together they would happily travel between Tipperary and Limerick. On occasion, they would even travel as far east as Waterford. It was in Waterford, in the summer of 1848, that Cormac heard about Guernsey and the stonecutters.

The actual move, the linchpin that gave rise to the concepts of before and after, took place in October of that same year when God, after a long period of silence, decided to step in to save the O'Connors. The move began before dawn when they climbed up on to Cormac's cart, Cormac having agreed to take them as far as Carrick on the Suir river. Once there he would talk with a friend of his who worked on one of the lighters that moved between Carrick and Waterford: he assured them that there would be no problems getting downstream to Waterford.

Patrick remembered his father saying that everything went as planned: Cormac was true to his word, and from Carrick they floated down the Suir on a lighter belonging to someone who was already nameless by the time Micheál was recounting the story to Patrick.

The quarrying company, desperate for the workers, had arranged transport from Waterford to St Peter Port. When the O'Connors boarded the ship in Waterford, it was about to embark on its fourth trip from Ireland to Guernsey.

Although the story would always be Micheál's, Timothy had his own special memories of the trip to Guernsey. He told Patrick that what he remembered most was the darkness of the night and closeness of other people. He recollected the sounds of strange voices and of water hitting the sides of the ship. He remembered the smell and taste of salt water. Even after so many years, he could still call to mind that he was both very cold and very excited at one and the same time.

But it was Catherine who helped Patrick understand what it was like when they turned their backs on their homeland.

'We had never meant to stay away so very long,' she had told him. 'It was just meant to be a little while. Until everything had righted itself. It had always been our intention to return to Tipperary.'

Then she had talked about Grace and how it had felt leaving her there, alone, in the graveyard. 'Of course, the old people, and even Brendan and Eileen, were there with her. . . ' she had mused, more to herself.

She told her son how she had visited the graveyard several times in the days before they left Ballinure, and on the last day she was there, she had taken a small pebble from the grave. No matter where she was, she would be able to hold the pebble, close her eyes and be back in the churchyard at Ballinure, watching over her daughter's grave.

Chapter Twelve

Kneeling on the floor next to her sister, Bridget repeated her question. 'Is it Oswald? Has something happened?' She was exhausted, but woven through the fatigue, she could feel her anxieties and fear quickly mixing with something else, something intangible, something she did not yet understand.

Sarah got up, walked into the second room and opened the box that Bridget had seen earlier on the sofa. Moments later, she returned with a letter in her hand.

'This letter arrived,' she said, handing Bridget a rectangular beige-coloured envelope that had been carefully opened with a knife. 'Two days ago.'

Bridget, who had seated herself on one of the chairs near the table, turned the envelope over in her hands: it almost looked official. She removed the one-page letter — the letterhead was definitely military, but the letter itself looked otherwise — and skimmed it quickly. She then went back to the beginning and reread it more carefully, in case she had carelessly missed something or misunderstood what it was trying to say.

'Pulmonary disease? Bronchopneumonia? I didn't know... ' She looked back down at the letter. 'He's in England, a military hospital,' she said, simply confirming what she had just read. 'At least he's... ' she began, her voice trailing off. She had been going to say that at least he was not dead, but it sounded so dreadfully harsh. 'At least he's being taken care of, and they're doing everything they can,' she added, wondering just how much care there could be in the middle of a war with so many men needing help, wondering what 'everything they can' actually implied. Pneumonia was a death sentence, just as much as a bullet in the chest.

Bridget decided that the letter was not official but had been written by some kind, compassionate person, someone who understood what it was like to be a wife needing information. It was difficult to say whether the kind-hearted person was a man or a woman: the name, P. Evans, at the end of the letter gave no indication of the writer's sex, but the letter had most probably been written in their precious spare time. Perhaps it had been a five-minute respite they managed to grab between patients, or perhaps it was written in a meal break, or even at the end of a frantic shift. A nurse? A doctor? An orderly? Someone who knew that Oswald had a wife who would be worrying. Did they write what they guessed Oswald would want to have written had he been able to write himself, or did Oswald, in the spaces between fever and persistent coughing, tell them what he wanted written? She was not sure, but she was moved by the person's kindness.

While she was considering the word *kindness* and everything it encompassed, she was thinking about what was written in the letter. Oswald had not been well for most of the voyage to England; by the time he reached Southampton he was so ill that he was immediately moved to the military hospital. No one expected him to recover.

Was he already sick when he left Sydney, or did he get sick on the way to England? Bridget wondered why he had been sent halfway around the world if he was not well. She did not know a lot about bronchopneumonia, but she knew that it usually meant that the person died.

'Did you know that he had pneumonia?' she asked her sister.

Sarah shook her head and then shrugged and said, 'I saw him. Before he left. It must have been the Sunday before he sailed. Now, when I think about it, he didn't look well: he'd lost weight, and there was something about him that just wasn't right. He kept telling me that he was okay, that it was a cold he'd picked up somewhere.

They'd begun to replace some of the tents with buildings, but many of the men, including Oswald, were still living in tents. I felt that everything looked cramped, though he told me that it had been much worse before he came there. He said that the sea air would fix him, and he told me not to worry.

'The visit wasn't very long. We met in what was probably a community hall, but there were many other wives and families there, so we took a walk outside just to be on our own. He promised he'd write. And then, a few days later, I heard that he'd sailed.

'You know how troubled I've been since he enlisted. I was worried sick about him being killed and never coming home again, but this is something else entirely, isn't it? It's not really the same: he's probably going to die, and it's not as thought he's done any fighting. He wrote a postcard to me from the ship. I guess a mate must have seen that it was posted. He said they'd be going first to the south of England, to some kind of a training camp. I thought they'd already done all of that, training and suchlike, but obviously I was wrong. From what he'd written on the card, I guessed that they would then be moved to France or wherever it is that they are fighting. He didn't write much, and I didn't think about it, him not writing much, until this letter arrived. Then I understood that he was probably sick even when he wrote to me.

'I can understand that he didn't want to worry me, more than I was already worrying, otherwise he'd have told me before he left that he was sick. Really sick. But now I know that he's dreadfully sick with this pneumonia, and he's in a hospital on the other side of the world, and I'll probably never see him again. It's all pretty meaningless, wouldn't you say?' Fighting against an undertow of mixed emotions, Sarah put her head in her hands.

For a moment, the room was completely quiet. No one spoke. Even the sounds beyond the window seemed to have stopped. Then Sarah raised her head and, leaning across to where her sister was sitting, hugged Bridget close. 'I'm really sorry, Bridget. I shouldn't be talking about such things. I should be thinking better, but that's what I'm not doing at the moment. You know what it's like. I mean, look at James. But you got him back. That's the main thing, isn't it? To get them back.'

Bridget did not know what to say. She agreed with her sister that war was completely without meaning, and she could understand how much she wanted Oswald to recover and return home, but she was not sure about James. Was it the main thing that she got him back? In the state he was? She pushed the questions from her mind, thinking that in actual fact the questions about James were now effectively academic, given what had happened.

She let her mind return to the waste and the stupidity: the whole thing, the War, the killing, the hate, everything, was without meaning. Oswald lying in a bed in a hospital thousands of miles away was definitely meaningless, but it was caught up with all those other senseless things. She returned her sister's hug, wondering yet again if the main thing was as simple as getting them back. When she thought of James she had to admit to herself that it had been better for both him and her had he never returned home. At least that way she would still have had her memories. Untainted, unblemished memories.

Pushing her thoughts back to Oswald, she decided that there was really nothing she could say, and she felt utterly ineffectual. 'He *will* get better, Sarah; he has to. And then, when he's better, perhaps they'll send him home,' she added, feeling that something still had to be said, in spite of there being no words for what she needed to say.

There was no question of Bridget and Joseph not remaining in Redfern with Sarah. Even though there were a lot of things that did not fit together, Sarah only wanted to believe that Bridget had come to Sydney to give her some support, and Bridget neither confirmed nor refuted this belief. That she should have turned up so soon after the letter from England had arrived and without knowing anything of its existence was something that neither of them discussed: Bridget, because it would have hinged on all the things that she was attempting to forget, and Sarah, because it would have drastically altered the story she had told herself: Bridget came because she somehow knew that her sister needed her.

As far as Bridget was concerned, the assumption that she had come to Sydney to be with her sister immediately solved a number of problems. It did not solve the biggest problem, but it made it just a little easier to live with.

While Sarah woke every morning eagerly hoping to receive a new letter telling her that Oswald had made a complete recovery and was on his way home, Bridget focused all her energies on building an invisible barricade against *any* kind of letter addressed to herself, or (a possibility that terrified her even more) against an unwanted visit from the police.

At night, lying in the bed next to her sister, those hours back in the house, before she finally left, kept replaying like a piece of theatre in front of her mind. Her efforts to replace the images with other, different, images failed miserably, and she felt like a prisoner chained to an enormous rock. At times the rock was what she had done; at other times it was simply a heavy, grey, immovable piece of stone. Occasionally she gave in to the relentless thoughts and fears, and then she went through the events of that evening bit by bit, trying to analyse what had happened and why, and whether or not she had overreacted. Following the law of cause and effect, she was quite certain that had she acted differently then everything would have turned out differently, and she would not now be in Sydney.

She could not change what had happened, even though she would have liked to have been able to do so. Most nights she fought against the nightmares that forced her back into the cottage where she was confronted by what she had done. But occasionally she dreamt of James, remembering what he had been like when they first met, before he went to war, before he had been completely destroyed.

In between the nightmares and the dreams about James, there were other terrifying dreams where enormous, serious-faced police officers were pulling her away from her sister and her son, before pushing her down slimy stone steps into a dungeon without light. Always, overhead, there was a hangman's noose, casting shadows, waiting patiently just for her.

Most nights, scared to a point of wakefulness by the dreams and images, she would then lie tossing and turning in the darkness, trying to forget what it was that had terrified her. Eventually, totally exhausted, she would slip, little by little, into a dreamless sleep.

The days passed, and in spite of Bridget's night-time agonies, no letter asking her to explain herself arrived, and no police came knocking on the door. Gradually, her uneasiness lessened just a fraction, and she began to believe that perhaps everything was going to be all right after all.

Sarah, on the other hand, became more and more convinced that Oswald had already succumbed somewhere on the other side of the world and that she was never going to see him again.

Chapter Thirteen

Oswald Reginald McCarthy was the ninth, and youngest, child of Connor and Florence McCarthy who arrived in Sydney with five children in the late 1870s. Four more children were born after the family settled in Surry Hills and Connor began working as a carter. Connor, originally from Dublin, had met Florence — Irish mother, English father — in Liverpool, where his family had fled during the famine of the 1840s.

As a child, Connor McCarthy was small with untidy straw-coloured hair that in certain lights hinted at both brown and sandy, grey-green eyes and a quietly determined attitude. Wiry and streetwise, he had learnt from an early age to focus all his energy and wits on one essential objective: survival. Poverty could easily have annihilated him, gradually stripping away his defences, but he found that he was able to weather its attacks, by turning negatives to advantages or else ignoring them altogether, while picking through all physical and metaphysical refuse to grab at anything and everything that was vaguely positive and possibly useful.

He had learnt a lot about being independent and self-reliant by the time he met and married Florence. He had also managed to stretch out to almost-average height, a fact which furthered his increasing feeling of self-worth. Then, after several years of marriage, he took the remarkable step of moving with his wife and four children to Sydney, Australia. During the following decade, two children died and several more were born. He mourned the children who were no more, but experience had taught him that life is a lottery and not everyone can be a winner. His hard-earned attitudes regarding survival and life in general were eventually picked up by his three surviving sons, while his four daughters all took after their mother, Florence, who was placid, submissive and neither attractive nor unattractive.

Connor's youngest son, Oswald Reginald, inherited not only his father's colouring and attitudes, but also his physical stature. While his brothers had all managed to surpass their father in height, Oswald stopped growing when he, like his father, was almost average. This could have upset him, but Oswald simply accepted it as yet another of Life's incomprehensible aberrations.

In 1907, he turned twenty, by which time he had already had a variety of jobs: on the docks, at a local blacksmith, in a market garden. He had even worked for a few months catching rats, during an outbreak of the plague. But seven years into the new century he finally joined his father and his two brothers in the family's carting business, Connor McCarthy & Sons. The family never questioned why it had taken Oswald so long to join the business: they knew what he was like. He was naturally restless and constantly on the outlook for new experiences.

It is said that the paths of people who are supposed to meet will eventually intersect, even though, looking at each path separately, the possibility of this happening may appear to be negligible. In August 1911, Sarah O'Connor moved from Molong to Penrith, west of Sydney, where she had found employment as companion and housekeeper for the newly widowed friend of one of Sarah's aunts. Mrs Aileen Byrne was a somewhat overweight and idiosyncratic woman in her late seventies with a friendly and talkative disposition. Childless, she found living in a large house in the centre of Penrith to be both lonely and demanding, especially after the unfortunate and recent demise of her husband. Although Sarah's first impression of the house was that it was intimidating, she soon discovered that by closing off the rooms that were no longer being used her workload was not particularly onerous. Mr Byrne had been one of the managers at the quarry, and as such both he and his wife were respected members of the community, despite the fact that both of them had an Irish background.

Mrs Byrne had confided in Sarah that she had been amazed when her darling Fergal was selected from among many applicants, most of them Protestants. 'I really don't know how it could have happened,' she smiled. Sarah had no idea either: the labels *Irish*, *Catholic* and *manager* did not normally go together, but perhaps someone on the Board had an affinity with one of the first two, or perhaps God had simply decided to give Fergal Byrne a decent break.

In early September, Mrs Byrne asked Sarah to take the train to Parramatta and fetch some curtain fabric for her from Murray Brothers. A neighbour of Mrs Byrne's had used such fabric to sew a set of curtains for her sitting room, and Mrs Byrne had been most impressed, so much so that she decided to purchase a length of the same fabric, a fine French lace, for herself. She was already envisaging just how it was going to look in her own small sitting room at the back of the house.

Penrith was the closest Sarah had ever come to Sydney, and travelling just that little bit further east was an excitement in itself. She left on the early morning train, a letter, detailing the exact fabric to be purchased, carefully folded in her purse.

On the same day, Oswald and one of his brothers were to deliver some articles of furniture from a deceased estate in Surry Hills to the sister of the deceased in Parramatta. They had packed the cart the evening before and left early in the morning.

The destination of the furniture was only a few doors down from Murray Brothers, and after unloading the cart, and while his brother was attending to other business in Parramatta, Oswald stepped out on to Church Street to have a smoke and a look around.

At the same time, Sarah, having bought her fabric, exited the shop, thinking about train times and a hot cup of tea and whether the one might, or might not, cancel out any possibility of the other. Totally immersed in her thoughts she did not see Oswald until she almost ran into him.

The apologies were profuse from both sides. Oswald, usually quite hesitant with the opposite sex, felt that the situation definitely called for tea, which, though it may have solved part of Sarah's quandary, certainly had ramifications for the other part.

They found a small tea house near the river, and after the half-hour it took for them to drink tea and introduce themselves, the intersection was firmly in place. Oswald, naturally cautious and in many ways introverted, was firmly convinced that this was the woman with whom he wanted to spend the rest of his life, and Sarah, who, somewhat overwhelmed, had fully accepted the fact that she would be taking a later train, believed that she felt the same.

They married the following April in Penrith with Mrs Byrne and Oswald's eldest brother as witnesses, then the priest accompanied the small party to Mrs Byrne's home where she had arranged afternoon tea in the sitting room with the new lace curtains. Sarah returned to Sydney with her husband and her brother-in-law, and in May, Sarah's sister Catherine came across from Molong to housekeep for the elderly lady.

Oswald had managed to find a couple of rooms in a house in Redfern, and it was there that he and Sarah began married life together.

Reserved and somewhat obstinate, Oswald was not only shorter than average, he was also an uncomplicated man with simple needs. Most of his needs had much to do with him being left alone to do things in the way he wanted to do them. Nevertheless, in spite of his reclusive manner, he was always straightforward and honest. He may have been shy, but he was always very clear about what he liked and what he did not like: he liked honesty, and he disliked all kinds of ambiguity. He loved his wife. At the same time, but in a completely different way, he also loved the noise, dirt, excitement and unpredictability that was so much part of the city where he lived. He loved the constant change that was a natural part of his job; he loved the sounds of the horse and the creaking of the cart; he even loved listening to the easy banter between his brothers and customers. He was not completely sure how he should interpret the word *love*, but assuming that it was simply a higher degree of *like,* he could say that he loved many things, things that were often black and white in comparison to each other but which were all individually essential to him, being the person he was.

Like Sarah, he had expected that there would be children, but delivering new McCarthy children, even just one, did not seem to be something that was very high on God's list of things to do. Neither he nor Sarah had completely reconciled themselves to a life without children, and they continued to pray, and they continued to hope.

As married life fell into an unavoidable daily routine, Oswald could occasionally feel irritable and even depressed. Not for a moment did he question his love for

Sarah, but on those days when he experienced the unstoppable and terrible slide into the yawning, dark pit within him, he became aware of a need that he could not really explain. Regardless of the word *love* and all it implied, he suspected that part of him was hankering after something else.

His uncertainty and feelings of disquiet worried him, because he knew without a doubt that he loved Sarah. She gave him a sense of purpose, a sense of belonging. He wondered why he always needed to be looking beyond that which was considered safe and normal to other things that seemed both exciting and unpredictable.

Then August 1914 arrived, obliterating what everyone had considered normal, and re-evaluating the meanings of words like *mateship* and *loyalty*, even life itself. Oswald, believing that he may have found what it was he was looking for, and discerning an unexpected opportunity for new experiences and excitement, while possibly seeing enlistment as his patriotic duty, presented himself at the recruitment office.

Given his slightly smaller-than-average stature, his application was instantly rejected, which merely reactivated and worsened his earlier depression: not only was he being denied the adventure he felt was lacking in his life, he was also being branded as not suitable.

Twelve months later, Oswald plucked up his courage and made a second attempt to join the army. Casualties had been high, and more men were desperately needed, so many of the earlier prerequisites had been quietly removed. However, to Oswald's dismay he was knocked back a second time, something that made very little sense to him when he knew that after the first rush of enthusiasm there were not as many men trying to enlist, and that the government was already discussing the possibility of conscription.

His surprise and disappointment were only accentuated by his conviction that people around him were condemning him for not having enlisted. He persuaded himself that all condescending looks and mumbled words were directed at him and him alone. Were people wondering why he was still in Sydney while their own husbands and sons and brothers were somewhere on the other side of the world, hideously wounded or possibly dead? Did they perhaps believe he was a pacifist or even a coward? Did they not understand that he had tried to enlist, twice, and that he had been rejected both times?

By this time most people were beginning to understand that war was not a game, it was something else entirely. It was deadly serious: men were being wounded and even killed. Sarah hugged him and told him that she was pleased he had not been accepted. She did not want him to be killed. She wanted him to remain with her. When he mentioned everyone else and what they most probably thought of him, she told him not to think about such things: the people who knew him, the people who mattered, knew that he had tried to enlist, and they knew that he had been rejected.

But Oswald *did* think about such things, and, in July 1916, he applied a third time. This time he was accepted, the necessary conditions for enlistment having been reduced even further. Excited by the prospect of everything ahead of him — the challenges, the change of scene and the adventure — all previous feelings of depression and despondency very quickly disappeared. At the same time, he was uneasily aware that Sarah was unhappy that he had been accepted, despite four of his five shillings' weekly pay being sent directly to her. She thanked him for his thoughtfulness, adding that her disapproval had nothing to do with money and everything to do with him. She made him promise to stay safe: a promise he gave, knowing that there was no way he could be certain that he would be able to keep it.

Within a week he was moved to the recruitment and training camp in Liverpool, where he was given a khaki tunic and breeches, a flannel shirt without a collar, underclothes, puttees and a pair of tan ankle boots. He was also given a pair of socks, a khaki greatcoat and a felt slouch hat. His days then fell into a routine of different military drills where he was taught to march, obey orders, use a rifle and manage a machine gun. Discipline was the very firm thread holding everything together.

He enjoyed the new structure that was shaping his life, and the feeling that he was about to do something that was important; something that caused strangers to look at him with admiration and, at times, with a slight hint of jealousy. It made him feel as though his height was no longer compromised, even though he could appreciate that he had not suddenly grown overnight, and probably for the first time in his life, he felt that he was doing something meaningful.

Conditions in the training camp were not particularly good, although he had heard that they had been much worse prior to his arrival. Oswald was not too concerned about living on top of thousands of other recruits: he was used to cramped, primitive conditions from his time in Surry Hills as a child; while the discipline, at times excessive, was definitely no worse than the scoldings he and his siblings had consistently experienced, growing up.

But not everyone was quite as magnanimous and accepting as Oswald. By the time he enlisted, Oswald knew that the discontent at the camp had already caused riots, and he was aware that the conditions and the violence had been responsible for a strike in February 1916. The news about the strike had been in the newspaper, and when he read about it, months before he actually enlisted, the thought had occurred to him that had he been in the training camp he could have been unwittingly caught up in the demonstration. It struck him then that he might even have been killed.

After the striking and the brawling, the rioters, in their hundreds, were rounded up, but to court-martial and discharge, or even gaol, them would have seriously depleted the country's fighting force. They were desperately needed overseas, so most of them escaped punishment. While the military and the government were coping with the dilemma of what to do and how to do it, the finger-pointing and blame-throwing continued.

The demonstrators were eventually packed on to ships and sent to individual hells that made many of them wonder what they had actually been complaining about in Liverpool, while, at home, conditions in the camp improved a little.

When Oswald arrived at the camp a few months later, there was slightly more room for the would-be soldiers, and the discipline was less aggressive. Then, after three months, Oswald and all the others, now acquainted with the rudiments of warfare, left Sydney for England.

Chapter Fourteen

Although Sarah's energies were focused on Oswald and whether or not she was ever going to see him again, there was something else niggling her: why was Bridget *really* in Sydney? It was tempting to believe in psychic connections and to believe that Bridget had made the journey from Gilgandra to Sydney simply because she had some intuitive feeling that her sister needed her, but she was dubious.

Sarah, who was a practical, rational person, did not believe that this could be true. She really wanted to believe it, but part of her knew that there had to be some other reason for her sister's sudden appearance in Sydney.

In spite of her pragmatism, she was aware of the special connection between herself and her younger sister, but there were limits to everything: three hundred miles was a long way for a feeling to travel when there was no reason for alarm or anxiety. When she last wrote to Bridget everything had been normal, or as normal as everything could be in the middle of a war. She wrote that she was concerned about Oswald, but Bridget knew that she had been concerned about him since he left Sydney, and when she wrote to Bridget she had not yet received the letter saying that he was ill. When Bridget wrote back to her, she mentioned that James was working again, doing farm work on a small property nearby, and that Joseph had been chased by the turkeys on a couple of occasions. Her sister did not give any indication that she was overly worried about either Oswald or Sarah.

Despite her oversupply of common sense, Sarah could understand that feelings, being inanimate things, probably followed special rules of their own. Perhaps Bridget *could* have picked up on her anxiety despite the many miles between them, and become worried about her even though she had not been given any reason to do so. Perhaps she was complicating things unnecessarily.

Or perhaps it was God who had decided that Bridget needed to be with her sister? Sarah may have been practical and realistic, but her reliance on God and His many saints was much stronger than her sister's. Talk of psychic connections may have caused her to question the likelihood or the credibility of such a story; God's influence was something else altogether.

Sarah sighed and let the scrubbing brush fall back into the bucket of dirty water. Having finished the two floors, she allowed herself a couple of minutes to enjoy the results of her work, and then she emptied the bucket into the sink and let the tap run, washing away all remnants of the dirty water. Having water at the turn of a tap in her own kitchen was something that she never failed to marvel at, even after living in Sydney for several years. She believed that some people also had hot water coming from a tap, but such a luxury was something well and truly beyond her wildest expectations.

Once the bucket and scrubbing brush had been stowed away, she removed her apron and began peeling potatoes. Bridget had taken Joseph with her to buy some cheap mutton chops for the evening meal, and she expected the two of them back shortly.

Still, her mind would not let go of Bridget and why she had suddenly turned up in Sydney. She could not honestly say whether she believed in the magic that allowed feelings to cross plains and mountain ranges (which a small voice inside her kept saying was not possible), or whether it was God who understood that she needed support (which was more likely). Intuitive feelings or God or something else entirely, there had to be a reason for Bridget turning up at her door, and the reason, should she remove God from the equation, had nothing to do with either herself or Oswald.

For some months she had been trying to read between the lines of her sister's many letters, and she had suspected that Bridget was not particularly happy. Sarah, being a realist, knew that no one was completely happy. She herself mourned the children she was unable to bear, but she was certain that everyone had something, or even someone, in their life that they would like to change. As far as Sarah was concerned, that was how life was. She admitted that things had probably not been easy for her sister, especially not since James came home more than a year ago, frail, wounded and so different to the man who had enlisted in 1914. But he was finally working again, so things must be improving, for him and even for Bridget.

She ran the knife around the potato, while at the same time she tried to find a small opening among all her memories and all the things she knew about her sister, an opening that might shed some light on the real reason Bridget was in Sydney.

Chapter Fifteen

Now, when Bridget was in the relative safety of Sydney and her sister's flat, she was able to think about what had happened in a more considered and logical manner. It was already five days since she arrived, and there had been nothing to indicate that there was anyone looking for her. There had been no police, uniformed or otherwise, knocking on the door, no frantic letter from her parents. There had been no questioning article in the Sydney Morning Herald. She could not let go of the implausible thought that no one had yet discovered what had happened; if they had, then they had as yet not managed to join the dots, connecting her to the crime. The more she thought about it, the more she was convinced that no one had been to the house.

James' place at Gilgandra was a good mile in from the main road, nestled behind an outcrop of rock at the end of a track that was not completely straight. A meagre stand of eucalypts acted as a kind of lookout near the entrance to the property, guarding the gate that no longer shut properly, and obscuring the house itself.

No one came to the Jackson place unless they had a reason for doing so: it was, after all, the end of the road. A house at the end of its own, somewhat meandering, track. Bridget pondered on the fact that she might not see anyone for two weeks, sometimes even longer, when James was away on a job. The more she thought about it, the more certain she became that the house had stood there alone and unvisited since the night she left.

Standing safely at a distance from everything that had happened, she thought of the animals: the few red hens and the belligerent turkeys, the skinny dogs, the cow and James' horse. She wondered how they were surviving; she wondered why she had not given them any thought earlier. The animals were used to being on their own, she thought. After all, James had always spent periods of time away from home, even before he met her, but when he was away Dave, who lived close by, would call by occasionally and see that everything was as it should be. He would milk the cow; he would give the animals food and water; he would talk to them. When James first told her about Dave she wondered what the elderly man could talk about with unruly turkeys and surly dogs.

Having let her thoughts wrap around the cow and the horse, she became anxious, almost guilty. Why had she not thought of the animals before? A small part of her was hoping that Dave would look in on the animals, the bigger part of her hoped that he did not. Her relief when she understood that no one might have been at the house had dissipated, and panic came creeping back.

What if they all died? Would that also be her fault?

Thinking of fault, and everything associated with that word, her thoughts accelerated towards what was likely to happen. When they eventually found out. They would naturally believe she was guilty, but could she still be held responsible if she had been provoked? She had never set out to do such a thing, it had never been her intention. She wondered if she could claim self-defence, and a small sliver of a thought threw up the possibility that she might be spared because she was a woman. The thought faded almost as quickly as it had come, she knew all too well that women had been executed in the past. Whether she would be saved or not would doubtlessly depend on the jury. She sent a silent prayer to God, asking for a compassionate jury. Then she remembered that juries were only made up of men, and she doubted that God would be able to accommodate her request.

If a man did what she had done, would he then be convicted? Executed? She decided that the male jury would have to be merciful to one of its own. It would argue extenuating circumstances. The defence counsel might even go so far as to present the accused man in the dock as the *real* victim; the presumed victim, now dead, having cruelly and slyly deluded him. In his summing-up, the judge would most likely say, 'It was self-defence, definitely self-defence,' his eye firmly fixed on the twelve men in the jury box.

While trying to arrange a sympathetic jury and an understanding judge, in spite of the gender problem, she recalled hearing about a woman who had killed her three stepchildren. At the trial, which was only recently, the woman was sentenced to be hanged. Bridget sighed and decided that the woman was most probably guilty: it would be difficult for anyone, male or female, to plead self-defence in such a situation.

When Bridget was nine or ten, an article in *The Molong Express* caught her eye, but she had no sooner begun reading it than her mother, suddenly aware of what her daughter was doing, confiscated the newspaper. Later, when she was alone with Martin, she asked him if he had read the article, and he told her that it was about a woman who was hanged because she had poisoned two husbands.

Nine-year-old Bridget had wondered how it was possible to have two husbands and why the woman had decided to poison them: she could have poisoned one and kept the other one. But now she was not thinking about why a woman might have two husbands and why she might have decided to rid herself of both of them, she was thinking of the aftermath: the court case and the hanging.

Although she did not want to enter such a murky place, Bridget's imagination was forcing her to face the likely reality of having the noose placed around her neck. She tried not to imagine what it would feel like, though she could not help wondering if the person doing it would be gentle or not, and whether the rope would be coarse or smooth. She thought how suffocating it would be in that little room with the executioner and several gaolers. There would probably also be a priest and a doctor.

Just thinking about her probable execution was making her feel ill. A coldness had crept into her body, and she was trembling. More than anything she wanted to discard the image, but it had taken complete possession of her. The rope was around her neck, the priest was saying a prayer, and the trapdoor beneath her feet was opening—

While trying to move away from the image, she wondered whether she would experience a split-second transition from life to darkness. She wondered if it would be painful, or if it would simply be the sensation of the rope around her neck and then, nothing.

She was trying to decide what 'nothing' would feel like, and whether there would be a period of *nothing* before she was plunged into eternal damnation, or whether the dreadful sensation of the rope tightening would continue through several stages of painful asphyxiation before she finally woke up in hell.

Since she was a child she had been told that hell was the underworld, a place of fire and torment, the opposite of heaven, and residing over this place of terror and pain was the devil. The word *eternity* would not leave her mind, but she was unable to picture something, anything, that went on and on forever, without a break, without an end. While torment without end must be unbelievably unpleasant, she wondered if, as the only possible reality, it might eventually become tolerable.

Her mind, attempting no doubt to soften the image and to even offer her a way out, threw up the word *purgatory*, and she gratefully grabbed hold of it. She felt that she could possibly accept such an alternative, given the fact that it described a finite amount of time. A week? A month? Two months? She wondered how much purgatory time she would have to endure, having killed someone when the killing was accidental, not premeditated.

Her mother did not give a lot of credence to the idea of purgatory, even though, since before her marriage, she had changed sides and was now a Catholic. Realistically spiritual, she did not talk much about religion at any time, but Bridget knew that her belief in God was an important part of who she was; she also suspected that she had her own personal way of viewing the afterlife.

A view that did not always include an easy way out.

Bridget wished that she could discuss it with someone who was already there. Catherine was already there: heaven, hell or purgatory. With God or elsewhere. She would definitely be the one who could advise her, who could explain the nothing after the rope and the drop. She would probably even know if there might be a reprieve, she would have to know if God was merciful, understanding or otherwise.

Perhaps she might even say a few words to God on her granddaughter's behalf. The fact that Catherine never actually knew her granddaughter did not have to be a problem. Bridget felt that such a small inconsistency was scarcely of any consequence. They were family, and surely that must account for something.

Purgatory was probably the best she could hope for, no matter how eloquently her grandmother might plead on her behalf or how benevolent God might be feeling. At least it would be temporary: she would not be caught up in a for ever and ever scenario where there would be no respite, no parole, no chance for an appeal.

Bridget sighed deeply, sensing that her thoughts were possibly beginning to verge on the blasphemous. She tried to steer them in some other direction: she could not afford to have even more misdeeds recorded against her. But, as she forced her thoughts down other, different, paths, she could not let go of the thought that she would really like to be certain about what was waiting for her beyond the terror of that sudden, endless drop.

Chapter Sixteen

The first time Bridget set eyes upon James Jackson was an afternoon in one of the last weeks of 1912 when he walked into the pub in Molong. She came into the bar just as the front door closed behind him, and she hesitated for a moment, sensing his presence and feeling that there was something about him that was interesting, without knowing exactly why. In a glance that lasted no longer than a microsecond, she noticed that he was tall and thin with a long face, and that his hair was somewhere between brown and fair. She did not consider whether or not he was attractive: she was captivated by the sense that he was different. 'Interestingly different', she would later say.

Whether he was aware of that microsecond's glance or not was difficult to say, but he smiled in her direction, and she felt herself being pulled into his gaze, a sensation that may have been similar to what a roly poly might feel being propelled forwards on a strong westerly. If anyone had asked her, which was most unlikely, she would have guessed that his eyes were pale blue or blue-grey. The colour, she later told herself, was really of no importance, it was the pull behind the gaze that was everything. It was what exploded into that split second and made her forget completely why she was where she was and what she was doing.

He came back, a few days before Christmas, and this time he asked to speak with her: the girl with the dark curls and the beautiful smile. She was in the small kitchen out the back with her mother, frying eggs and sausages for one of the pub patrons, when she heard that someone wanted to speak with her. Later she told herself that she had known who it was, although she had no idea how she had known. Or was it that she simply imagined that she understood who it was? She was not sure. She was fascinated by the idea that she might have been aware of his presence before she had even seen him: perhaps he had also felt the same kind of pull? Or perhaps not.

Her father watched her as she stood at one side of the bar, answering the man's polite questions, listening to his comments about the pub, the summer, the drought: comments that went nowhere in particular, but which kept her in his space. The pub, the drought and the summer no longer existed for her. Everything had been collected together into the person standing in front of her.

She had no trouble ignoring her father's glances as she hung on to the feeling of captivation and a sense of the two of them, the man in front of her and herself, being the only two people in the pub. Although the conversation was innocent, even casual, she knew that she felt complimented and special, though she was not quite sure why. When she returned to the kitchen, she mentally drew several lines under her first impression of James Jackson, confirming that he was most definitely both interesting and different.

He came back several times, and then on an afternoon in January he arrived just before closing time, wanting to take a short walk with her. She was certain that her father would refuse, but perhaps the day was one of his better days. Whether his approval was motivated by a feeling of generosity, a sense of well-being or something else entirely, Patrick nodded absently, and Bridget fetched her hat and gloves.

It was a relief to get away from the pub where people drew conclusions based on hearsay and boredom, and where nothing was private and everything, every word, glance or even a partially formed thought, could be pulled apart and reassembled into unfamiliar new shapes and new realities by anyone and everyone.

They walked as far as the dairy, where they stood for a while, looking out over rolling hills that the summer had already turned varying shades of brown, their eyes occasionally faltering past sentinel-looking shade trees and groups of cows clustered around the half-empty dam. For want of something to talk about, they talked a little about the summer that was and compared it to summers that had been. Then, more at ease and before returning to the pub, they talked a little about themselves.

Like so many of the men who came into the pub, he moved from place to place, following the work. A couple of times a year he might pick up a job droving: sometimes he was away for a few weeks, moving a mob of cattle from one property to another property. Sometimes it was a bigger job, stretching over several months and taking him across the border into Queensland.

Besides his horse he said that he also owned a small cottage surrounded by a few acres of land on the edge of Gilgandra. Then he backtracked a little and said that the property actually belonged to his father, but his father had moved into Dubbo some years back, and the cottage had been left standing empty. It was fairly run-down, not having been lived in for several years, but he hastened to add that it was sturdy and kept the rain out. After a slight pause, he said that one day he might do something with it; for now he was moving around too much: droving, labouring, doing the rounds of the shearing sheds, picking up all kinds of farm work. He crushed some grass seeds between his fingers, scattering them on the ground below. For the last couple of months he had been in Molong, helping a friend with some fencing.

Bridget was thinking about Gilgandra: she had never been there, but she knew it was about one hundred miles north of Molong. Apart from Orange and Dubbo, she had not seen much of the world beyond Molong. Of course, there was Cudal and Manildra, but she wondered if such small places actually counted.

She swept aside her thoughts about places she had seen and reflected briefly on the fact that her older sister Anne lived in Dubbo. She must ask her next time she wrote if she happened to know anyone by the name of Jackson. The thought, that Anne might have met James' father, disappeared almost as quickly as it came, but then she became aware that James was listing off the names of his siblings, all of them older than he was. Five? Six? She was not sure and did not want to ask. From the little she heard, she gathered that they were all spread out and at least two were living in Queensland.

She was still trying to form a picture in her head of the scattered siblings when James told her that his grandparents had come from England and Germany.

As far as Bridget was concerned, James' siblings and ancestors were of very little interest to her: they were simply indistinct grey shadows, lurking somewhere in the background, while the more she learnt about James, the more appealing he became.

Over the next couple of months, Bridget saw a lot of James Jackson in spite of the fact that the fencing job outside Molong finished, and he had begun working for a farmer in Manildra, fourteen miles to the south-west. Their meetings gradually evolved into a casual, friendly relationship that had undertones of something more serious and perhaps even more permanent. There had been no talk about marriage, but there was an unpronounced feeling or understanding that wrapped around them like an invisible cloud.

Patrick, normally protected by his mantle of male obtuseness, had a vague sense of that which was often still invisible to many others. For a brief moment, he considered suggesting to his daughter that a Catholic boy with connections to the old country could be a better choice, but before the thought had fully formed he was uncomfortably aware that such a suggestion was without any kind of merit and would not hold much weight given his own situation.

Bridget's mother, Mary Boyd, short with fair hair that in certain lights was almost red, came from Gunning in southern New South Wales, a small place with rolling hills, sheep, a handful of people and an irregular patchwork of paddocks. For the first two decades of Mary's life, Gunning and farm life was all she knew. Mary's father, Thomas, a quietly-spoken, introspective Scot, had always been a farmer, while Mary's mother, Elizabeth, was an orphan from Cork.

In 1850, Elizabeth Anne McNamara, the sole survivor of a family of eight, was removed from a workhouse in Cork and told that she was to be given the chance of a new life in Sydney, Australia. The news must have been overwhelming for the poor girl who had only just turned fifteen. She could read but not write, and all she had ever seen of the world was contained within a five-mile radius of her village. On the ship carrying her and more than a hundred other female orphans to Sydney, she was given a wooden box containing basic clothing, linen and a prayer book: a box that could be locked and for which she, and only she, had the key. To own anything of even minimal value was something completely new for Elizabeth, and it is possible that it was then that she began to believe that Sydney might actually be the new beginning she had been promised.

On arrival in Sydney she was immediately taken to the Female Immigration Depot in the recently converted Hyde Park Barracks. She was assessed physically and spiritually and was then placed in one of the undecorated and sparsely furnished dormitories. The austerity did not worry Elizabeth: she had a roof over her head, a bed to sleep in and food to eat.

Even though the girls were allotted various chores around the barracks, it was never expected that they would remain where they were, scrubbing floors, preparing food or unravelling old ropes for wadding: the aim was for them to be hired as domestics as soon as possible. Having been saved from further misery in their homeland, it was also hoped that they would eventually even out the gender disparity in the colony.

Elizabeth had only been at the barracks a couple of months when, one morning at the beginning of spring, she and a large number of other new arrivals were escorted by the matron down a couple of flights of stairs to the hiring room on the ground floor. Before leaving the dormitories, the girls had been instructed to make themselves as presentable as possible: it was, they were told, essential that they should make a good impression.

Information may have been sparse, but Elizabeth was aware that the hiring room was where prospective employers inspected the girls before selecting their house servant, nursemaid, farmhand or even wife. She did not like the idea of being put on display, but she had no choice, and she knew that she should be thankful: had she remained in Ireland she would have already been dead. As she walked down the stairs and along the long hallway, she forced herself to concentrate both on the noise of shoes connecting with the timber flooring and on the sounds made by the group of nervous girls walking together. She did not want her thoughts to dwell on likely images of the men waiting in the room at the end of the hallway, no matter how positive or negative the images might be.

Outside were the many street sounds of Sydney: cartwheels turning, horses neighing and carters calling, to their horses, their mates, an unobservant pedestrian. There were also the muted voices and footsteps within the building itself. When the matron finally opened the door to the hiring room and indicated that the girls should enter, Elizabeth's thoughts were still caught up with the many invisible things, things that existed both within and beyond the building.

There were many people in the room, and Elizabeth's first impression was of disorder, almost chaos. From her place at one side of the room, she looked out at the people, mainly men, milling around, and she wondered to herself which of them would decide that she was the domestic he was looking for.

Several of the men were red-faced and pompous-looking with top hats and impeccable clothing, while many others were dressed in the nondescript jacket and trousers of the worker. Elizabeth's eyes glanced quickly over the men before settling for a moment on a man standing by the window. He was tall with red-tinged hair and beard, and her first impression of him was that he was around thirty years of age, serious and, if she were to judge him by his clothes, respectable.

A short, plump man with a maroon double-breasted waistcoat and a long jacket caught the matron's eye and nodded loftily in the direction of Elizabeth. Elizabeth's heart dropped: this was not the man she had imagined she would be working for: he seemed arrogant and unkind. She tried to make herself as small as possible, hoping that a miracle might allow her to disappear into the wall behind her. Then, as the matron beckoned her to step forwards, the man with the red-tinged hair left his place by the window.

Thomas Boyd, a Scottish farmer from Gunning, crossed the room, ignoring the man in the double-breasted waistcoat, and directed his attention towards the thin, pasty-faced girl in front of him. It is possible that he noticed the couple of mousy strands of hair that had escaped from beneath her bonnet, and that her grey eyes were unable to hide her nervousness and anxiety. He asked her a couple of questions about herself: where she was from and whether or not she would be able to take care of a simple household.

She was so relieved to have been saved from the man with the waistcoat that she would have answered that she could take care of anything or anyone. Thomas told the matron that he was looking for a housekeeper and that he was certain that the girl in front of him would be quite suitable.

Elizabeth returned to Gunning with Thomas Boyd, leaving Sydney and the barracks behind her. It was a long and arduous coach journey, and she had no idea what to expect when she finally reached her destination. A down-to-earth girl, she told herself that nothing could be as bad as the workhouse in Cork and that her first impression of Thomas Boyd was that he seemed decent, if somewhat quiet and uncommunicative. Much later, she told him that she had liked that he treated her with respect. She had also decided, when she first saw him, that he was not unpleasant in appearance, although she did not tell him so, keeping such thoughts completely to herself.

Back in Gunning, it did not take long before Thomas was sharing her bed, and when she became pregnant, he offered to make the union legal. The marriage before a minister of the Scottish Church was perfectly legitimate, but for Elizabeth, a Catholic, it was not spiritually valid, and she hoped that God would understand. If she had refused Thomas' offer, she would have been sent back to the Immigration Depot, and with a bastard child her outlook would not have been particularly optimistic. She consoled herself with the thought that Thomas was, all things considered, a good man, and that she could do much worse. While the minister recited his unfamiliar prayers, Elizabeth silently prayed a Hail Mary, and trusted in a God who, she hoped, was able to see things from many different, and sometimes opposing, perspectives.

Mary, born in 1857, was Elizabeth's third living child, and while Mary's relationship with her father was quite ordinary, both uncomplicated and untroubled, her bond with her mother was special. When Elizabeth unexpectedly died in childbirth fourteen years after Mary's birth, the girl was left not only to mourn the one person who stood her close, but also to take on the responsibility for five younger siblings and the Boyd household itself. Apart from having to cope with profound grief, life had not changed so drastically for her — she was used to looking after the younger children — but now there was no mother to guide her, and she could expect no help from her father or her two older brothers as they had the farm to attend to. Life for Mary soon became wrapped around an ill-defined space that was very much part of the household, and which, in so many ways, still belonged to Elizabeth.

When Mary was about to turn sixteen, Thomas married Margaret Grey, a governess. Margaret and Mary took an immediate dislike to each other: Mary, because she saw Margaret invading not only that which she regarded as her territory but that which, before her, had belonged to her mother; Margaret, because Mary was a constant reminder of the woman she was attempting to replace.

As the family grew with small half-siblings, the enmity between Mary and her stepmother only increased, and Mary became more and more miserable. With her father siding with his new wife, the girl had no support and nowhere to turn. Then, by chance, she met Patrick Francis O'Connor. Not only was she attracted to the talkative Irishman, but she also saw in him an answer to her prayers: he was the liberator she had been hoping for. He was the rescuer, the knight on the white horse, the hero who would sweep her into a life free from conflict and bitterness.

Liberation, however, did not come at all smoothly. Thomas may have been in two minds, but Margaret, still haunted by the ghost of Elizabeth, was adamant that she would not accept an Irish Catholic into the family. Given an ultimatum — her family or the Irishman — Mary decided that she had but one option: she turned her back on Gunning and followed Patrick O'Connor. She never saw her family or Gunning again.

Had her mother still been alive, it is unlikely that Mary would have looked upon Patrick O'Connor as a way of escape. There would have been no need to escape: there would have been no difficult stepmother, and her father would have had no need to quarrel with her. Mary would not have left Gunning, Patrick O'Connor would have met and married a Catholic girl, and Bridget would not have been contemplating some terrible future. In fact, she would not have been contemplating anything at all.

It was an evening in Molong, more than three decades after Mary had made her escape from Gunning on the arm of Patrick O'Connor. The late-summer warmth was refusing to make way for early autumn, and a full moon was marking a path across the soft grass in the orchard on the edge of town, when Bridget took the first step in a chain of events that led to her eventually wondering whether or not she was going to be hanged.

Whether that first step had anything to do with Bridget's growing infatuation with James momentarily overshadowing all reason, or whether it was a simply a reckless flirtation with chance is difficult to say. Whatever the reason, she did not object when his kisses became more determined, nor did she protest when his caresses caused her to briefly ignore those small anxieties of which, in her inmost being, she was still aware.

Later, it took her a while to grasp that she was actually pregnant. Her body sent out small, silent signs, attempting to make her aware of the fact, but either she had no way of interpreting them or else she did not want to admit that they were there. Then, when she began to suspect that something was not as it should be, and it was no longer possible to pretend that nothing was out of the ordinary, she understood that there was no one to whom she could turn. She would have liked to have confided in Sarah, but she had no idea how or where she should begin: a letter could never convey all the things she needed to say.

As April wended its way towards May, Bridget noticed that many of the smells in the kitchen would turn her stomach. Though the nausea was unusual for her, she instinctively did not believe that she had eaten something that disagreed with her, which was the explanation she gave her mother when the latter had come upon her vomiting at the back of the pub. Eventually she decided that the only person she could turn to was James, and James gave her the answer she had suspected but had not been able to put into words.

Much later she attempted to recall his reaction. Had he been surprised, annoyed, perturbed? She was not sure. In her mind, she re-ran the conversation several times without finding the answer she was looking for. Perhaps she was being unnecessarily apprehensive: he had, after all, offered to marry her, adding that it had been his intention all along. She was not sure about the afterthought, wondering if it could have simply been a collection of words to make them both feel at ease with the situation. She tried to convince herself that there was a reason for things happening as they had; he assured her that he was happy with how everything had turned out: obviously, they were meant to be together.

Bridget really wanted to believe that James was happy that she was pregnant. She really wanted to believe that *she* was happy she was pregnant. She was quite sure that she liked James, even loved him, but things had got ahead of them both so quickly. Part of her wanted to hold back and get to know him better, something that was now impossible, while another part continued to be enthralled by everything about him that was different.

She knew that there was something special about James, and she kept telling herself that he must feel the same about her, otherwise he would not have asked her to marry him. She avoided the thought that he had only asked her out of a sense of chivalry or because he felt he had no other choice. Blocking out all such negative thoughts, she concentrated on telling herself that this was what they both wanted. It was supposed to happen, and just like in the fairy tales, they would live happily ever after. Whether or not it was supposed to have happened, she was very aware that she now had no option: as an unmarried woman with a bastard child she would be relegated to the perimeter of society, in fact she would probably find herself somewhere in the wasteland beyond. Keeping her focus on happy endings, she told herself that this is what she had wanted right from the moment she first saw James. That things had moved a little quicker and in a slightly different manner to what she had imagined was really of no importance.

Within a month, Bridget was married, for better or for worse, and had moved with her husband to the run-down cottage in Gilgandra. Her life had abruptly changed, and she was still attempting to catch up with, and fully understand, this new version of herself. James was still the James with whom she had fallen in love, but if he felt things had moved quicker than he had anticipated, he did not say so.

Patrick might have had some regrets that his daughter had married a man who was a bit of a mystery, and he might have also regretted that her marriage was not so much a matter of choice as of urgency. Whether or not he seriously regretted that James was not part of the flock is dubious: the situation was far too similar to his own. Also, Patrick was not particularly devout: he had his own way of interpreting God's word, and the parts that were confronting or that refused to fuse together with how he wanted to live his life had long since been discarded or altered. He considered Father O'Grady a good mate, but both of them knew where the boundaries of their friendship, and even their religious convictions, went. They chose to close their eyes to the differences and concentrate solely on the similarities.

Patrick, sentimental but also often impetuous, usually managed to keep both parts of himself somewhat separate while, in some situations, a small drop of sentimentality could sometimes curb or tone down an otherwise ill-considered and poor decision. It was difficult to say whether the mixing and the quantities of the parts had much to do with Patrick himself, or whether the formulation and the dispensation was due to Divine intervention.

No matter how much, or how little, God involved Himself in his life, Patrick had not forgotten the impact that his marriage had had on both Mary's family and his. He remembered thinking at the time that the same God was being invoked from both sides to stop something that was considered to be the ultimate wrongdoing, and he remembered taking his thoughts a step further, thinking that even if there were three persons in God it was hardly likely that they would hold conflicting views on topics of importance. He was aghast at the lack of logic, but somehow managed to retain a belief in a God who did not take sides with Himself, and who was able to appreciate the goodness in all people, Protestant or Catholic. In many ways, he was thankful that his mother had died several months before his marriage to Mary almost managed to split the family.

By the time Bridget married James, attitudes had softened a little, but secretly and not so secretly, there were many O'Connors who felt that Bridget had wandered from the path of the righteous and that she could have, and should have, done much better.

Regrets were not confined to the O'Connor side of the family. James' father and his two sisters, the only siblings who lived anywhere remotely near the Central West, made it very clear that James had chosen below his status. The word *Irish*, like the word *Catholic*, was a synonym for society's underclass, and although the two words were almost always connected, as they most definitely were for Patrick, James Jackson's father and both his sisters felt that Bridget's being Irish *and* Catholic simply underlined the fact that she was no good.

All three admonished James for being so foolhardy. The rebukes, coming loud and strong, made him feel as though he had expressed an intention to launch on a life of crime and not that he had simply notified his family of his intention to marry.

James disagreed with his family's hastily concocted theories, but he was not at all interested in trying to win any of them over to his way of thinking. He made it clear that if Bridget was not welcome then they could exclude him as well, an option that his father actually considered for a couple of days. Jackson senior was, like his son, not a particularly religious man, and eventually he decided on a truce: as he pointed out, it was unlikely that everyone from the bottom of society was bad, and an understanding of sorts was achieved between the father and his youngest son. James' sisters, united in their dislike of anyone who gave off the slightest whiff of the Roman church, severed connections with their brother, hoping that his reckless decision to bring such a distasteful person into the family would not eventually reflect back on them. As good Anglicans, with a reputable English background, they definitely did not want to be associated with the riff-raff of society.

Joseph arrived at the beginning of 1914, and when war broke out in August of the same year, James immediately enlisted in the army. Unlike the many other women who felt that it was the duty of their men to fight for their country, Bridget did not want James to go to war. No one was making him enlist: it was his own decision, but it was a decision with which Bridget could not agree. James understood that he had obligations to her and Joseph, but though he was fully aware of her opposition, his mind was made up. As far as he was concerned, it was his duty as a British subject, and as an Australian, to go to war.

When he came back home a year later, he was no longer the same man with whom she had fallen in love.

Chapter Seventeen

lthough Bridget was now and then still worrying about a knock on the door that might come at any time of the day or night, her panic had subsided a little. She had had time to think through things, forcing her mind back to the place where it did not want to be. Attempting to look at what happened with the eyes of an outsider, she believed that there was a slight possibility that people might assume that she had not been at home: she was visiting someone in her family; she was staying with one of her aunts; she had left Gilgandra several days, even a week, before anything had happened. Perhaps Sarah would be prepared to support her by saying that she and Joseph had arrived in Sydney earlier than they actually had.

On second thoughts, she doubted that Sarah would lie for her, not with a stern-faced uniformed policeman standing in her kitchen, looking at her directly and asking, 'Now, Mrs McCarthy, when did you say that your sister arrived in Sydney?' Even Bridget, adept at giving two opposite answers to the same question, would find it difficult to lie in such circumstances.

She needed to believe that no one had been to the house. She needed to be confident that no one knew what she knew and was now trying to forget.

While attempting to quell her own concerns, Bridget was being swept up in her sister's uncertainty about Oswald. Having something else on which she could focus at least part of her attention was helping her forget why she was in Sydney. Concentrating on Oswald blurred the frightening image of the policeman knocking on the door, and placed the possibility of having to confront a hangman's noose just that little further away.

Both Bridget and Sarah were hoping for the letter that would tell them that Oswald was on his way home or that he was well again and that he was being moved to the front. Without mentioning it, they also knew that instead of such a letter there could be a letter full of official regret, containing only a few well-formulated lines. It would tell them that everything possible had been done in an attempt to save him, but that everything had not been enough.

Bridget knew for certain that Sarah was praying for the first of these three possibilities.

While Bridget was doing all in her power to forget what had happened and to focus her attention elsewhere, Sarah was becoming increasingly suspicious that something must have happened between Bridget and James. The more she thought about it, the less it made sense that her sister had appeared on her doorstep before she had had a chance to write to her. Her relief at having Bridget so close when her life was filled with uncertainty, and everything around her was threatening to implode, had overshadowed what would have been normal concerns punctuated by question marks. She understood now that she should have been more curious, more aware, right from the beginning; she should not have been quite so trustful. She could not remove her own worries, but she was sufficiently astute to see that they not only obscured but also altered perspectives. If she wanted, she could easily let herself feel hurt by her sister's possible deceit. Instead she told herself that Bridget obviously had her own reasons for not being completely truthful.

It had been comforting to hang on to the belief that their psychic connection was so strong that Bridget 'just knew' that something was wrong, 'just knew' that her sister needed her.

Now, when Sarah had had several days to reassess her sister's miraculous arrival on her doorstep, she was beginning to wonder if Bridget had possibly taken Joseph and left her husband. She knew that the idea was ridiculous: as far as she knew, Bridget loved James, and she tried telling herself that she was being foolish and unbalanced. But, while she was attempting to push down all her imaginings and concerns to a place where she could not hear them, she knew that she would have to say something, if only for her own peace of mind. She needed to know whether Bridget 'just knew' or whether there was some other reason for her sister being in Sydney.

A couple of nights later, after Joseph had been put to bed, the two women were sitting at the table drinking tea when Sarah finally raised her concerns, not knowing whether her sister would be angry, hurt or something in between. Whatever she had been expecting her sister to say shattered into one thousand tiny, disconnected pieces when Bridget took a very deep breath and said, 'I really wanted to say something sooner, but I didn't know what to say or how to say it, and then there was, and still is, all the worry about Oswald. James is dead, Sarah.'

While incredulity and sympathy were nakedly visible on Sarah's face, there were also all the unasked questions: why had she not said anything? How had he died? Why did no one else know? *Did* someone else know? Bridget only had to look at her sister to get some idea of what was exploding through her head.

'I killed him.'

Sarah stared at her sister, her mouth open, obviously unable to give verbal form to anything that could or should be said. In those few seconds, Bridget imagined that Sarah was most probably testing a myriad responses for their suitability and discarding all of them.

'It was an accident. You really must believe me, Sarah: I never wanted to kill him, but he wouldn't stop, and it just happened,' Bridget said, the words tumbling over each other, her voice shaking.

She could understand her sister's silence: where was she to find the appropriate thing to say, the words that might give some expression to her shock, her distress, even her love? What would *she* have said or done in the same situation? In spite of all her understanding, she desperately needed Sarah to say something, anything. The silence was asphyxiating, and Bridget was on the point of regretting that she had said anything at all when, after what seemed like forever but was probably only a fraction of a minute, Sarah pushed back her chair and stood up. Bending over Bridget's chair, she held her sister tightly in her arms while floundering after words, stringing the ones she found into sentences that somehow sounded incomplete and wanting. 'What did he do? What was it he wouldn't stop? Why didn't you say anything?'

Relieved that the silence had finally been broken, but ignoring her sister's questions, Bridget wondered, 'I'll be hanged, won't I?' Her eyes were brimming over with tears. 'People are not supposed to kill each other, even if — '

'Even if?' Sarah was clearly looking for an opening, any opening, into what had happened.

If her sister was going to be able to give her any kind of support, it was important that she knew exactly what had happened. Bridget was aware of this even though she was certain that Sarah would take her part, no matter how much or how little she knew: she would not want her sister to be hanged.

Sarah had released Bridget from her embrace and, having moved her chair closer to her sister's, was sitting with both hands resting on Bridget's knee. 'What happened? What did he do, Bridget? Did he hurt you? You must tell me what happened.'

Bridget thought for a moment, closing her eyes. When she again opened them, she said, 'He's so different since he came back, Sarah. I don't know... he gets angry; he loses his temper for no reason... ' She emphatically shook her head and then corrected herself, '*Was, got, lost*. Lost

179

his temper. I keep forgetting. It's silly, isn't it? James is the only thing I think about, but I still forget he's… '

She managed a weak smile and then continued, 'It was as though the James I knew and married had died over there, and this stranger had come back home in his place.' Bridget took hold of one of Sarah's hands and held it tightly. 'I didn't understand him any longer, Sarah. He was so changed; he was erratic. He would get really angry for no reason, and sometimes, often, he hit me. I tried to tell myself that it wasn't his fault. I didn't know what to do, but I was hoping that he would get better. I kept believing that my James, the James I married, would come back. I thought that with time... but it never happened. Everything just got worse.'

She let go of her sister's hand and ran her fingers through her hair. An expression of complete exasperation crossed her face as she inwardly blamed the War, the Empire, the Germans and politics. She even blamed people's inability to think for themselves, though she was not quite sure what such a state of affairs had to do with either herself or James.

'You should have told me, Bridget. I'm your sister, for God's sake. You should know that I'm always here for you, always have been. I'd do anything for you. Surely you know that?'

Knowing full well that Sarah was right, Bridget was uncomfortably distressed by her sister's words. She had been pulled in two directions: wanting to keep James' abuse a secret while wanting to be able to share it with someone, someone who might understand. Now that Sarah knew what had happened, Bridget was relieved, but she did not believe that her sister would be able to remove the anxiety and terror that had plagued her for days and nights on end. All she could possibly hope for was that her life might now be just that little bit easier.

Bridget retrieved her sister's hand and sat holding it between both of her own, relieved to have finally reached the point of being able to share her fear and dread with someone.

'I really wanted to tell you everything as soon as we arrived, but you mentioned Oswald, and... ' Bridget's voice trailed away a moment before continuing, 'I didn't feel that I could say anything to you; it wouldn't have been fair. I guessed that you had more than enough to worry about, even though I didn't know then why you were so worried.'

Bridget paused, thinking of everything she had wanted to say to Sarah and of her disappointment when it became apparent that she would not be able to say anything. She sighed and continued: 'As I said, it has not been easy since James returned. He was different. He was not the same man who went away. It was the injury, Sarah; it destroyed him. It didn't kill him, but it destroyed him. It was the injury and this awful, senseless war. He was so unpredictable when he came back. He could be calculating and cruel, but some days he was just the same as he'd been before.'

Sarah squeezed her hand in an attempt to make her aware that she understood. 'I am so sorry, Bridget,' she said. 'I really am.'

Bridget was thinking how it was, afterwards, after it was all over, when she had mentally crossed the line between her past and her future, and she had been hesitating about what to do next. She remembered that her mind and her body had been numb: there was no next, nor was there any before; she was not even sure if there was a now. The now that she was attempting to hold on to kept moving backwards into the past, and she was unable to stop it from moving. She had stood for what seemed like an eternity in the middle of the room, shivering in spite of the heat. She had been unable to move. All she could do was stand stock-still, looking at the inert body lying on the floor.

At first, she was terrified that it would get up, that the 'it' that used to be a 'he' was not dead and that she had simply imagined everything. Then she was terrified that he actually *was* dead and that she was the cause of his death, and part of her was hoping that he *would* get up and that everything could revert to how it had been before. The past with all its imperfections and question marks was ever so much more attractive than the terrifying future that was rapidly looming up in front of her.

Even if he was the cause of the situation in which she now found herself, and even if his miraculous return to life, if such a thing were possible, would simply reinstate her previous reality, a reality she had attempted to free herself from, part of her still hoped and prayed that he would open his eyes and stand up.

She remembered the jumbled words of prayers mixing with promises to God, the God who, for all she knew, had allowed such an awful thing to happen.

Thinking back, she was convinced that she was not thinking of consequences. Not then. Not immediately. As she stood in the room, looking at the man stretched out on the floor, she did not think about what was likely to happen to her. She did not think about police and trials and execution. Those thoughts came much later.

She was transfixed, dazed and focused completely on the form that only minutes before had been noisily moving towards her and was now lying motionless on the floor. She was horrified that she, Bridget Mary Kathleen O'Connor, now Jackson, the person who detested killing in all its forms, had killed someone.

It was late afternoon, almost evening, and beyond the house the crows were cawing. There was a weak shaft of end-of-the-day light coming in through the kitchen window, and it was in that shaft of light that the body was lying. She remembered thinking that there was something religious about it, seeing parallels between the light coming into the kitchen and the light that she had seen streaming through the stained-glass windows of the local church.

He was lying in an unwieldy manner, one arm above his head, the other caught somewhere beneath his body. He had fallen forwards, and his face was hidden. There was already a dark stain on the back of his head, and she tried to ignore all the thoughts telling her that it was blood and that it was she who had caused it to be there.

She forced herself to kneel next to him, placing her head near his. There was no sound, no breath. Nothing. Now that he could not harm her, memories came rushing back at her. She remembered his smile and the way he could pull her into that smile and everything that was behind it. She remembered the touch of his hand on her arm. She remembered the sound of his voice and his warmth and his smell. She wanted to bury her head in his chest; she wanted to forget everything except the 'before'. She wanted him to stand up and take her back to where everything had begun.

But she also remembered the fear. She remembered the painful uneasiness of 'not knowing'. Not knowing when he might suddenly become angry without reason; not knowing when or if he might want to hurt her; not knowing whether the man crossing the threshold was her James or the unwelcome stranger she had learnt to detest.

The child stirred in his cot, and his stirrings reached into her consciousness. Soon it would be night and then it would be morning. With the new light, people would be up and about. Something was telling her that she should leave.

But after she had stood up, knowing that she had to do something, she was still unable to move. It was as though a spell had been cast and she was now sentenced to be forever tied to that particular part of the floor.

The crows cawed yet again and then, as the sky darkened, they became quiet.

A loose shutter on a window somewhere in the house banged back and forth. She started, fearful that there was someone outside, before becoming aware of what it was and only then was she able to relax just a little.

But it was in that moment that she knew for certain that she had to get away.

An understanding of the consequences was finally beginning to push its way to the forefront of her brain: people who killed other people were hanged. More than anything, she did not want to be hanged.

The child stirred again.

She suddenly became aware of the iron poker: she must have dropped it afterwards, after it was all over, and now it lay on the floor, not far from where James was lying, not far from where she was standing. She tried not to look at the blood already congealing on the tip.

She did not have a plan, it had all happened so quickly. While she was looking at the poker lying on the floor, she wondered if unpremeditated murder was also a hanging offence.

Having acknowledged the poker, she felt a strange sense of release. It was as though she had moved some of the guilt and responsibility to the inanimate object. Within moments, whatever it was that had kept her rooted to the spot relaxed its hold. She remembered feeling that she was not real, just a figment of someone else's imagination, and she wondered in whose imagination she had managed to lose herself. For the first time in more than twenty minutes, she turned away from the figure on the floor.

She collapsed on to a chair, her head in her hands. She had absolutely no idea what to do next. She felt as though the whole room, in fact the whole world, was moving in on her, suffocating her. What she wanted most of all was to be able to remain where she was while the body, the poker and the blood floated off into space, but she knew that such things did not happen. After what seemed like forever, but was probably only a matter of minutes, she pulled herself to her feet.

The darkness had come quickly while she had been caught in a state of numbness. It had wrapped around her and the house, cutting off that small part of the world from all that was sane and normal. For all that time, and even afterwards, she felt alone, isolated, apart; she was no longer part of the normal world. She was a woman with a dead husband, and a hangman's noose swaying above her.

Taking a bag from the bedroom, she shoved a few clothes into it before returning to the kitchen, where she wrapped the remainder of the day's loaf with a few pieces of cold meat. As she added the parcel to her bag her hands were trembling. She knew that there were other things she needed to take, but the dark, confused images rushing through her head were telling her to go. They were telling her that she needed to be gone.

She snatched her coat from the hook behind the bedroom door; took the money that they always kept in a battered tea tin above the stove, trying all the time to avoid looking at what was on the floor; hoisted the bag on to her shoulder; lifted the child from his cot; slammed the door and walked out of the house.

She had no definite plan: all she wanted was to get as far away from the house and the farm as possible. For a moment, she stood outside the house, wondering what she should do next. The idea of walking into town in the middle of the night terrified her, but she knew that she needed to get away. She could not stay where she was. It was still uncomfortably hot, but the moon had risen, and the track leading away from the house was lit up with a bright, almost eerie, light. She took a deep breath, and without looking behind her, began to walk away from the house. Away from what she had done; away from the body growing cold on the kitchen floor.

Before she reached the main road, she stepped off the track and took a detour across a couple of paddocks, occasionally following an all-but-dry creek. When she felt that she had put a reasonable distance between herself and the house, she rested with the child in a thicket of small trees. Then, as the darkness very slowly began to give way to the inkling of a new day, she stood up, and with her bag on her shoulder and Joseph on her hip, she crossed from the paddock to the road.

In the distance, she could already see the shapes of the buildings she knew as Gilgandra.

She ran her fingers through her very tousled hair, took a deep breath and began, 'I had been so happy when I knew that he was coming home, almost two years ago now. You know how I felt, Sarah, I had written to you, counting the weeks, days and then hours. I knew that he had been wounded. He had written, but there had been so few letters, and the ones he did write did not tell me much. Not the things I wanted to know. He did not go into detail: he simply told me that there had been an attack somewhere and that many men had been killed and even more had been wounded. He wrote that he was getting better and that he was looking forward to being with me and Joseph again.

'When the train pulled into Gilgandra — it was sometime in September — Joseph and I were on the platform, waiting for him. That he was able to walk off the train on his own made me believe that everything must have been all right with him: there were a couple of other men being lifted off on stretchers and several being helped by medical staff. One man had lost a leg and another had bandages covering most of his face.

'James seemed to be unharmed, but I could not believe how weak and haggard he looked. You might remember that I wrote to you then, telling you how much he seemed to have changed. When we were back home in the cottage, I burst into tears, dismayed and disturbed by his appearance, but he brushed away my concerns, saying that some decent food and lots of Australian sunshine would soon have him fine again.

'But, Sarah, it never happened. Not really. His physical wounds had already healed by the time he arrived home, and over the following months he kept his promise and put on most of the weight he had lost. He even got back some of his energy, but there was something about him that had changed. There were times when I felt he was a different person, someone I did not know, someone I did not want to know. In between, he was the James I knew and loved, the man I could talk to and laugh with, the man I was able to trust. But without warning he could suddenly become someone else, someone who was cruel and violent, a complete stranger.

'Once I accepted that this stranger was now part of our life, I had to learn not to upset him. I became very good at weaving myself in and out of his moods and his irritation.

I learnt how to fade into the background when something upset him and he came storming into the house. I always tried to remain one step ahead of him, guessing what it was he might want or not want. It was like walking through a room of broken glass, trying to avoid getting cut while trying, at the same time, not to make any sound. It was utterly exhausting, Sarah. I wanted to tell you, but I did not know how. I did not know where to begin.'

While Bridget was talking to her sister, a thought that she stumbled upon earlier once again took shape and then refused to go away: perhaps she had been expecting too much, and perhaps she was being unreasonable. Men often punched and hit women. It was nothing new. It was not something that only she had experienced. Most people would have said that it was to be expected; it was the norm. She had grown up hearing how men needed to keep women in their place. It was commonplace: it was what men did and what women put up with.

She stopped the thought abruptly in its tracks: James had been different. He had never been that kind of man, the kind of man who would hit a woman. Although it was considered normal, she had always had the feeling that it was wrong. She was not sure why she thought it was wrong. How could something be wrong when no one seemed to object? Or was it that one half of the population did actually object, but the objection was overruled by the other half? No, it was not a question of half and half. There were even women who felt it was to be expected: men were naturally superior to women; the Church said so, everyone said so. While other men, men like James, agreed with the women who silently objected. They respected women; they would never raise a hand against them. Such violence had not been something that Bridget needed to worry about, not until the stranger entered their lives.

Although she had never fully accepted the idea of men being naturally superior to women, she found herself sitting on a fence between what was an established belief and what she felt was fair. She had grown up accepting that women were somehow inferior to men, and though some small part of her might have occasionally railed against the belief, society left her no other choice than to acquiesce. Whether the idea was connected to the accepted image of God as male, or whether it was simply that men were physically more powerful and therefore more suited to being in charge, she found herself pulled between what she felt was logical and just, and what society wanted her to accept. Although she would never dare put her thoughts into so many words, she was certain that if women were occasionally given the chance to make important decisions and say what they really thought, then things would most probably be very different.

But regardless of the absence of gender equality, James had never shouted at her or hit her, not before he went away.

While thoughts about fairness and what was logical and illogical were still swarming around in her head, she continued talking to her sister: 'Sometimes, more often than not, he was completely normal and gentle and kind, and it was then that I wondered if I might have misunderstood him, and if, perhaps, I was actually the cause of his temper and his violent outbursts. Sometimes, I even wondered if I was imagining it all, and he was not violent at all.'

She paused for a moment, thinking of the bruises that told another story. She had often looked at the bruises and could not find any correlation between the man who had caused them and the man who sometimes put his arms around her and told her that he loved her; the man with the magnetic blue eyes with whom she wanted to spend all the years of her life. She was caught between two men, both with the name James: one of them was the man she loved, the man she had married; the other was the stranger.

He could move between charming and terrifying in the short time it took for him to walk across the room. When he was home, she was never really at ease. She could never know when he was likely to explode.

Like that dreadful day that was still foremost in her memory.

Sarah was obviously waiting for her to continue. There was no turning back now, no possibility of saying that it had never happened. She knew that her next words would condemn her completely, but with condemnation there was also an element of acceptance and even relief.

'I had been ironing in the kitchen,' she said, thinking of the coarse grey blanket spread out over the kitchen table, and the two heavy irons heating on the stove. 'Joseph was asleep. It was quiet in the house.' She remembered how, every now and then, she would suddenly become aware of the crows cawing outside. Through the window, the heat was shimmering.

The room was hot, summer hot. All day there had been a burning wind moving in from the west, colouring the sky orange, sucking up the final drops of moisture from wilting crops and grasses. The noise and the dust and the shimmering heat were all pressing in on her, cocooning her, making her feel vulnerable. She remembered pulling her hair back and tying it with the first thing that came to hand — a piece of black cord that had previously been tied around a box containing an assortment of papers — before picking up the heated iron. She believed that she could have been thinking of moist green grass and sparkling waterfalls.

'The kitchen door swung open,' she said, while her thoughts recalled the hard, frightening, unexpected noise, and how, in the door opening, silhouetted by the angry orange sky, was her husband, first filling the doorway and then filling the entire kitchen. 'It was James; he was obviously angry. He slammed the door shut and then knocked over a chair. A cloth that I had finished ironing and had carefully folded was picked up and thrown on to the floor.

'I dared not complain, Sarah. I was sure that he was provoking me, hoping that I would say something so that he would have a reason, a legitimate reason, to strike me.' She stopped talking for a moment, thinking how her hand had been shaking as she placed the iron on the side of the stove.

'He crossed the room and took me by the wrist. He had been drinking. I could smell it on his breath as he moved in closer and squeezed my arm tightly.

'My arm hurt, but this was nothing new. I remember that I closed my eyes and prayed that he would let me go.

He pushed me across the room.' Could she possibly go on? Could she possibly explain what happened next?

'What happened then?' asked Sarah softly, cradling her sister's hand, her eyes intently watching her face. 'Could you have possibly got away from him?'

Bridget shook her head, remembering the sudden pain that soared through her leg as she collided with the heavy table. 'He grabbed me before I even had a chance to stand up, and then he threw me back towards the stove.'

Had he actually been intending to kill her? She did not know. She could still remember how she was trembling as she finally pulled herself to her feet. He was not looking at her, his attention having been caught by something beyond the window. The sky? The billowing dust? Intuitively she must have understood that this was the only help she was going to get, and a primitive need to survive pushed away all other emotions and any moral qualms she may have had. Without analysing the situation, without thinking about she was about to do, without even knowing what she was about to do, she picked up the poker leaning next to the stove and swung it as hard as she could.

'I hit him with the poker, Sarah. I didn't stop to think about what I was doing. I just did it. I knew that I had hit him when the room once again became quiet.'

Chapter Eighteen

A couple of weeks after Bridget arrived in Sydney two things happened. They were quite separate from each other, yet they were still in some way connected, and they both happened on the same day.

The first thing that transpired was that Bridget received two letters, one from her mother and the other from Thomas. When she saw that the letters were for her, and not for Sarah, she was both amazed and disconcerted: no one was supposed to know that she was in Sydney. But then it occurred to her that Sarah would most certainly have written home and would have naturally mentioned that Bridget was in Sydney.

Bridget's immediate instinct was to be angry with her sister, but before she was able to act on this instinct, her more reasonable self intervened, pointing out that Sarah had done what anyone would normally have done in such a situation. It was clear that Sarah had written home before Bridget had told her exactly *why* she was in Sydney. Before Sarah had been given all the details, there was no reason why she would not have expected everyone to know what she knew: Bridget and Joseph were with her in Sydney, and James was still in Gilgandra.

Standing inside the front door, the letters in her hand, Bridget was certain that she needed to retain a sense of the ordinary. Previously, she might not have been so intent on creating a feeling that everything was normal — she had had too many other things on her mind — but now that it had been thrust upon her she understood that it was something worthwhile hanging on to and believing in. It was normal that she should come to Sydney when her sister needed her. It was also normal that her sister should write home and comment on the fact that she was in Sydney. That Sarah now knew the real reason why her sister was in Sydney did not have to eradicate the need for this façade of the ordinary. If she was somehow going to survive the situation she had unwittingly brought into being, she could only do it by embracing everything that still had some shred of normality, however small.

Mary O'Connor spent the first part of her letter describing her astonishment on learning that Bridget and Joseph were in Sydney. This was followed by a few lines asking about James and how he was managing, lines that Bridget skimmed quickly, concerned that they could easily call up the images she was trying to rid herself of, images that would almost certainly destroy the very fragile balance she needed to survive. The fact that her mother wrote about James in the present tense gave Bridget a small rush of something that could be equated with joy: the O'Connors had, as yet, not received any unwanted news. Obviously, Mary did not know that James was dead. As far as Bridget's family in Molong was concerned, Bridget was in Sydney with Sarah, and James was alive and well in Gilgandra.

In the second part of the letter, there was mention of a late burst of oppressive summer heat and that the farmers, including Martin, were hoping for rain before they commenced ploughing. At the very end of the letter, Mary wrote that they had still not heard anything more regarding Daniel, but she trusted God was watching over him, wherever he might be, and that he would soon be found and brought back home.

The letter from Thomas was relatively short, two pages in length, and Bridget put it to one side, like a chocolate in silver paper wrapping, waiting for just the right moment to read it. She had a special place in her heart for her unconventional and warm-hearted little brother, whose loud laugh usually proceeded him, and who managed to turn the ordinary into something that was, more often than not, extraordinary.

She would have liked to have escaped to some quiet place with the letter, but knowing that this was impossible she finally slit open the envelope with a knife from the kitchen. Sitting on her own at the kitchen table, she read Thomas' letter:

Dear Bridget,

There's been no more news of Dan, so we have to assume that he's still missing. As long as he's simply missing then there's hope that he's still alive, somewhere. We're all praying that he'll be found, that he's safe and well and that he'll soon be coming home.

More than anything I want this to be true, but it has been so many months now. If he's alive, then why hasn't he written? I don't want my thoughts to run in such a direction, but I'm no longer sure if there's any other direction for them to run.

Ma is taking it all really bad. You know what she's like: she doesn't say much, but she worries constantly. I tell her that missing doesn't have to mean the same as dead while deep down I kind of agree with her. I'm not sure, but I think Ma has already decided that he's dead, and all she's waiting for is to find out that she's right. At the same time she's praying that he's still alive. Both options are completely real for her, his being dead and his being alive.

Perhaps that's the same for all of us?

How is Sydney? I was truly blown away when I heard about you and Joe being in Sydney with Sarah. It would be grand to be there with both of you, and Joe, but I can't leave Molong what with all this with Dan, and Ma and Da needing me.

And now there's Oswald. When Ma received Sarah's letter, she went straight to Father O'Grady and asked him to say a Mass for him and Daniel. Let's hope that God was paying attention. I'd say He's working overtime, trying to help so many at once, being asked to find and save lost husbands and sons. And brothers. I don't suppose we can expect Him to listen to everyone.

When I read Sarah's letter, I did wonder what kind of help Oswald might be getting. We've no idea what hospitals are like over there, not with all the wounded and the dying. At least Sarah has received a letter: that has to be a good sign. Perhaps he's already on a boat and he'll soon be arriving back in Sydney. Or am I too hopeful? I feel that it's important to remain hopeful, to remain positive; the alternative can't help anyone.

Dearest sister, I fear we all gave you a hard time with everything about the War, but perhaps you were right all along. I know, I did agree with Martin and Daniel. Felt it was a duty, going to war. Now I'm not so sure. So many men have already died, and I've been thinking a lot about the point of it all. Is there a point? What does it take to win a war? Are there any winners? Or, in the end, are there really only losers?

Ryan Clancy and Billy Goodman — remember them? They're both dead. Billy wrote to me, it must have been only days before he was killed. He was somewhere in France, and I guessed from what he wrote that things were pretty bad. I understood that he couldn't write much of the truth, but it was clear from the few lines he did write that men were dying both in and out of the trenches. He wrote that there were things that he was not able to put into words, things that he would never be able to forget.

Well, he won't have to worry about that now, will he?

Did James mind you taking Joe and going to Sydney on your own? Or perhaps that is really not a concern? I know it's none of my business but I often feel that life has not been particularly easy for you since James returned. If I'm wrong, ignore what I have written...

Bridget read the whole letter, treasuring the *'love in abundance from'* at the end. She then returned to the beginning and reread it, in case she had missed something of importance. That Thomas suspected what others obviously had not (or perhaps they suspected but dared not question what they thought they suspected) was comforting to her, but his concern, if it existed, was already past tense. No matter whether the concern was about James' reaction to her being in Sydney, or whether it was a concern that went deeper, delving into how James might, or might not, have been treating her, it could no longer be considered of any relevance. Not for Thomas and definitely not for James. Bridget was very aware that her brother's consideration was directed at herself, and she wondered vaguely how Thomas was going to feel when he learnt that his sister was to be hanged.

She shook her head as if to rid her mind of such thoughts, and having returned the letter to its envelope she stood up before placing Thomas' letter carefully with the other letter in her bag.

They had been invited to call on Nora Murphy in the afternoon. Nora, who lived in the flat on the ground floor, was a couple of decades older than Sarah, and she had taken a liking to the young couple on the top floor. Occasionally she would knock on their door with some freshly baked soda bread or a few pieces of bruised fruit that her husband had managed to pick up cheaply at the market. If Sarah sometimes resented the older woman's probing and nosy nature, she was mostly grateful to have someone with whom she could talk about ordinary, everyday things, especially with her mother and siblings so far away. She had gradually become aware that Nora had a kind heart; it was just a matter of being very selective about what to tell her and how much to tell her.

When, one of the first days after she arrived in Sydney, Bridget heard Sarah mention the name *Murphy,* her thoughts immediately flew to the young man she had met outside Gilgandra more than six months ago. She heard the name while washing up after dinner in Sarah's kitchen, and she had felt a strange feeling surge through her body, thinking that perhaps Sarah was talking about the same Murphy. The young man with the name Murphy had seemed like a pleasant person, and, had her life been different, she would have liked to have got to know him better. But, on second thoughts, Murphy was a common name, and the chances of *her* Murphy living in the same house as her sister were highly unlikely. It was more credible that Callum Murphy was still somewhere in the north-west of the state, that he had not returned to Sydney as he had intended, and that he most definitely did not live on Wells Street in Redfern.

Bridget gathered that Nora Murphy, in spite of the prying, which could perhaps be interpreted as a kind of misguided concern, had actually been a great help to Sarah, especially since Oswald left. Her thoughts took a small detour, and she wondered if compassion and friendliness could be *Murphy* characteristics. A couple of times, she was on the verge of asking her sister if Nora had a son called Callum, but she shied away from doing so, knowing that a negative answer would have contained more disappointment than she felt she could handle at the moment. It was better to be able to dream until it became obvious that the dream was, in fact, no more than a dream.

Nevertheless, Bridget's mind refused to let go of the word *Murphy* or of the image connected with the name or of the possibility, microscopic as it might be, that Callum Murphy could actually be living downstairs, in the same house as she was now living. Eventually, she let her mind have free rein and suddenly, like a time traveller, she had moved backwards almost six months. Remembering the fresh smells and the ditches filled with wildflowers, she thought that it could have been late September or possibly early October.

She had walked the three miles into Gilgandra to buy a few groceries and was now on her way home. There had been rain earlier in the day, but it had dried up, leaving the air fresh and the dirt road reasonably dust free. The first yellow and purple wildflowers of the season were already filling the ditches, while a gentle breeze had picked up the smells of both the rain-touched earth and the scattered blue-green eucalyptus trees lining parts of the road. For the first time in ages she felt that she could separate herself from her anxieties concerning James, and concentrate on simply feeling good. Her worries would be waiting for her when she got home, but for a few hours she would be a different, less anxious person. She would have liked the present moment, filled with spring and soft, warm breezes, to go on forever.

She had Joseph and her parcels in the high-wheeled pram. Except for the occasional noisy cockatoo or crow, the world was very quiet. In the distance she could see a mob of kangaroos.

Rounding a slight bend in the road, she noticed, slightly further on, someone at the side of the road. It was apparently a man, and he was lying under a large, spreading red gum, clearly unaware of Bridget's slow progress along the road. Close by there was a horse grazing.

As she came closer, the horse lifted its head, looked at her and then continued with what it had been doing. She was not sure whether or not she should make herself known to the man: it seemed somehow rude to simply walk past when she and the man were clearly the only two people in the world or, at least, the only two people on that stretch of isolated road. On the other hand, she did not know the man. She had no idea if he was trustworthy: he could be anyone at all, a rogue, an outlaw, even a murderer.

People were usually trustworthy. Nevertheless, she had heard some awful stories, and while she could not get the stories out of her head she was clinging to the belief that they were only made-up stories. Imaginations, she knew, could often run wild. A few isolated facts could easily mix with fears and fantasies to produce something quite alarming. Shadows could fill out and become both concrete and substantial.

She was still wondering what was the right thing to do when he opened his eyes, noticed her and scrambled to his feet. 'How's it going there? Must say you startled me just a little,' he said, smiling, brushing some pieces of grass off his shirt.

Bridget stopped in the middle of the road and smiled back, her hands resting lightly on the pram. She decided that most probably he was trustworthy and that she had nothing to fear from him. The shadows backed away, silently.

'Grand,' she replied. 'And yourself?' Having bravely crossed out the words *outlaw* and *murderer*, she felt that she should say something more, and searched in her mind for words that might be suitable. 'You're not from around here?' she finally added.

At the same time there was a small, nagging thought that would not leave her alone. The shadows had not completely disappeared: they insisted on lingering, somewhere in the background. He seemed pleasant, but imagine if he was not as he seemed. Imagine if he actually *was* an outlaw, one of those wicked men she had been so intent on removing from her mind. Trying not to pay too much attention to the nagging, she found herself returning to the thought of them being the only two people in that part of the world. Then she thought of Joseph and corrected herself: the only three people.

She had heard of the man who had murdered a whole family somewhere near Gilgandra, but that was years ago, and from what she had heard, the family was at home, doing normal things, not expecting to be killed.

Bridget took a deep breath, trying to rid herself of such thoughts, but, in spite of her best intentions, her head began to fill with snippets of the talk about the boundary rider who had assaulted—

She stopped the thoughts before they managed to take hold and looked directly at the man. She guessed that he was possibly a few years younger than she was. Now that he was standing, she could see that he was also slightly taller and quite compact, with a head of untidy fair hair that made Bridget think of the fields after harvesting. His skin was obviously pink, *sunburnt* was the word that ran through Bridget's mind, and it did not have the weather-beaten appearance that was normal for someone who spent all his time outdoors.

'I'm up from Sydney,' he said, 'but I've been in Coonamble these past three weeks, helping me Uncle Vic. By the way, the name is Callum. Callum Murphy.'

The nagging was rapidly becoming more indistinct. The image of herself and Joseph being left dead at the side of the road had more or less disintegrated. He did not seem the type who would randomly kill vulnerable women and children.

Then he added, 'Uncle Vic's sort of crook at the moment.'

Bridget listened to Callum relate how Victor Murphy had fallen from a roof he was mending only a month ago, and how, having only young daughters, four in total, and with the harvest season already looming, he had sent for Callum. She wondered how Callum could possibly be free to travel to Coonamble or Gilgandra or wherever, and why he was now lying in the grass at the side of a road in Gilgandra. Against her will, and while she was still wondering about Callum, she thought of all the young men being shot at and killed in places the names of which no one had ever heard before. For a brief second, she even thought of Daniel and then she blushed, understanding that her reaction was no different from the reactions of those who were aggressively advocating participation in the War.

Bridget was still guiltily regretting her reaction, which was so unlike everything she felt was right and just, and wondering how she might be able to make amends, when Callum continued, 'Uncle Vic's place is south of Coonamble, not so far from Gilgandra. His neighbour's been helping out as well, and it's been pretty hectic these past two weeks,' he paused for a moment before continuing, 'and then Uncle Vic said I could have the day off.'

Pieces of the puzzle were slotting together: she now knew why he was in Gilgandra, but there were still pieces that did not fit.

Whether it was a psychic connection or whether it was simply that he had an uncanny ability to relate to her unexpected and unwanted reaction, he said, 'I got the consumption real bad last year, they reckoned it was the end of me. I guess I was lucky, others aren't as lucky.' He stopped talking, obviously thinking about the others and why they were or were not lucky.

Bridget did not want to pursue the topic any further, fearing that it could be leading in a difficult direction. She was still upset by her thoughts, which were so contrary to everything in which she believed. She told him her name and moved the pram into the shade under the tree. She had made up her mind that Callum was not a murderer and that her name was not going to be splashed across the front of the local newspaper.

'I've never been to Coonamble,' she said, simply for the sake of saying something that sounded ordinary and safe.

She asked him how long he thought he might be staying with his uncle, and he told her that he would stay until after the harvest and probably a week or so longer. Then he told her that he hoped to return to his job at the Railyards when he got back to Sydney. His father had been at the Eveleigh Railyards for years, he added before going on to say that he had been working on track maintenance, but that was before he got sick.

Somehow he reminded Bridget of her two younger brothers, and she wanted him to keep talking so that she could pretend, for a moment, that she was at home and that everything was as it had been before. Before Daniel went away. Before James came back.

It was no problem for Callum to keep talking. Perhaps, like Bridget, he was also finding some kind of solace in their meeting, or perhaps he simply liked having someone willing to listen to him.

Bridget was looking at Callum, thinking of Daniel and Thomas. She was not fully aware of what he was saying, but then she scattered the images of her two brothers, and she became aware that he must be talking about his work at the Railyards. It was like walking into a room and into a conversation that had already begun.

'... in the yard,' she heard him say. 'It was me break, and one of the engineers were there with wife and kid. Not sure why he'd his family with him, but he were off duty so perhaps that was why. He's talking with one of the boilermakers, and it's noisy as usual, and then the kid disappears. I'd no idea what was going on. I was jus' having a smoke and thinking of other things, and then these people started calling out, and out of the corner of me eye I saw this kid in front of the loco shed. There he is, crossing the lines that go in and out of the shed, and there's a loco backing out. Could be the kid was in no danger — the loco driver might've seen him — but it could've been too late. So I dropped me smoke and dashed across the yard to where the kid's picking up stones from between the lines and grabbed him.

'They all thanked me. The engineer, his wife, the shop manager... I told them all that it were no more than anyone would've done, but the manager insisted on giving me something. Of course, I was thinking money, but I could see him consid'ring it, very carefully, and then he says he'd give me a grand certificate to hang on me wall. You know, with a signature and a frame.'

Bridget smiled but said nothing. Waited for him to continue.

'It weren't long after that that I got crook, and I guess the manager had been thinking a little longer, 'cause he came 'round to me house a couple o' months after I'd stopped working, and he gave me Ma...' He stopped talking, abruptly, and actually blushed a little through his sunburn. 'I've been talking too much,' he said. 'It's a Murphy thing.'

Bridget shook her head. She did not feel he was talking too much. In fact, she was enjoying listening to the sound of his voice while thinking about Daniel and Thomas. For the first time in months she felt like an ordinary woman doing ordinary, everyday things. 'No,' she said, 'not at all.' Then she added, 'If you really think you talk too much, then you should meet my father.'

Thinking back, she remembered how natural it felt, standing there at the side of the road, the spring sun warm without being intrusive. Apart from mentioning his illness and giving a few anecdotes from his time working for the railways, Callum did not reveal a lot about himself. He talked a bit about the work with his uncle and asked Bridget what her husband did. He was clearly sympathetic when Bridget told him that James had been wounded somewhere in the Middle East but relieved when she told him that he was now back home.

Callum talked about Uncle Vic's accident, his family, Sydney and Coonamble. Bridget mentioned Daniel, and then moved quickly on to topics that were safe and more or less devoid of question marks. She appreciated the unfamiliar, but very welcome, sense of calmness and serenity that had settled over the place, and she wanted the moment, the moments, to go on forever. Finally, though, she had to say goodbye, because she knew that James would be expecting her. Even though she might have felt that time had stopped, she knew that it was still ticking resolutely towards the future.

He helped her push the pram back out on to the road and then tipped his hat, saying that he really hoped they would meet again, although he would have known that it was most unlikely. She had felt an enormous urge to hug him, as if he had been one of her brothers or even the James from before, but she had restrained herself, and once she started walking she did not look back.

While Sarah talked about Nora Murphy, the Murphy flat downstairs and the visit planned for the afternoon, Bridget's mind continued to dig out images of Callum until she understood just how ridiculous she was being: there was no way that Nora Murphy could be the mother of Callum. She returned the images whence they had come and tried to concentrate on other things instead.

Bridget had imagined Nora Murphy as being a woman somewhere in her mid- to late forties, short rather than tall, and, like so many other women of her age, weary-looking and disenchanted. When Nora opened the door to the three of them — Bridget, Joseph and Sarah — Bridget saw that she had been right with some things but wrong with others.

A little more than medium height with brown hair already heavily streaked with grey and pulled back into a severe bun, Nora was obviously well into her forties and both tired and careworn, but as she opened the door her face lit up with a bright smile. Bridget was no longer sure about there being any disenchantment. In fact, she mentally deleted that word from the collection of words she had bundled together to describe Nora Murphy.

As the door closed behind them, blocking out the dismal hallway and the existence of the staircase, Bridget saw that they were in a room that more or less resembled the rooms in her sister's flat and, in all probability, most of the rooms in the building. Apart from it being sitting room, kitchen and sleeping area (there was a sofa bed against the long wall to the right), it had the same brown walls and the same grey, sun-deprived atmosphere that had surrounded her for the past couple of weeks. During those weeks, when the uninspiring constraints of the flat became too much, she would let her thoughts escape to places where the horizon and the sky blurred together and the sun was part of everything. Standing in yet another confined, colourless room, her imagination was already yearning to take her to a place where the scope was unhindered and the colours were infinite shades of blue and yellow.

She became aware of people speaking, and she reluctantly brought her attention back to the flat and its position in relation to everything else in the house. Although the main part of the ground-floor flat was at the back of the building, accessed from a door to the left of the stairs, Sarah had already mentioned that the room near the front door was part of the downstairs flat. Bridget wondered what it would be like living in a flat split by stairs, a general access area and a back door, and then she thought of the pub in Molong and decided that there was probably not that much difference.

The flat was long and narrow, stretching out behind the main part of the house and running parallel to the path on the left. The pathway, which led away from the back door of the house, was made of flat, grey stones. It was also very narrow and filled the space between the Murphy flat on the right and a tall brick wall on the left. Its main purpose was to provide a general passage to the open laundry building and, at the very end of the long, confined property, the communal toilet. Bridget had used the path many times in the few short weeks she had lived with her sister, occasionally wondering about the people living in the downstairs flat while reflecting on the fact that the neighbouring house beyond the solid wall was doubtlessly very similar to the building Bridget was already calling her sister's. A lush green vine with purple and pink flowers covered a large part of the wall, sending out long tendrils towards the Murphy flat and, in places, threatening to enclose the pathway and turn it into a tunnel.

Standing inside the flat with her back to the front door, Bridget noticed a window on the left, which looked out on to the stone pathway and the greenery. She had seen it before, from the outside, and had wondered what might be behind it. Now she knew: a brown, gloomy room. The very few anaemic rays of sun that somehow managed to fight their way into the space via the small window were shaded with green and grey and, in most cases, had lost any brightness they might have had before they arrived. On the far side of the window, the back door of the flat gave access to the narrow pathway.

The somewhat cluttered room, with its accumulated melancholia, was obviously the main room in the flat. There was a closed door on the short wall opposite, and Bridget assumed that it led to a bedroom. A stove filled the space between the door and the long wall on the right, while a sink, a tallboy, a chest of drawers and a small wooden chest were lined up along the wall next to the sofa bed. In the centre of the room there was a rectangular table surrounded by several assorted chairs. Bridget wondered, somewhat absent-mindedly, if the crocheted tablecloth had been placed there in preparation for afternoon tea or if it always covered the table.

While Nora was greeting her three guests and Sarah was making the necessary introductions, Bridget's eyes had been moving quickly around the flat. As they completed the circle, Bridget noted the sewing machine under the window on her left, and Nora, following her gaze, explained that she did piecework for a clothing company on George Street.

Bridget nodded politely; after a cursory glance at the pile of finished bodices and the carefully prepared pieces of textiles that had not yet been sewn together, she acknowledged Nora's invitation to sit down and followed Sarah across the room to the sofa. Lifting Joseph on to her knee, she would have preferred to have been doing something, anything at all, but there was nothing for her to do. Instead, she sat nervously on the edge of the sofa, her arms wrapped around her son, and watched while Nora positioned the cups and plates and placed the sugar bowl and milk jug at one end of the table near the teapot. In the centre of the table there was a dough cake, which Bridget suspected would have been made specially for the afternoon tea.

Nora had just invited everyone to move to the table and was about to pour the tea, when there was the sound of footsteps outside the front door. They all paused what they were doing and looked in the direction of the door as it swung open, and a man walked into the room.

Nora turned to Bridget and said, 'Bridget, I'd like you to meet my eldest son.'

Chapter Nineteen

Seamus Murphy was a big man and several inches taller than Bridget. He was solid with thick, black hair cut short, parted on the side and slicked back with some kind of oil. On entering the room, he nodded to his mother and Sarah, and introduced himself to Bridget. Catching sight of Joseph, who was once again sitting on his mother's knee, he smiled and made a terrifying monster face at him. After initially wondering whether or not he should burst into tears, Joseph, safe in his mother's arms, decided that the monster was obviously a fake and began hesitantly to laugh instead. Seamus patted the child on his head and sat down on the only free chair at the table, his green eyes dancing with some private amusement.

Nora bustled around, fetching an extra cup and plate, expressing regret for not having remembered that Seamus would be home early. In spite of the disruption, it was obvious that she was delighted to be able to show off her eldest son.

Although Bridget had never really expected to be reunited with Callum Murphy, she could still not help but be just a little disappointed. A very small part of her had been looking forward to a possible, but highly improbable, reunion. Now, when that possibility was completely overruled, she removed the fading images of Callum from her mind and concentrated on the man sitting at the table opposite her.

If Callum believed that he talked too much, and if Bridget had decided that Patrick was miles ahead of him on that front, she now had to concede that Seamus would definitely have to be the winner. He moved easily from one complicated and, most likely, fabricated story to the next, from one elaborate description of a person, an event or a political idea to a description of something entirely different.

As the tea was poured and the dough cake was sliced and placed on plates, Bridget felt herself being unwillingly pulled into the orbit of something completely beyond anything she had experienced before. Callum had given her some respite: he had let her feel normal again, and she had enjoyed that feeling. During that brief breathing space with Callum, she had been able to forget everything that was pulling her life to pieces. For a short space of time she had been permitted to be herself. Any attraction that she may have felt had not been to Callum but to the wonderful suspension of time he had inadvertently given her.

She believed that she had always loved James even when she kept telling herself that he had changed and that her feelings for him had also changed. Now when he could no longer hurt her, she loved the memory of him, a memory of him being gentle and kind. She had no intention of being attracted to another man. Should she avoid being hanged, she found it difficult to imagine that anyone would be interested in being involved with a woman who had killed her husband.

Like Callum, Seamus could never be more than a brief respite or distraction, but in spite of her resolve, Bridget had to admit to herself that there was something about Seamus that made her wonder, ever so vaguely, about the possibility of second chances. For the duration of the visit, she forgot her anxieties, and gave herself over to the exhilaration of the experience.

Later, when Bridget and Sarah were alone in the flat upstairs, Bridget wondered about Seamus and the War and enlistment, and whether Seamus, like Oswald initially, had been rejected or whether he was a pacifist with the courage to hold on to his convictions. Sarah answered that Seamus came from a family that could never have reconciled itself with any one of its members going anywhere to fight for England.

According to what Sarah had been told by Nora, Seamus' grandfather, John Rian Murphy, alias Rian Liam O'Toole, alias Liam Gallagher, had fled Ireland in 1878 with the British close, but not sufficiently close, on his heels. Sometime in the 1860s, when he was in his early thirties and angry at England's refusal to grant Ireland home rule, John joined the Irish Republican Brotherhood. England's response to the activities of the Brotherhood was to make a number of arrests, which through an unfortunate series of events led to the hanging of three Brotherhood members in 1867. Revenging themselves with a bomb did not help the Brotherhood's cause and only managed to push the movement further underground. In spite of these seemingly insurmountable obstacles, John did not lose his dream of an independent Ireland. In the mid-seventies, he and a small group of like-minded members secretly began publishing and distributing a small nationalistic pamphlet, describing Irish independence and the ways it could be achieved.

Although the group believed that it had been careful, the English authorities managed to round up two of the men, and John, already married with several children, became Rian and then Liam in quick succession. He wanted to continue the work for Ireland's independence, but he also wanted to continue living.

In 1878, under the name of Liam Gallagher, he accompanied his wife (to all intents and purposes his widowed sister) and his children (that is to say, his nieces and nephews), on the three-month journey to Sydney, Australia. John's son Colm, ten years old when the family arrived in Australia, had already learnt enough in the few years he had so far lived to know that life was not fair. He had gathered that England did not want Ireland being in charge of anything or anyone, and most definitely not herself.

Colm grew up and eventually married Nora, settled in Sydney and had four children: Seamus, Patrick, Anne and Brendan. By the time war broke out in 1914, John Murphy, and all his aliases, had been dead ten years. His death by drowning in a river south of Sydney could have been an unexplainable accident, or it could simply have been the final act in a life that had been hurtling in that direction since the curtain rose on his birth in Tipperary more than sixty years previously. There was also a small chance that the links in the long chain that connected the English crown with its colony in the southern hemisphere had all pulled in the same direction at the same time and, without explanation or justification, had finally caught up with

John Rian Murphy, alias Rian Liam O'Toole, alias Liam Gallagher.

By 1914, Colm had worked on the roads as a pick and shovel worker; he had spent a few months at the abattoir on Glebe Island; he had worked as a builder's labourer; and he had spent a year constructing sewerage tunnels in different parts of Sydney. Now in his late forties, he was working as a fettler at the Eveleigh Railway Yard. Seamus, his eldest, was also working there, as a packer.

In 1914, twenty-two-year-old Seamus was old enough to enlist, but although he was fully prepared to fight for his country, with the blood of John Murphy running through his veins there was definitely no chance of him putting himself forward to fight for the English King and the English Empire.

When Bridget heard that Seamus worked for the railway she wondered if he knew Callum, and, as she was falling asleep later that evening, she decided that she might ask him next time she saw him. She was already quite certain that there would be a next time.

Chapter Twenty

Seamus was aware that Sarah's sister was married. He also knew that Mrs Jackson's husband had been badly wounded in the War, somewhere in the Middle East, and that he had spent many months recuperating. A sense of there being lines of etiquette that should not be crossed stopped him from asking Sarah and, later, Bridget herself more about Mr Jackson, even though he wanted to know the nature of his injuries. However, having now met and spoken with Bridget Jackson, he very much regretted that there was a Mr Jackson, injured or not.

He was also aware of all the lines between himself and Bridget Jackson, lines that followed the moral law rather than any law related to social convention, but awareness of the lines could not stop him from being fascinated by her. He did not think of her as being beautiful or not beautiful; the thing about her that enraptured and charmed him was something intangible. Whatever it was, it radiated life and purpose. In fact, if he had to equate it with something physical he would have said that it reminded him of water surging over a waterfall. Long, glistening curtains of water, twisting and changing shape, all the time catching the sun's colours in a thousand different reflections. He wanted to wrap himself in her thick black curls; he wanted to breathe in everything that made her who she was. He wanted to be able to do nothing more than to gaze upon her, immersing himself in her smile.

She may have caused him to think of sparkle and life, but he had noted that there was also a sadness about her, something that he had, as yet, been unable to unravel. He guessed that it must have had something to do with her husband, which he found puzzling, seeing as he had heard that Mr Jackson was improving and that he had even started working again. While trying to find some kind of harmony in these opposites, Seamus kept his eye on all the different lines surrounding Bridget, lines that he wanted to be able to erase.

He was twenty-four, and he had spent all of his life in Sydney. There had never been any reason for him to go beyond the boundaries of the city: his life had always been shaped by family and work, both of which were gathered together neatly within those boundaries. There had never been time over for anything else that might have taken him further afield. For him the world had Redfern at its centre, even if he was aware that there were many other places and even many other countries. Several polite, safe friendships with local girls had been easily forgotten as either he or they moved on. He had not met anyone who had enchanted him, who had had the ability to sweep him into some new, exciting universe — that is, not until now.

In spite of his very best intentions to acknowledge all lines, both moral and otherwise, he and Bridget kept encountering one another. The meetings were always arbitrary and unintentional: they were not in any way planned. Seamus told himself that the fact that they happened without any planning, meant that they were supposed to happen. The idea that they were supposed to happen made him wonder if there might be a small shred of something there that could give him cause for optimism.

At the same time he was concerned that the God who had to be manipulating all the strings was possibly mocking him. That same God would have to understand that there was a growing attraction between the two of them: the provocation, he decided, was nothing if not cynical.

The first time they met after the afternoon tea was outside the laundry behind the house on Wells Street. Bridget was on her way out of the laundry with a basket of washed clothing to hang on one of the two lines running between the laundry and the communal toilet. Seamus had been about to open the door to the Murphy flat when he saw her and, in the space of a nanosecond, changed his mind about the door and stepped back on to the path.

Her hair, which she had made a half-hearted attempt to pull back from her face, had partially escaped its ribbon, sending thick, black curls in all directions. From where he stood, it appeared as though the curls had wrapped themselves around the bright rays of the afternoon sun, or was it the other way around? Whichever way it was, the combination of sun and black curls gave her an other-worldly appearance. He wondered whether he had ever in all his life seen anything so beautiful.

As he walked down the narrow path towards where she was already hanging items of clothing on the line, he was wondering what he would say to her. Would he call her Mrs Jackson, or would he use her name as she had insisted he should? Would he comment on the weather, her washing, the state of the path, the afternoon tea... ?

Before he had a chance to decide, she called out to him, asking him if he could help her prop up the line. But first she needed to finish hanging the washing, she added, wondering if he could just wait a few minutes. Then, as though she had asked or expected too much, she quickly went on to say that if he was busy, if he needed to be doing other things, she could manage on her own, but she had seen him, and she had thought—

Seamus was not only enchanted by her hair and the sunlight dancing in it, he was fascinated by everything about her. He was quite sure that he could wait for her forever if it was necessary. He offered to help her hang the washing, but she shook her head and said that it was sufficient that he was willing to wait. While she quickly pegged the few remaining articles of clothing to the line he watched her, thinking that it was such an ordinary, everyday situation, and yet it was something else entirely. Seamus was unable to say exactly what it was, but he knew that it was something extraordinary. He was quite sure that his life had taken some kind of turn, but whether it was a turn for the better or the worse he was not sure.

When she was finished, he helped her with the heavy prop and then they remained where they were, uncertain of what to do next, the empty washing basket at their feet. Needing to fill the uncertain space with something, anything, he mentioned the opening of an obelisk at Moore Park, of which Bridget was completely ignorant, and they talked about sacrifice and politics until Seamus recollected Daniel and James.

Somewhat flustered he changed the subject and asked her how her day had been, and then hearing how feeble the words sounded when they were all packed together in a line, he spoke for a few moments about Ernest Shackleton, who only a few days earlier had given a talk at Sydney Town Hall. Although he had never been outside Sydney, Seamus had been fascinated with Shackleton's attempt to cross Antarctica. That the ship had become icebound and that Shackleton and five companions were finally forced to set out on a dangerous sea voyage to find help simply added to the fascination.

When the topic came to a natural close — Bridget was relieved to hear that Shackleton and his men successfully managed what they had originally set out to do — Seamus offered to return the basket to the laundry. She smiled at him, nodded her thanks and then followed him back along the narrow path.

The second time they met was on Redfern Street. He was on his way home from work, thinking about nothing in particular, when he saw her standing outside the butcher's shop. He assumed that she had been shopping: he could see that she had a couple of paper-wrapped parcels in her basket. When she caught sight of him, she waved, hesitated and then crossed the road. As they were both on their way back to Wells Street, they walked together.

She asked him how his day had been, and he answered with a smile that it had been all right, much the same as always. Then, on his insistence, she talked a little about her afternoon, adding that no matter how one dissected the collection of fairly mundane afternoon happenings, it could hardly be considered an interesting topic of conversation. They had both then laughed: he at the drab images of butcher and grocer shops hoping to inspire conversation; she at— he was not sure why she laughed; he wondered if it could have been for the same reason.

She was still laughing when he insisted on taking her basket on his free arm, his other arm already linked with hers. It was the closest he had ever been to her, and while a small part of him questioned the moral implications, the larger part of him exulted in his being Seamus Murphy, walking through Redfern with such a woman at his side. Like Bridget, but for a completely different reason, he was doing his best to ignore all the images the future was trying to place before him, and he was only concentrating on the present moment.

Instead of turning into Pitt Street, and without actually discussing their change of plan, they continued along

Redfern Street to Chalmers Street. For Seamus, Bridget's compliance was a sign that perhaps, in spite of being Mrs Jackson, she was not against spending time in his company. Nevertheless, the signs, though positive, did not remove the awareness that his enchantment with her was doomed before it could even have time to blossom. He shook his head, banishing all unwanted thoughts, and focused on the fact that in the now, the only moment of which he could be completely certain, she was walking next to him.

Across the road, he could see the mixture of greens and yellows and greys that blended together to create Redfern Park, and more than anything he wanted the 'now' to last as long as possible. It was late afternoon, but still warm, and the slanted sun, running in long uneven fingers that stretched from the park to where they stood, was beckoning them to visit.

In the park they found a bench beneath a large fig tree. There were very few people in the park, and the emptiness and the silence were almost meditative. Seamus was grateful for the 'now', but he could not stop thinking about lines and how they were probably there for a reason and why they should not be crossed.

Sitting beneath the dark green leaves with the afternoon sun playing across the grass, Seamus wanted the moment to go on forever. He was quite sure that at least one line had been crossed, but as far as he was concerned it no longer mattered. Being alone with the woman who embodied everything he had ever imagined about love, beauty and, indeed, life itself was an experience he knew he would not forget. He knew that the experience could never be anything but temporary, that he would soon have to recross the line and pretend to himself that the experience had never happened, but just for the moment he wanted to absorb it, feel it, immerse himself in it.

Bridget did not seem to be aware of his inner torment, and while he juggled with the present and the future, wanting to be able to hang on to a present that was threatening to move into an impossible future, she talked about Sydney and Redfern and asked him polite questions about his family and what he had done. Before. Before they met.

Had his 'before' always included Redfern? Had he ever wished to live somewhere else, rather than in a city with streets filled with buildings and noise and people?

He was not sure: he had always lived in Redfern, and he could not imagine living elsewhere. The buildings and the people and the noise, and even all the things that were worn and tarnished, gave him a sense of security, a sense of belonging. As the conversation moved on to Molong and even Gilgandra, he told Bridget that he found it difficult to envisage spaces without buildings and roads, but he let his imagination be carried along, like a seagull riding on the top of a wave. Listening to her talk, he decided that he could probably live anywhere at all, even on one of those ghastly plains speckled with a few trees and flocks of placid, and possibly stupid, sheep, as long as Bridget was there with him.

But, of course, that was not going to happen, so he continued, like the seagull, simply enjoying the thrill of the moment.

By the time they met up for a third time — Seamus was on his way into the house on Wells Street and Bridget, holding Joseph by the hand, was on her way out — Seamus was no longer thinking about lines. He was not even thinking about impossible futures. He took a step back to let them pass, but not before he smiled, catching her eye, noticing the heightened colour on her cheeks. As he stood at the door, watching them turn into the street without looking behind them, he wanted, more than anything, for time always to remain in the present.

He had decided that God was neither tempting him nor provoking him. Instead He was giving him an inkling of what life could be like. The only problem was that there were far too many things blocking his way.

Chapter Twenty-One

When war was declared on the 4th August 1914, James Jackson was one of the first from Gilgandra to enlist. Ignoring the fact that his grandmother had been German, James considered himself totally British, even if it was a Britishness that had been carefully moulded under an Australian sun. If the Empire needed him, he argued, then it was his duty as a citizen of that Empire to put himself forward.

After enlisting, he and hundreds of others were sent to Liverpool on the outskirts of Sydney for training. He was taken aback by the conditions in the camp, there being too many men and no privacy. Also, with winter refusing to yield to spring, sickness was rife. James, like most of the other young men rapidly filling the camp, was used to physical hardship, but the close quarters packed with bodies trying to mark out something that resembled a small piece of personal space was almost too much for him. He was used to wide open landscapes, and in spite of his resolve to do his bit for the Empire he found himself already longing to be back in north-west New South Wales.

But before his longing was able to become a major problem for him, he found himself with hundreds of others on a ship heading towards Egypt. The adventure was finally about to start: his longing subsided. He was tentatively excited and more than a little apprehensive.

In Cairo, chilly but with the clear blue skies that did their best to remind him of home, there was more exercise and training, and he felt that the adventure was being moved back a few steps every time he moved forwards just as many steps. Finally, just as he had begun to believe that he would never get further than Cairo, he found himself on one of several ships heading towards a place called Gaba Tepe on the western side of the Gallipoli peninsula.

It was a night somewhere towards the end of April when he and hundreds of others were moved from the warships on to steamboats and then into small rowing boats. There was a restrained sense of excitement: they had all finally taken several steps forwards and none backwards. At long last, something was about to happen.

The steamboats pulled the rowing boats to within a hundred yards of the shore, and then the men were left on their own. Packed into the rowing boats, two men to an oar, they strained their eyes, hoping and not hoping to catch glimpses of the enemy in the hills in front of them. The sound of oars dipping into the cold, black water was all that could be heard.

Later, much later, James learnt that he and the men he was with had landed further north than intended. Whether it was because of ambiguous instructions, or whether it was simply the difficulty of making a landing in the dark he was never told. By then it really made no difference, and he often wondered if it would have changed anything had they landed where they should have landed.

The dark, the suppressed tension and the muted sounds of boats and water and men suddenly erupted into confusion and noise: the noise of gunfire, shells exploding, men screaming. The men tumbled out of the boats into the cold water, their sights set on the small beach, but the Turks, commanding the ridges, had no difficulty firing on the men swarming from the water and on to the beach below.

James barely felt the cutting coldness of the water as he jumped out of the boat and threw himself towards the beach. Two men who were with him fell forwards, one after the other. Intuitively, James turned, thinking to help them. Even in the shadowy almost-light, he could see that they no longer needed help: they were both dead. A knife-sharp understanding of just how quickly life could be extinguished remained with him as he zigzagged further up the beach towards the base of the cliff.

With three other men, he scrambled into a gully filled with thick, matted vegetation and began to climb towards the first ridge. Barely twenty yards above the gully, he felt the searing pain, a pain like a thousand nails being hammered into his head, a pain that expanded within him, filling every part of him, taking away his ability to think properly. His eyes were still fixed on the ridge above him, and something inside him was telling him that he had to keep pushing on. But as the pain took an even greater hold, everything around him became surreal. For a brief moment even the noise stopped, and all he was aware of were hundreds of strange shapes moving slowly against a background painted with nuances of grey and black. Then someone switched on the sound again, and James staggered and fell, the sound grabbing at him and pushing him first one way and then another. His one thought was to survive but that did not seem to be an option any longer: men were screaming and dying all around him.

He could feel the rough sand beneath him. If he could manage to pull himself up, perhaps he could still reach the ridge. It was not that far. He had to reach the ridge.

Afterwards, James did not remember much about the time he spent on the small rise beyond the beach. For all he knew, he could have been there for days. He slipped in and out of consciousness, and when he was vaguely conscious the only thing of which he was aware was the noise. He wanted it to stop, but there was nothing he could do to stop it. In the very beginning while his mind was still ordering him to reach the ridge, his head had been throbbing as though it would burst; blood was running down his face and neck, blocking his sight, filling his mouth. It was plain to him then that he was going to die, like everyone else around him. His instructions were to reach the ridge above him, but he knew that it would not be possible.

At some point he became aware that the throbbing had stopped and that all he could feel was an absence of feeling, a numbness. He was cold and then he was hot. He dreamt of water: lakes and rivers filled with cold, clear water; water falling down cliff sides; even water pooling in ditches at the side of the track. He dreamt that it was raining, but when he stuck out his tongue to catch the drops there was nothing there. Only the noise: the explosions, the shooting and the screaming.

He knew there were dead men lying all around him and men like himself who could only hear the noise.

When he was finally lifted on to a stretcher to begin his trip back across the water, he was no longer conscious. In fact, he later learnt that he had almost been left behind, because those with the stretchers believed him to be dead. But then he made some small sound, his body needing, no doubt, to be saved, and the stretcher-bearers understood that he was still alive, and they took him with them.

The hospital ship, like all the other hospital ships, was crowded and there was very little medical help. James believed that someone may have held his hand while a bandage was wrapped around his head, the head that was no longer a physical part of him but, instead, a blurred, heavy cloud of raw pain, like a balloon on the end of a long, taut string. The morphine was saved for someone else, someone who was not falling in and out of consciousness, someone who needed help to be able to escape the pain and the misery. The screaming had given way to moaning, and the sounds of fighting had been replaced with the sounds of people trying to be of help.

In Cairo, the balloon slowly drifted away, or burst, and the haze eventually lifted. The doctor told James that had the bullet been a fraction of an inch further to the right he would not have had any use for a hospital in Cairo or anywhere. He was placed on a crowded ward with other men, some of whom had only minimal use for the hospital and whose beds would soon be emptied and then refilled. James could not decide if it had been a kind gesture on the part of some Divine Being, in whom he did not believe, to allow these men to imagine, at least for a few days, that they were going to survive, or whether it was simply part of the general malevolence that he had gradually come to understand was at the heart of this thing called war.

His wound slowly healed; the headaches that made him wonder if sudden death had been a better alternative became less frequent and less severe; the bright, flashing lights disappeared and he found that he was able to focus again. But the psychological damage showed no improvement: sudden noises caused him to lose his equilibrium, and his nights were hacked to pieces by nightmares, each one worse than the one before. If something, or someone, cut into his daily routine, creating confusion and uncertainty, James would become hysterical, even violent. The doctor had initially hoped to be able to discharge him as battle-ready and have him sent to France, but after two months it was decided to send him home instead.

James arrived back in Sydney in early September 1915 and was given an honourable discharge and a train ticket back to Gilgandra. War had not been the adventure he had hoped for, and returning home without having achieved anything for King, country or anyone else only added to his feeling of failure.

Those who had not been there could never come anywhere close to understanding what he had experienced: the indescribable noise, the fear, the screaming, the confusion and the pain. Those same people had not seen the faces of dead men, mates and strangers, where life had been extinguished in the space between one word and the next, one footstep and the next. People who remained safely at home did not know what it was like to sit in a small boat in the dark with artillery fire all around, not knowing whether or not there would be anything on the other side of that small, confined space which was attempting to mark out a position between the past and the future.

When he alighted from the train at Gilgandra that September, he was relieved to see Bridget standing on the platform with Joseph, waiting for him. She was the thread that connected everything from before the War with what might be, now that he was home. He hoped that she might be able to erase the immediate past. He wanted to be able to forget everything that had happened to him since he left Australia. He wanted to be able to begin again.

But the marks were too strong, too substantial, and no one could have erased them. Physically, he seemed perfectly normal, and in spite of the indelible, invisible, but heavy, marks he was soon working again. He was happiest when he was in the saddle, droving cattle or checking fences. He had always enjoyed the quietness, the vastness and, most of all, the freedom of being totally on his own. On those occasions when he was away from home for several days, he would lie on the ground at night, watching the stars moving across the sky until he fell asleep, breathing in the smells of cold night air and eucalyptus. He was very aware of just how much those nights meant to him, when everything was quiet, and when the sky enveloped him like a dark blanket with small, small gaps in the weave through which he could gaze at infinity.

But life was not all quiet nights and infinity, and at times the nightmares and the pain became too much to bear, or else the noise and the memories would not turn off in his head, and it was then that he turned to drink. He had always liked a drink, but he now found that it helped him put things into perspective. At times, after a few drinks, he almost felt normal again.

Chapter Twenty-Two

Although it had been a relief to talk to Sarah, Bridget knew that the situation as such had not changed: James was still dead, and she was still likely to be hanged. Her revelation had not done anything to change those two facts. It was implausible that James had somehow suddenly, and mysteriously, returned to life; as soon as people worked out that it was she who had killed him, the outcome, as far as she was concerned, was indisputable. There was a slight chance that some consideration might be given to the fact that she did not mean to kill him and that she had been provoked into killing him, but she could not be sure. There were no witnesses who could vouch for her. Furthermore, she was sufficiently astute to know that men would believe what they wanted to believe, especially in a case like hers.

In the interim, she waited for the official knock on the door and the trip to the State Reformatory at Long Bay in Sydney's south. It would not be a case of her being put there to be reformed; it would simply be a place where they would keep her under guard until the awful day of her execution.

She could already see the headlines in the newspaper: 'Cold-blooded killing of war hero', 'Self-sacrificing patriot killed by heartless wife'. She forced herself to erase such images from her mind, and she concentrated on focusing completely on the present. Thinking of either the past or the future was both futile and distressing.

But it was difficult to remain firmly in the present, with the past, and all it implied, pressing up behind her while a terrifying future was already rushing towards her. She tried to imagine a number of different scenarios free from the dark shadow of what had been, scenarios that were painted with a more positive brush, but her imagination failed her. Secretly, she would have liked to have felt free to imagine a future with Seamus Murphy, even if such a fantasy would, of moral necessity, have to remain somewhere on the periphery of her mind. Her imminent execution made any such thoughts completely meaningless, and if there should be the slightest chance of her avoiding the noose and even gaol, she could not envisage someone like Seamus wanting to be involved with a murderess.

In spite of how she imagined Seamus might react to what she had done, her few meetings with him, though random and unplanned, had given her the incentive to keep going forwards. She was not quite sure, in the circumstances, what *forwards* actually implied: she had not seriously considered ending her life, but she was no longer quite as anxious, and she no longer spent her days completely fixated on what was likely to happen. Even though Seamus was not in any way aware of her predicament, being with him helped calm her, and while she was with him she even dared consider the infinitesimal possibility that she could be wrong about everything, including the future and what was likely to happen.

Their meetings were usually short and uncomplicated, but each time they happened upon each other Bridget felt a growing attraction, which, were she not to be hanged within a reasonably short space of time, she would have definitely encouraged. Given the extremely negative situation in which she had unintentionally placed herself, she decided it was safer, and probably kinder, to maintain a reasonable distance. Eventually, she hoped that he would understand.

Three weeks after Bridget had knocked on her sister's door in the early hours of that morning in February, a letter arrived for her. Although she immediately identified her mother's handwriting, she had at first thought to put it to one side to read later in the day. Then something, she knew not what, compelled her to open it.

The envelope contained a short note from her mother and a separate letter in its own envelope. The envelope and its contents had been carefully folded in half, and as she unfolded it she gasped as she saw the handwriting, and with the letter in her hand she sat down heavily on the closest chair.

The letter was from James.

Chapter Twenty-Three

She read through the letter several times, not able to believe that it could be from James. She was confused and shaken: dead people did not, could not, write anything. But it was definitely his handwriting, and in spite of everything that was telling her that it was completely impossible, she finally had to accept that the written communication she was holding in her hand was from her husband.

He began by saying that he did not know if his letter would find her: he had no idea where she and the boy were. He could not even be sure if they were still alive. He was taking a gamble on their being in Molong, but where else could they be? The thought that they might be dead was something he did not want to dwell on, and if he did not allow the idea to take root then perhaps it would not be true. Something kept telling him that he should have gone to the police, but the situation was complicated: there were too many things that would have to be explained.

He had woken up on the floor in the early hours of the morning, and one of the first things that struck him was that the house was empty and quiet: his wife and child were nowhere to be seen. It took him a while to assemble a small part of the puzzle, the part that involved blazing heat and clouds of dust. Then he vaguely remembered himself somewhere at the centre of all the heat and the suffocating orange dust. He had been into Gilgandra — that much he could remember — but he knew that he should probably have stayed at home. As the picture became stronger he believed that something had made him angry, but whether it was the heat, the dust, something else entirely or a combination of everything, he was not sure. Bit by bit the confusion evaporated, things became clearer and he remembered hitting his wife.

Later, he searched everywhere for Bridget and Joe. He had even gone down to the dam and looked for them, wading out beyond the rushes along its edge. Had she simply run away with the boy, or had something happened to the two of them? Had the same person who struck him also hurt them? Had they been killed and their bodies hidden somewhere? He had no way of knowing.

Initially he avoided even contemplating that it could have been his wife who had struck him, but as the days passed he had to admit that it was possible. He was certain that he had hit her, and perhaps she had hit back. Whether she had been intent on hurting him or whether she had simply been defending herself was something he could not answer, did not want to answer. He knew that he loved her, but at times there were other emotions, emotions he was unable to control. Feelings of love and hate and even irritation fell over each other, until he no longer knew exactly what it was he actually felt. In a moment of acute insight he wondered if the hate and irritation were actually directed at himself.

During the days after the dust storm, thoughts kept moving through his head, like energy passing through water, creating waves. The thoughts were always jumbled yet relentless: one moment he felt he understood why Bridget might have acted the way she possibly had. The next moment all such understanding evaporated, and he felt both angry and resentful.

After he had woken up on the floor and slowly regained a sense of who and where he was, he had become aware of the awful throbbing in his head. His fingers, searching for the source of the throbbing, found blood, clotted and sticky, spread throughout his hair. When he finally managed to sit up, he saw the patch of dried blood on the floor and the poker lying close by. It was not difficult to work out what had happened. Somewhere in the background of his awareness was the uncomfortable feeling that everything had doubtlessly been his fault; a feeling that he gingerly acknowledged before discarding it.

James did not feel that he was a violent man. He had always kept to himself and avoided confrontation; he had never had a need to push himself into another's space. At least, that was the way he used to be. As he attempted to hold on to the image he had of himself as relatively kind and forgiving, he became conscious of the fact that the uncomfortable feeling was still there and that it was slowly moving from the background into the foreground.

After he accepted the reality that he was on his own, his thoughts began to focus on what might have happened and why his wife and child were no longer in the house. Days later, as he attempted to pick through all the pieces and rearrange them, he understood that it must have been Bridget who wielded the poker, and he had no choice but to ask himself *why*. It was not a question or a place he wanted to visit, because on some hidden level of himself, he knew the answer, and he understood that it was all his own fault. He could not blame her. He wanted to, but he could not.

Was it possible that the bullet that had pierced his head, almost killing him, should take the blame, or was everything connected to some darker side of himself, a side he had never wanted to acknowledge? Either way, it was not easy for him to admit that whatever it was that had happened in the cottage was most likely his fault. He had spent months trying to tell himself that his injury had not altered him in any way. If it was the bullet that had changed him, then he was forced to concede that it was the War that had to take the ultimate responsibility. He was confused: he had supported the War as the right thing to do, the patriotic thing to do, and now he was no longer certain. He had watched so many men die; he himself had almost died. Bullet or no bullet, he knew that he was not the same man who, in 1914, had willingly signed his name at the bottom of the enlistment form.

Had it all been worthwhile? Had it achieved anything? Was the world now a better place, a fairer place? Were those young boys who died cruel deaths with their guts hanging out, or with gaping holes where their eyes had once been, satisfied and rewarded by knowing that their sacrifice had not been in vain?

While finally able to admit that the war experience was insane, he knew that he was still equivocating: he felt pulled between his horror at all he had experienced and his belief that war was somehow good and honourable. He found himself agreeing with Bridget that it *was* England's — and Germany's — war but part of him still clung to the idea that Australia needed to be supportive.

He had always believed that fighting for one's country was the noble thing to do.

But, at the same time, he could not be completely sure of anything any more: he was confused and disillusioned. His time at the front might have been short, yet in those hours and days he had seen and experienced things that would remain with him for a lifetime. Later, after the terrible days on the beach, he had spent weeks enveloped not only in his own horror but also in the dismay and the pain of other men; a disillusionment which they were trying, usually unsuccessfully, to dissect and explain. To themselves; to others.

His experience had reshaped him into a person he could not always identify with and, at times, did not like. When he was being totally frank, he would occasionally ask himself if it had been worth it: if he had not gone to war then nothing would have changed. But no one can control the future, and perhaps things would have changed anyway, perhaps he would also have changed, even if he had never gone to war.

As Bridget read James' letter, she understood how difficult it must have been for him to articulate such things for himself, much less put them down on paper. Since his return from overseas he had always been insistent that he was still the same person who had left in 1914: he had not suddenly transformed into someone else.

The letter showed that he was clearly trying to balance things that were in opposition, though on different levels: his belief in a fair and just war, and his self-image as a decent person. During those long, drawn-out days, having no real idea as to what had happened or why, he had slowly begun to comprehend that it was difficult to rediscover and re-establish any kind of balance, in spite of knowing that a balance was necessary.

In the letter, James finally admitted that though his injury had not killed him, it had clearly altered him. He wrote of constant pain and of the anger and frustration that surged up from a place deep within him and over which he had no control. He admitted that when he became angry he became another person: a person he did not know, did not understand. He wrote that there were times when he no longer felt like the man he once used to be and that this feeling, together with his pain, fuelled a self-hatred that could only be subdued by drink. The drink numbed the pain, but it often fed the anger.

Part of him, like an objective onlooker, had been aware of what he had been doing to her, but the disconnection was vast, and the piece of him that understood was so very small, and it was forced to comply with the other, larger, part of himself that was constantly resentful and angry.

He mentioned the times in between when things were still the way they had been in the beginning. He wrote that, more than anything, he wanted things to be the way they once were. It was all he hoped for. He loved her, and he wanted to be given another chance.

Even after reading the letter for the third time, Bridget could not forget how she had truly believed that he was dead, and how she had listened for a heartbeat and found none. She wondered if her mistake was because of her own stress: in her mind he *was* dead. She had killed him. Facts and reality were no longer important: they no longer had anything to tell her. There would have been a pulse, a hint of breath, the rise and fall of his chest, but they were not part of the reality of which she had already convinced herself. As far as she was concerned, he was already dead.

While she was amazed by her ignorance and her willingness to believe what was not true, she thought to herself: 'I could have killed you, James, though I didn't set out to kill you. I don't believe I was thinking, not then. I was terrified. *You* know what it is like to be terrified, so you must understand what I mean when I say that I was terrified. Afterwards, I really believed that I had killed you. The last weeks have been a nightmare while I have waited to be arrested.

'Even if I am trying to understand what it is that pushes you into these dark, violent places, and even if I accept that it is not completely your fault, some of the responsibility is still yours. You should never have gone away. You should never have allowed them to destroy you.'

For no obvious reason, her thoughts moved off on another, absurd, tangent as she pictured James' sister Mavis. Mavis had never liked her, and Bridget wondered what the woman's reaction might have been had things turned out as she had first believed they might: James was dead and his Irish-Catholic wife was to be executed.

She pulled her thoughts, which were obviously unfocused and wandering, back to the letter, letting them continue their own silent monologue. She thought: 'I believed you were dead, and I was so sure that I'd be punished. I'm extremely grateful, relieved, overjoyed to hear that you are still alive. I did not want to kill you; I just wanted you to stop. I wanted you to stop hitting me; I wanted you to be like you were before. You are not the same person who went off to fight for God knows what. We both know that. I never wanted you to go. Remember how I had pleaded with you to stay, for my sake, for our sakes? Imagine if you had listened to me and stayed at home. Things would have been so different now. I don't believe that there is any way back. I'm not sure that "going back" is even possible. The past is a place behind locked doors, and as we move on we keep locking doors behind us. There are so many doors, and there is no way back, because we keep losing the keys. We would like to be able to go back and change things or fix things, but without the right key we can't open any of the doors.

'But you wrote about wanting a second chance, James. Should we try to find that key, the one that will open the door to how things were before? Can I really believe that you are willing to change and that you are willing to try all over again? Is it possible for you to forget the person you have become and remember the person you used to be?'

As she pushed the two pages back into the envelope, she decided that she had no other option than to give him that chance he wanted. Perhaps he was prepared to change, and perhaps things would be the way they were before everything lurched out of control. She was dubious, but she did not feel she could refuse him when he had more or less taken the blame for everything that had happened.

Somewhere in the back of her mind, behind all her good intentions and her dubious hopes for a brighter future, she was uncomfortably aware of Seamus. Even while she was trying to concentrate only on James, she was conscious of Seamus' sometimes baffling smile, his voice and his kindness. In Seamus she had discovered a stability that she could rely on. With Seamus she doubted that there would be any need for keys to unlock even part of the past: the past, the present and the future would blend into each other, creating something that was both secure and normal.

After losing herself in her musings for a while, she remembered that there had been a second letter in the envelope, and she glanced through the short letter her mother had written. It had been written merely as a cover for James' letter, but one sentence stood out.

I cannot understand why James should be sending a letter to you at this address. Surely he knows that you are in Sydney?

Chapter Twenty-Four

March was beginning to give way to April, and Bridget was preparing to farewell her sister and return to Gilgandra. Although Sarah was mostly supportive of her sister's decision, now that she had all the pieces of the puzzle, she did not feel that James would be able to change, he was too damaged. She could understand that Bridget felt she had no other option than to give him a second chance, but the terrifying James was someone over whom the real James had no control. When Bridget told her that she was determined to give her husband the chance he wanted, Sarah had shaken her head and smiled faintly through her tears: she did not feel that things could possibly end well.

On the other hand, Bridget, greatly relieved that she no longer had to worry about her life coming to an untimely end, was prepared to look upon the future as being framed in light rather than darkness. Having pushed Seamus to the back of her mind as far as was possible, she was concentrating on a new 'before' with James. She had managed to convince herself that it was possible. Like her grandfather before her, she was extremely grateful to God for the small mercy He had shown her. As far as she was concerned, giving James a second chance was more than reasonable payment for being saved from the gallows.

After much discussion between the two sisters, it was decided that Joseph would remain in Sydney with Sarah for a few months. Catherine would be returning to Molong in August — Mrs Byrne having decided to sell her home in Penrith and move to live with her sister in Newcastle — and she would be able to take Joseph with her. Sarah argued that it would be better for the child to remain in Sydney in the meantime: he and Sarah had formed a close bond, and he was loved by everyone in the Murphy household. The three-year-old might not have been worried by the prospect of a noose tightening around his neck, but over the past eighteen months he had witnessed some frightening things. He did not need more anxiety and uncertainty.

Although Bridget initially tried to counter her sister's arguments, she knew that Sarah was right: no one could read the future. If James was unable to keep to his side of the bargain, there was a good possibility that everything would once again descend into chaos. Bridget was doing her best to remain positive, and she was trying to shut out all images that wanted to say anything else, but she had to admit to herself, and also to Sarah, that it made sense for

Joseph to remain where he was. Perhaps it was better that Joseph could be with ordinary, uncomplicated people for a longer period. It would also give Bridget time to work things out with James.

At the same time, Bridget was fully aware that Sarah was not being completely altruistic: she was lonely. She had still not heard anything from either Oswald or the hospital, and with Bridget returning home she would once again be on her own. Joseph would help fill a very deep gap in her life.

The day before Bridget was to leave Sydney a letter arrived from Thomas. Daniel was no longer missing. The people who Thomas trusted were searching for him had finally found him. He had been found, but he would not be coming home.

With words that were lacking and inadequate in every way, Thomas tried his best to pass on the information contained in the telegram on pink paper that had arrived in Molong only two days ago.

The words on the paper, '... previously reported missing in action now killed 25th August 1916 (...) deep regret and sympathy of their Majesties the King and Queen and the Commonwealth Government... ' wiped away the hope, negligible as it might have been, that they would be reunited with Daniel.

Thomas wrote of his own and his parents' heartache, and how he was unable to fully grasp the unalterable reality behind the black words on the pink paper. He wanted to ignore the words and what they were trying to tell him, because he needed to concentrate on Daniel as he was before. Before the War; before France; before the distressing telegram.

The King and the Queen and the Commonwealth meant nothing to Bridget. All she could think of was that Daniel Brendan O'Connor had been killed in France on the 25th August 1916 at a place called Pozières.

She had a vague notion where France was, but everything that she understood to be connected with that country was now gathered together in one word: *Pozières*. She cried because Daniel was dead, but she also cried because he was dead in a place that was already, for her, synonymous with death. Did it have hills and valleys? Were there trees and forests and streams of water, now coloured red with the blood of those who had died? Were there streets of houses or was there just some large, endless, treeless expanse where boys like Daniel went to die?

When they heard about their cousin months ago, they learnt that he was just one of thousands; now she would have to add Daniel's name to those thousands.

Neither Bridget nor Sarah wanted to believe that their brother was dead. As long as he had been missing, there had always been a glimmer of hope: they had been able to cling to the belief that he was still alive. Somewhere. That delicate hope had now been stamped on and destroyed. Their brother would not be coming home. They would never again hear his laugh, nor would they be pulled into his impossible arguments. Never again would they see his round, freckled face with the unruly curls falling across his forehead. When he left them more than a year ago, telling them that he would 'see them soon', he did not know that he would not be coming home. He had not been coming home since August. Hopefully, he and his cousin had found each other amidst the dead and the dying. Bridget wanted to think of them both together in a happier, kinder place.

Sitting in the kitchen with the autumn sun forcing its way through the dirty window, Bridget was barraged by all the emotions that had built up inside her over the past months and over which she now had no control. Although she was relieved to know that she was not a murderess, she had spent several weeks believing that she was, and all the time she had been worrying about what was likely to happen to her she had also been worrying about Daniel, willing him to be alive, willing him to be found. He had been found, but it was not at all as she had hoped.

Bridget was heartbroken to hear of her brother's death, even if there was some relief in finally knowing what had happened and being able to mourn him as dead. While he had been missing he had been neither alive nor dead; he had existed in a twilight zone that was neither one thing nor the other. During all that time she had been unable to let her thoughts and feelings move completely in either a positive or a negative direction. She had been constantly flung between hope and despair.

All the thoughts and feelings for her brother, and even those for herself, feelings that she had denied or held back, now surged to the surface and threatened to rip her into thousands of small pieces. She wondered if this was how Catherine felt when her children died, when her parents died, when everyone around her died. Was it at such moments she remembered her connection with her God, and did she then turn to Him, seeking answers or consolation, or did she blame God for what had happened?

Bridget did not feel that Catherine blamed God for all that happened to them, and she did not feel that *she* could blame God for Daniel dying on the battlefield. A battlefield was not much more than an enormous chessboard where soldiers were chessmen who could be knocked over and removed. The men moving the chessmen could afford to lose pieces that were less important in order to attain their goal, in order to win. It was the goal that was important, no matter whether the pieces were black or white. Both sides had the same goal; sacrifices along the way were to be expected and could be tolerated.

No, it was not God who had destroyed James. It was not God who had killed Daniel and all those other thousands upon thousands of men who were simply being moved around on immense chessboards. God must have have felt frustrated and depressed (she wondered: is it possible for God to feel depressed?) as the two sides, the white and the black, threw all their energies into checkmating the opponent's King or Kaiser or Emperor while pawns, who were actually men, were left dead or dying.

God may have created mankind, but He did not start the War. He did not take sides against Englishmen or Germans or Turks or Russians. As far as He was concerned, everyone was equal — equally responsible, equally guilty, equally innocent — in spite of the prayers of the one side for help in vanquishing the other.

Bridget felt that she could not stay in that cramped little kitchen with Thomas' letter still open on the table. She hugged her sister, pulled on her gloves and grabbed her hat. She knew that she needed to get outside where she could feel the air against her face and see people, ordinary people, going about their everyday activities. She needed to know that the world had not changed simply because Daniel was no longer part of it. She needed a sense of normality to resurrect some kind of balance in her life.

She walked down Wells Street in the direction of the railway and had almost reached the end of the street when she saw Seamus coming towards her on the other side of the street. It was one thing to get outside and feel the air and see the people and hear life going on around her, but what she wanted even more was to feel another human being next to her, someone with whom she could, just for a moment, share her immense sorrow. Sarah was standing on the same side of the chasm as she was. She needed someone on the other side, someone who could grab hold of her and pull her to safety.

She did not need to say anything: Seamus could immediately see that something had happened, and without asking any questions he was there for her, offering her his hand and then both his arms to lift her across the abyss.

Chapter Twenty-Five

Back in Molong, Bridget and her family were pulled together as the deluge of sadness and mourning swept over them and churned up many, often contrasting, memories of Daniel. Some of the memories were accurate; others were not. But all the memories, true and false, anchored Daniel firmly to the centre of the O'Connor home. While he might have died in a place no one had ever heard of, his spirit had returned to Molong.

The Memorial Mass was celebrated on a Thursday afternoon by Father O'Grady in the presence of a full church. The priest, a man in his late sixties with white hair and an arthritic hip, was genuinely overwhelmed by the loss of one of his young parishioners, and he spoke at length, mentioning that he had known Daniel since he was a boyeen with a glint in both eyes. His homily was both emotional and scattered as he remembered things, both real and imagined, small fragments that he hoped would add some optimism and comfort.

As well as the many who had known and loved

Daniel, and were now filled with grief, there were those who attended the Mass out of curiosity or from a need to be part of something that went beyond the borders of the small town and which made it, and them, briefly important.

Because there was no body, there could be no casket. Instead there was a simple, unadorned table with a candle where the casket should have been, and a photo of Daniel in uniform next to the candle, taken a few days before he embarked. On the same table, in front of the candle and the photo, and somewhat to one side, there was a small bunch of wildflowers and Daniel's work boots.

No one could be certain who had placed the flowers on the table, but the work boots were Patrick's idea. They were, he insisted, a sign that Daniel was still with them. He had always believed that his son would come back home, and now he was grappling with the fact that his son had not only died, but done so fighting for England in a place the name of which he could not pronounce. When Martin attempted to explain to him that Daniel had essentially been fighting for Australia, Patrick just shook his head, pushed back his chair and stormed out of the kitchen. In the small hallway that allowed access to both the kitchen and the stairs to the floor above, Patrick noisily opened the door to a shabby, brown cupboard and pulled out the boots. Running his fingers over the worn leather, feeling the indentations, the scars and the crisscross pattern of the laces, he could almost believe that Daniel was there in the room with him. He almost believed that he might get an answer to the all-important question *why*: why had his son felt the need to go to war?

Mary sat silently next to her husband at the front of the church. Although everyone was now talking about Daniel in the past tense, she was positive that the authorities had got it wrong. Despite the fact that Daniel's belongings — his prayer book, a penknife, a half-finished letter, a few coins and a photo of someone no one could identify — had arrived, together with a short note regretting what had happened, she could not, would not, accept that he was dead. She acknowledged her son's possessions, which arrived a few days after the telegram from the Commonwealth, but she refused to believe that Daniel would not be coming back to her; this was in spite of her having spent months believing and fearing that such was the case. Now that it was a confirmed reality, she changed her mind completely and insisted that her son was not dead at all: he was still missing and would eventually be found. Such mistakes had been made before, many times, and men listed as having died had later turned up alive and well. She held fast to her belief that he had been taken prisoner, without those in charge knowing, or that he had been afflicted with amnesia and was unable to remember anything. It made sense to her that he was somewhere, locked into himself, unable to remember who he was or where he was from.

Those family members who had been able to make the trip to Molong, or who were already there, sat in the two front rows of the little church. Sarah was not among them, having remained in Sydney with Joseph. She wanted to be with her family, but she did not feel that she could leave Sydney when she spent every day hoping to hear from Oswald. Catherine was also absent, being unable to leave Mrs Byrne, but Anne and her husband had made the trip from Dubbo, and Martin and his two eldest sons had come up from Cudal. James, who had been doing some work on a station south of Molong, sat in the second row. Next to him on the brown polished bench was Bridget.

Bridget had not been at all sure how she would react when she saw James again. The memory that was still foremost in her mind was of him lying on the kitchen floor in Gilgandra, apparently dead. She knew that she had to try to dispel the images that had been terrifying her for weeks and replace them with a living, breathing, moving husband. She needed to keep telling herself that nothing had happened: he was not dead. She may have been placed in a harrowing situation, a situation she never again wanted to experience, but thankfully life had moved on, taking her with it.

James had met her at Molong railway station when she alighted from the train from Orange. As she stepped down from the carriage, she could not help but be aware of a disturbing repetition of the meeting in Gilgandra all those months ago. But, on second thoughts, too many things were different, things had changed, life had taken a large number of twists and turns. The analogy, though possibly fitting, very quickly faded.

He was clearly delighted to see her; attempting to push aside her anxiety and her many doubts, she forced herself to believe in the James from before, the James she had loved and whom she had promised to be true to and to honour for the rest of their lives together. The James who had always been interestingly different; the James who had pulled her into his gaze and into his life.

He made no reference to what had happened, feeling, perhaps, that the letter had been sufficient, and he greeted Bridget at the railway station as if everything was, and always had been, normal: he had never attacked her, and she had not almost killed him. They had been apart a short while, and now they were together again.

But she was unable to act as though everything was completely normal between them. As far as she was concerned, there had to be some acknowledgement of what had happened, even if James felt that it had been conveniently relegated to the past. She needed them both to be able to accept the awfulness of all that had happened in Gilgandra and admit to themselves, and to each other, that there could have been terrible consequences. She told him that she wanted things between them to be as they were before he went away. For that to work they both had to be aware of how close they had come to destroying each other. More than anything, she wanted to be able to rely on him and trust him, but if he were ever to hit her again, she would leave him.

A good deal of her anxiety had dissipated when she received James' letter, but she still felt like a split person: part of her was relieved that he was alive (though she was not sure just how much of her relief was self-serving), while another part was terrified of what the future could hold for her; indeed, what it could hold for both of them. She kept willing him to be as he had been when they first met, before he went to war, before he had almost been killed. If she believed strongly enough, then perhaps it could be possible.

But there was an uncertainty lurking in her musings. If she was completely honest with herself, she was no longer certain that she wanted her life to include James; she was not sure that she had the energy to keep both of them afloat. As far as she was concerned, her husband had somehow mutated into a person who could not be trusted, someone who was dangerous. She believed that she knew how it had happened, but such an understanding did not remove the anxiety, the bruises or the loneliness. She kept thinking of Seamus and, in spite of it being morally unacceptable, continued to weigh him against

James. She felt that she understood Seamus: he was reliable, kind, respectful. As much as she knew of him, he was a person she believed she could trust. Would she ever be able to trust James again after all that had happened? Would he be able to revert to what he had been when they had first met? She asked herself the questions, but she was not sure of the answers, and she did not want to think of the alternative if he was unable to keep to his side of the agreement.

In a secret part of herself, she wondered if it would not have been better for him, and for her, if he had been killed outright and not sent home as an unpredictable, violent stranger. At least then she would still have had something beautiful to look back on.

Such thoughts both troubled and frightened her, and when they pushed their way into her consciousness, she blessed herself and asked God to forgive her.

The familiar Latin words, the smell of incense and Mrs Geoghan's admirable effort on the organ came together momentarily to shut out all other thoughts and anxieties. For a small sliver of time, Bridget was able to forget why she was where she was. She was even able to forget James, and she managed to drift away without thoughts, wrapped in a peaceful auditory and olfactory blanket. Then the words of a poem that had something to do with a road and darkness pulled her back into the real world from which she had been only too grateful to escape. Woken from her reverie, she found herself thinking about the symbolism surrounding roads and darkness and death. She was still brooding over possible meanings when the verse came to an end with something about larks singing and never having to walk alone.

Moving her thoughts from darkness and death to a more comforting image of not being alone, Bridget was conscious of the fact that she had been alone for a long time, even more so since James came home. The words *May you see God's light on the path ahead* kept ringing in her head, and while the idea of God's light shifted through a number of different shapes and interpretations, she found herself wondering if such a light could be all that difficult to find and whether or not it could possibly remove at least some of her feelings of isolation and loneliness. She reflected on the idea of James returning to the person he had once been. Then, without consciously pushing her thoughts in such a direction, she found herself wondering about the possibility of a completely different path that did not include James.

There could be no proper wake: there was no one to watch over or protect. There would be no burial, no tears at the graveside, no proper place to visit where it might be possible to reminisce. But there had to be something to allow people to openly mourn and remember Daniel, and after the Mass everyone moved to the pub. Patrick placed the candle and the flowers, and even Daniel's boots, ceremoniously on the counter and family and neighbours raised glasses, calling to mind Daniel as 'a real mate', 'one of a kind', 'at home with the good Lord'.

Father O'Grady arrived late, the skirt of his black soutane flapping loosely around his legs. He made his way slowly through the throng of people, the majority of whom were his parishioners. When he came to where Mary was sitting, he sat down heavily on an empty chair beside her. At first he said nothing, then he sighed deeply and remarked, 'To be sure, Mrs O'Connor, it's a quare sad time, but, like all things, it will surely pass.' He shook his head sorrowfully and, after a few moments of contemplation, continued, 'It must be said, Mrs O'Connor, Dan, he was a good boy, that he was.'

Mary looked at him with the flicker of an indecipherable smile. 'Thank you, Father,' she said. 'I am sure that all of Heaven is watching over him right now, and they'll see that he's soon brought back home where he belongs.'

He sighed yet again, his hand lightly touching her arm. He knew that Mary was refusing to accept the news of her son's death. He also knew that this was not the time to try to convince her otherwise. Seeing Martin on the other side of the room, he excused himself and moved through the groups of people, stopping a couple of times to exchange a few words with parishioners, agreeing that Daniel had been an exceptional person and was now greatly missed.

Bridget moved around the familiar room, pouring tea and nodding acknowledgement as friends and strangers offered their condolences in accepted, overused phrases: *Sorry for your trouble, Deepest sympathy, So sorry for your loss.* She wondered what it would have been like had she actually killed James. Would people have been sorry for her troubles? She really was not sure.

Chapter Twenty-Six

She was not sure how much she missed not having Joseph with her. She knew that she missed him, they had gone through so much together, even if he was still too little to understand. Part of her, the part that she kept hidden away from everyone, admitted that it was a relief not having to consider his needs at a time when there were so many other confusing and difficult things demanding her attention. The last few months had been exhausting: she had been terribly worried that her crime would be detected, and she had spent much time contemplating all the possible consequences. On top of her own personal anxiety, there had also been the anguish and uneasiness connected with Daniel. Although she may have avoided the noose, and she now knew that no amount of concern or worry was ever going to bring Daniel back home, her tension regarding James still managed to swell and fill both her waking and sleeping hours. They needed time to find the calm that was buried somewhere in the 'before'. She was not sure if it still existed, but she believed that she had no choice but to look for it, and it was easier when she did not have to think of Joseph's needs as well.

Nevertheless, there had been many times since she returned to Molong, and more recently to Gilgandra, when she wanted to be able to look into Joseph's blue eyes and see the uncomplicated, more innocent world that she knew would be reflected there. On those days, when she was able to forget all the possible futures that could be waiting for both herself and James, her hand would often relive the softness of Joseph's small hand in hers, and her mind would remember his child's voice and everything that was good about him.

She comforted herself by knowing that Sarah was caring for him, and that he was well and happy. Sarah wrote several times a week, and in every letter she mentioned Joseph and what he had been doing. Bridget was forced to admit to herself that she was just a little jealous that Joseph had been able to attach himself so quickly and so perfectly to her sister. Sarah may be childless, but Bridget was beginning to believe that she was possibly a better mother than she was. She did not want to dwell too much on what might happen when it was eventually time for Joseph to return home.

But she did not have time to worry about things so far into the future: her main concern at the moment was whether or not things would work out with James.

Chapter Twenty-Seven

ridget and James had already been back in Gilgandra for a couple of weeks, and life was slowly beginning to return to some form of normality. James was doing some work for Dave, who owned a small property that ran across the main road and continued part of the way up the access road to the Jackson farm. In an attempt to banish the images that still confronted her in the kitchen, Bridget cleaned the room thoroughly, whispering a collection of prayers and uneasy requests, willing all terrifying images and any remaining vestiges of evil to depart the house. After her small purification ceremony, she felt that she had done all she could do to remove any traces of ungodliness from the house. She still needed to be able to erase the images from her mind, but she knew that such an undertaking would take time.

Towards the end of May, she received a letter from Sarah:

'... It's all so sudden, I still can't believe it. The letter only arrived this morning, and I've spent every moment since then thanking God and hugging Joe. The poor boy must certainly wonder what is going on.

'Oswald is alive. He did not die, Bridget, even though I was so certain that he had died. During all those weeks when I heard nothing from him, it was difficult to believe that he could possibly still be alive. He wrote to me from France. He said that it was spring, that he'd already been there for several weeks and that he was well.

'All that time when I knew nothing, while I was hoping and praying that he was somehow still alive, I was also hoping, if by God's grace he was alive, he'd be sent home. But this is what he wanted, he wanted to fight. We'd talked and argued about it so much before he went away. You know that I didn't want him to go, but at least I now know that he's still alive, though who knows for how long? I suppose it's important that he's finally doing what he believes he wants to do.

'He wrote that he wanted to write earlier but that things had been so hectic and chaotic. He said that the past few weeks were still a bit of a blur for him what with hospital and everything. Before he was discharged from the hospital back in March, they assessed him as being well enough for duty, and only a couple of days later he was on a ship heading for France.'

Bridget read through Sarah's letter, noting that since arriving in France, Oswald had already been moved once, and that he believed they were somewhere in the north of the country. Even had he known where they were, Bridget knew that he would not have been permitted to say exactly where, nor would he have been able to give any indication of where they might be heading. Sarah mentioned how strange it felt that he should be talking about spring, but it was evidently a spring that did not feel like spring, and although he had not yet been in battle, he had already seen some dreadful, unforgettable things, things of which he would never be able to write.

She wrote that though she had tried to read between the few lines that Oswald had written, it was like walking down a dark street with no light: there were things lurking there, but she could not see them, and they came alive only in her imagination.

While Bridget was reading her sister's letter, she was very aware that Oswald's being moved to the front was not at all what Sarah had wanted to hear. She knew that her sister had spent the last few weeks hoping and praying not only that her husband was still alive but that he would be returned home as unfit for duty.

After several paragraphs about Oswald, Sarah mentioned in the last part of her letter that both Nora and Seamus had been asking after her. While Bridget paused in her reading, wondering if the asking had been weighted equally or if the one had been more insistent than the other, she was aware that Seamus could never be anything more than a pleasant interlude. Had her life taken a different path and had she and Seamus met several years earlier then perhaps the interlude could have turned into something more permanent, but she knew that such fantasies were the stuff of dreams, not of reality.

As life took on an appearance of normality, Bridget became slightly more relaxed, daring to believe that the future might actually be a place worth looking forward to. Initially, she was apprehensive when she was near James, expecting him to suddenly lose his temper and turn into a person she did not understand and did not want to know. But James remained the James from 'before', and bit by bit she dropped her guard, believing that her husband may indeed have reverted to the person with whom she had fallen in love.

When James first returned home all those months previously, she quickly learnt that he needed a calm, safe environment free from abrupt bumps or unexpected happenings. Even now, when things seemed to be moving in a more positive direction, she did all she could to shield him from any kind of upset. In spite of all her efforts, she was occasionally bothered by the thought of sudden, unexpected turns and dead ends in what she was hoping would remain as a smooth, straight path. While telling herself that everything was going to be fine, she could not completely rid herself of the fear of the stranger who was lurking, ready and eager to take her husband's place.

In late June, the weather turned bitterly cold, with bleak, dry winds blowing across from the west. Bridget kept the windows closed and tried to maintain a smidgen of warmth in the house, but in spite of all her efforts the kitchen was the only room that responded. Over her normal clothes she wrapped herself in two large woollen shawls, the ends of which she tied around her waist, and she went about her chores as usual. Her hands and feet broke out in chilblains, but she knew better than to complain. She kept telling herself that the cold weather would soon move on and that the sun and the warmth would return. Soon she would be complaining because it was too hot and the water in the dam was sinking.

It was a Tuesday towards the end of June. James had left home early in the morning to help Dave with a disc plough, and the two men spent several hours working in

Dave's shed with its collection of farming equipment, discarded furniture, bags of feed, piles of farming magazines, various tools and several cats. The plough had not been cutting deep enough, and when nothing else seemed to work the two men finally decided to add ballast to increase the weight.

It was freezing cold and the wind was blowing a gale, doing its best to flatten the shed and everything else as well. Even the normally fearless turkeys were huddled together in a corner of their enclosure.

By early afternoon, the job was still not done, and James was struggling against feelings of inadequacy and the noise of the wind; he could feel his emotional stability beginning to disintegrate. Then, as they were lifting the back of the plough, he slipped and cut his hand on one of the discs.

He swore, pulling his hand away from the disc and cradling it with his other hand; the blood was already seeping through his fingers in long, thin rivulets. Dave rummaged in a box, looking for a rag to wrap around his friend's hand, but James shook his head. He had moved into another space. He knew that he needed to get away from the noise and the erratic wind. He needed to be somewhere where it was quiet and where things went to plan. His hand was simply the catalyst. Had he been able to analyse what was happening, he might have wondered why he had not seen all the signs. He might have even understood that some kind of explosion was imminent. But he was unable to analyse his actions, and he was unaware that he was already hurtling towards disaster.

He swore and shook his head at Dave a second time, mumbling something about 'having to get away' and 'another day', before overturning a couple of boxes and noisily crashing though a pile of junk as he hurtled towards the door. Dave had always understood that James could be moody, but he had never seen him lose his equilibrium. He had never before seen the stranger who could so easily push away the James he thought he knew.

James was already out of the shed by the time Dave had got over his surprise. He called his horse that had been sheltering at the side of the house, and with the wind shrieking around him he rode the short distance back to his own place. If he had been able to stop for a moment and question what what he was doing, he would have had no idea why he had left Dave and why he should now be hurtling home. Was it that he believed Bridget would be able to take away the noise? Did he think that she would be able to remove the frustration of things suddenly gone wrong? Or was it that he needed someone to blame, for his frustration, the wind, the confusion in his head and the pain in his hand? He did not know. He was not thinking.

His mind was not processing things in a logical manner: there were images of Bridget and all the things he was assuming that she would be able to do for him, but they were all converging on each other, forming new images. The new images were dark and threatening; he could not understand why. In some part of his mind he believed that he wanted them to disappear, but by the time he had reached the place he knew as home they had grown in size. They completely filled his mind with their darkness and their threats.

When he walked into the house, there was still a small sliver of him that wanted the darkness to go away and for someone, anyone, to make everything right. He was not sure why things were wrong or even if they were wrong, but he was very aware of the thick, opaque fog pushing in on him, suffocating him. The tiny part of him that believed in deliverance remained clinging to the belief that some kind of rescue was possible. But as the door closed behind him and the darkness closed in on him, the other James pushed him to one side and moved towards Bridget, his uninjured hand raised, his befuddled mind intent on harm.

Chapter Twenty-Eight

At the same time as James noisily closed the door behind him, Bridget felt her stomach clench and her mouth turn dry. Watching him cross the room towards her, she was shaking uncontrollably. The only thing she could think was that something bad must have happened, or was about to happen, and any dreams she may have had of a safe, normal future were rapidly disintegrating in front of her. The dreams were already escaping under furniture and into dark corners. The man who was bearing down on her was not the James who was 'interestingly different'; it was not the man with whom she had fallen in love. It was the stranger she had learnt to fear, the man she had once believed she had killed.

His eyes were altered by an emotion Bridget was unable to fathom but which she had seen before. Somewhere behind the angry haze was the man she loved. She was sure he was there, even though everything radiating from the man in front of her was screaming that her James no longer existed. She had to keep focused. Although the man now in front of her was not her James, *her* James was somehow locked inside. He had to be: *her* James had always been kind and considerate; he had never been violent. Not until he returned home. The thought of a kind James locked inside a violent James fascinated her for a millisecond, but she did not have time to expand on the thought; she was frantically trying to decide what she should do. There was nowhere to run to: it was impossible to escape.

The man who looked like James, but could not possibly be James, raised his hand, his face twisted in anger.

Terrified by the certainty of what she knew was about to happen, she froze. It was possible that somewhere in her brain she was asking herself what it was that she had done, but the bigger part of her brain was shouting at her to do something and to do it quickly.

What had happened? She had been so careful not to upset her husband, but in some rational part of her brain she knew that whether he exploded or not had nothing to do with her: she could keep some of the demons away for some of the time, but they were clever, and they knew how to squeeze past all the barriers she believed she had placed in their way.

The blow almost knocked her off her feet, and she could feel something warm and wet running down the side of her face. She backed away, trying to get to the other room, hoping at least to put a door between herself and her attacker. Her efforts were futile: James lunged at her and hit her a second time.

He tried unsuccessfully to grab her by the arm with his injured hand while slapping her hard across the face with his other. Certain that she was going to die, she could only think of Joseph. She hoped that he would remain with Sarah. She also hoped that he would not forget her.

As James forced her into a corner of the room, she tried to find her voice, but it had completely disappeared. She wanted to tell James to stop what he was doing. She wanted to plead with him not to kill her. But what she wanted to do was impossible: her throat was dry and constricted, and she was unable to form the necessary sounds. Mute and terrified, her tears already mingling with the blood smeared across her face, she wondered if this is how everything would end. There would be a moment of acute pain, and then there would be darkness and nothing.

Unexpectedly, he stopped. It was as though, somewhere within himself, he sensed her silent pleas for mercy. For a moment, he looked confused, like a man waking up and not knowing where he was. He glanced at his wife and then at his hands. His injured hand was bleeding badly, and he was obviously searching in his mind for a connection.

Unable to find the answer in his hands, he backed away from Bridget, knocking over a chair as he did so. Swearing at himself, he began to rummage in the cupboard where he usually kept his alcohol. Bridget knew that if she was going to escape it had to be in that moment while his attention was elsewhere. She had only seconds to decide; if she hesitated she knew it would be too late.

Somewhere on the very periphery of her fear she could hear the loose shutter on the window rattling, and for a split second she wondered why it was still loose and why it had not been fixed. At the same time she was worried about it being torn from its hinges, and whether or not she should try to secure it. Then the second passed and she reflected on the absurdity of thinking about things like windows and shutters and wind. Nothing beyond the walls of the cottage was of any importance, not in the moment when she was about to be killed.

She moved slowly across the room, both her head and body pulsating with pain, and although the pain defined her at the moment, it was of secondary importance. She could only have one focus: to reach the door. She had to put something between herself and James; she had to remove herself from the house. His back was still towards her, but she was certain that once he found what he was looking for he would turn around.

By the time she reached the door, she had all but stopped breathing. The tension within her was both urging her on and petrifying her, and while relief surged through her body as she felt the smoothness of the knob beneath her fingers, she had no idea whether or not James had seen her. She dared not turn around, but instead turned the knob, throwing herself through the opening, pushing the door shut behind her as she did so.

Then she ran and ran. As she ran, she imagined an infuriated James opening the door, shouting at her, chasing her, but when she finally dared turn around the road behind her was empty and, except for the trees bending under the wind, and the swirling dust and debris, the world, her world, was completely devoid of movement and anything that even vaguely resembled humankind.

Dave, several years past sixty, widowed and reclusive, took her gently by the arm and led her into the house. Some time after James had stormed out of the shed, the older man decided to call it a day, and returned to his house to make some tea. Upset and rattled by James' outburst, he knew that he needed to be doing something ordinary in a place that felt safe and calm. When he heard the knock on the door, he had just lifted down the billycan from its hook near the stove and was about to fill it with water.

He opened the door and, taken aback by the sight of her face, was fixed to the spot, his hand still on the latch, unsure of what to do next. The moment passed and, released from his temporary paralysis, he led her into the house, moving a pile of clothing from one of the chairs so she could sit down.

Thoughts were rushing through Bridget's head, changing focus, changing direction. She attempted to slow her breathing, trying to tell herself that she was safe now, at least for the moment: James would never attack her while she was with Dave. All she needed to do was to concentrate on the present: Dave's kitchen, the table in front of her, the spiderweb in a corner of the window. She had no reason to move beyond the ordinariness of everything around her, but if there was the slightest possibility of success, however small, she had to be able to rid her mind of all troubling and terrifying thoughts.

She knew what she had to do, but her mind fought against the logic of discarding all, or even some, of the distressing images. If she did not hold on to them, then she would not be prepared should he suddenly burst in through the door. James was not likely to turn up on Dave's doorstep, but her mind insisted that she had to be prepared: now was not the time to be lowering her guard.

Confronted with the improbable image of her husband forcing his way into Dave's cottage, Bridget found herself regretting how the old James, the James she had married, had vanished. When he first returned from the War, violent and unpredictable, she had often caught glimpses of the attentive and caring James, causing her to believe that the anger and the violence were simply a passing aberration that would soon pass. But as the weeks became months, and the glimpses became fewer, she began to despair of ever finding the old James. On several occasions, she feared for her life, and even though she sought to downplay her distress, telling herself that many men beat their wives, she knew that James had never been one of them. She remembered how she had once considered herself fortunate in having a kind, understanding husband, but as that fortune rapidly disintegrated, she had found herself worrying about what would happen to Joseph if, and when, James finally killed her.

Several months after James returned home and long before she finally fled to her sister in Sydney, she had written to both her mother and Sarah, but had been indecisive as to what she should or should not say. She had written that James had not been himself since he returned: could it possibly be the injury or was it difficult for some returned soldiers to readjust to normality? She had carefully avoided writing about the cuts and bruises and black eyes, mentioning that James occasionally shouted at her and Joseph. She had written that he was sometimes angry (or perhaps it was that he was simply despondent?), thinking to herself that *sometimes* was a better choice than the word *usually*. Bridget knew that she needed help, but to ask for it required her being more open about her reality, and she did not feel that she could be disloyal to her husband. When she had finished writing the letters, she almost tore them up, frustrated by what they did not say, could not say. Eventually, she had posted them, hoping that either her mother or Sarah would understand the things she had not written: the things that were not on the page.

Mary O'Connor had written back to her daughter, regretting that James was not himself. She had reminded Bridget that it would take time for James to move on from all he had seen and done: it was to be expected that he would sometimes seem bad-tempered; all Bridget needed to do was to be patient. Men were more easily irritated than women. They could flare up over small things; it was important not to displease them. That was how things were and there was little anyone could do about it.

Even back then, when she knew nothing of the truth, Sarah had been able to catch sight of some of the unwritten words. She had asked just what *sometimes* actually implied and whether James' anger was confined to ranting and shouting or whether it was more physical.

She had written that Bridget was possibly right in suspecting that her husband's experiences in the War were a cause of his temper outbursts. She had read about something called 'shell shock'; perhaps that was what was wrong with James?

So many times since then had Bridget regretted not being honest with Sarah right from the beginning. Had she told Sarah exactly what was going on her sister might have been able to help her before things spiralled out of control, perhaps much heartache and worry could have been avoided. But the past was the past, and though she might now regret what she had done or not done, Bridget knew that no amount of focusing on such regrets could possibly change all that subsequently happened.

Still and all, when she first wrote to Sarah, all those months ago, she had appreciated that Sarah had been able to read between at least some of the lines, but she had hesitated as to whether or not she should fill in the gaps. She now understood that she should have written back to her sister, elaborating on the bruises and the beatings. She could also have asked for more information about the thing called 'shell shock'. More than anything she had wanted to take her sister into her confidence, but something had stopped her from saying any more: there was still a chance that everything was all her own fault. Perhaps *she* was the cause of James' irritation and ill temper.

Finally, she had answered Sarah's letter, saying that the outbursts were really quite infrequent. She regretted having mentioned them, they would almost certainly disappear as James recovered his strength. Yes, he did occasionally hit her, but it was more than likely her own fault. She remembered how she had then placed the pen on the table and read through what she had written; it was definitely not the truth, but it was not a complete lie. She should have told her sister everything, but she did not want to discredit her husband, more especially if there was a possibility, however small, that she was the cause of his violence. Instead of being completely open with Sarah, she persisted in clinging to the fact that James was not always threatening: there were, after all, times when he was just as he was before he went away. Whether his aggression was caused by his injury, the War or herself she had no way of knowing. As far as she could see, there was nowhere to turn. She had felt totally alone and vulnerable.

Sitting in the untidy kitchen, wrapped in a grey blanket that smelt of horse and dank, stuffy rooms, Bridget tried her best to explain the impossible to Dave: James was unpredictable: he was no longer just one person, he was two. To her relief, talking to Dave about James was helping to discard at least some of the troubling thoughts. She could sense that she was safe: even if James were to suddenly appear at the door there would be someone between him and her.

With old-man awkwardness Dave fetched the water bucket that stood on the bench under the window, poured some water into a cracked bowl and handed it to Bridget with a cloth so that she could wash the blood from her face.

She moved the wet cloth over her injured face, instinctively avoiding the places that were sore and broken. She cringed at the pain, thinking to herself that it was inconceivable that she and James would ever be able to move on together from this moment: they standing on a bridge that she had told herself she would never stand on again. Beneath the two opposing directions that were held together by the bridge, she could discern the dark water below. She felt as though she was already falling from that bridge. Once she fell, there would be no way back up: either she would be swept away or she would drown.

It was staring at her: their reality. It did not matter that James talked about resurrecting the person he had once been. It did not even matter that he truly repented of his violence towards her. He obviously had no control over the situation. The more logical part of her brain was telling her that this is what would happen again and again. There was no going back to what had been: eventually, one of them would die.

She did not want to follow that train of thought. All she knew was that she was now standing in the middle of the bridge, and she needed to make a choice as regards direction. Something was telling her that it would not be a difficult choice to make.

Dave pushed some more wood into the stove and filled the billy from the bucket. As he moved around the room, making tea, Bridget watched him, secure in the knowledge that nothing could happen to her now. Her mind, however, was still in turmoil: James had said that it would not happen again, but it *had* happened. He had said he would not hit her again, but he had.

This is not what she wanted: she had desperately wanted them to be together, but she had also wanted everything to be normal. She did not feel that it was too much to want, and she was certain that it could be possible if the stranger, who looked so like James, did not keep intruding and creating havoc. She now understood that the stranger would not be going away: he had come to stay.

In the first weeks after James had returned home from the War, disorientated, angry and often unpredictable, Bridget had kept hoping that her kind, considerate husband was somewhere inside the man who was calling himself James. She had looked forward to his coming home so much, but now that he was home, she had become confused and troubled by his impulsive, and often raging, outbursts. Trying to find an explanation, she had told herself that he possibly needed time to rid himself of all the images and the pain. Now she finally had to admit to herself that the explanation was inadequate: the James she had once known and fallen in love with was no more.

Dave placed the two cups of tea on the table and then handed one of them to Bridget. She was welcome to stay the night, he said. She could sleep on the sofa. Hopefully James would have calmed down by the morning. He would talk to him then.

The following morning dawned still and quiet. The wind had almost completely subsided or else it had moved on elsewhere, and in its wake birds could be heard again. It was sunny but cold. Long bands of white frost across the paddocks were shrinking slowly.

Dave harnessed the horse to the sulky and he and Bridget travelled the short distance to the Jackson place. There was no one outside the house, which surprised Bridget a little as she would have expected that James was already up and about. Dave did not think it was so strange: in all probability he was sleeping off both his tantrum and the drink.

Bridget was glad to have Dave with her; she was quite sure that she could not have faced James on her own. Even knowing that Dave was next to her, she could feel her heart beginning to beat more rapidly, and as they approached the front of the cottage, she was uncomfortably aware of the disquiet that was already taking control of her body.

She breathed in deeply, trying to calm herself, and opened the door while calling to James. There was no answer: the house felt cold, uninviting and empty. She called again, this time more forcefully. Dave pushed open the door to the bedroom, expecting to find James asleep on the bed, but there was no one there. The house was deserted.

Bridget was not sure if she felt relieved or distraught. He was possibly checking on the animals, or perhaps he was in one of the far paddocks. There was always work to be done; Bridget knew that. He was not in the house, but he was probably not that far away.

Dave left the house to look around outside. Bridget noticed that the fire in the stove had gone out, and there was nothing in the kitchen that indicated that someone had been there and would soon be back.

She sat down on one of the chairs while her mind sorted through a litany of explanations. The empty bottles on the table told her that he found what he had been looking for, but the gratification must have been short-lived. It was becoming more and more obvious that her husband had left. Though there was still a small chance he was somewhere in one of the paddocks, Bridget was not at all certain this is what Dave would be telling her on his return. Deep inside herself she knew that James had gone.

As it became clear that he had left, she felt strangely abandoned and empty. In the same way as she had not wanted him to go to war, she did not now want him to simply step out of her life. She had wanted them to be able to remain together and for the stranger to leave. The part of her that was unemotional and reasonable knew that what she had wanted was not possible: these two men were conjoined, and if she accepted the one she had to accept the other. As if she had been on an out-of-control train plunging down the side of a mountain, she could see that her options had always been limited: either she could have stayed on the train and taken her chances, or else jumped.

James had made that decision for her.

While her thoughts were focused on the image of the out-of-control train, Bridget was also thinking of the bridge. Whether it was an imaginary train or bridge was of no importance: the outcome would have to be much the same. Jumping from a train or falling from a bridge would have a similar result.

She was beginning to understand that James had opened the carriage door and was now pushing her through the opening. Or was it that he was pushing her across the bridge? She was not sure. Her coherent self was telling her that leaving the train or bridge was the only sensible thing to do: if she did not, it was most likely that she would die when the train finally crashed or else, unable to make a decision, she would let herself fall from the bridge.

She wondered if he had been able to save himself as well. Did he also jump? Did he leave the bridge unscathed? He could have done either, holding her hand. They could have avoided the train wreck or the dark, angry waters and still remained together.

Ever since he returned home from overseas, she had been trying to understand why he sometimes exploded, and why he could become violent without any obvious reason. She now knew that it could not have been her fault. There was something inside him, pulling and pushing him in directions that he did not want to go. It was then that he became another person, or perhaps it was then that another person, the stranger, took over his body, and she was no longer able to reach him. She thought of how the James she knew and loved became another James, someone she did not want to know. She had wanted to be able to get close to him, she had wanted to be able to help him, but he had always pushed her away. Now he had pushed her even further away.

Bridget reflected that he had always looked so normal. He did not look violent until, suddenly, he was. She hated the stranger, the other James, the man who had come home with her James and had tried to ruin their lives. She understood that he had finally succeeded. She would have liked to have left the train or the bridge while holding tightly on to her husband. She would have liked to have seen the stranger fall to his death in the twisted wreckage of the train or in the raging waters beneath the bridge.

She had spent months hoping that things could return to what they were in the beginning, but she now knew that it was impossible to resurrect the past. Life was continuously moving forwards. She had always wanted James to be part of her future, but he had moved in a different direction. Like Bridget, he would have been aware of the horror waiting for him at the bottom of the hill, and he would have known that the only way of survival was to leave the train: he would have understood that there was no point continuing to the very end.

What if James had always been secretly violent, but the violence had not been obvious in the beginning? What if it was not the War that had caused the change in her husband? What if it had simply prompted something in him, something that brought his true nature to the fore? She found the idea distressing, but the more she thought about it the more she doubted that a person could change from good to bad so quickly. She understood that his experiences on the other side of the world would have impacted on him, changed him, but she was not so certain that they could have changed him into a person he had never been. Unless, of course, facets of that person had been there all the time, without her actually noticing.

She had to believe that it was a good thing that he had left her. The new James frightened her, and she needed to accept that her James, the James from 'before' was no more, and perhaps he had never really existed.

Dave was still outside, and Bridget could feel the tears welling up in her eyes. In spite of everything that had happened, the part of her still clinging to the memory of a kind and reliable husband did not want to lose James, but she knew that she had lost him a long time ago. She had to accept that she lost him when that Turkish bullet pierced his head and almost killed him. In her mind, the man she had known and loved had died on that beach somewhere on the other side of the world.

She sat, looking out the window at the new day. She wondered when he had left: was it after she had run away, or was it in the early hours of the morning? Did he sit for hours mulling over what he was about to do, or did he simply make the decision, pack his saddle bags, saddle up his horse and leave? Did he ever think of letting her know? Did he stand for a moment in the yard before swinging himself up on to his horse, remembering his wife, wondering what she would think when she found him gone? Did he leave with regrets, or did he feel a sense of freedom and relief? Would he occasionally remember what they had once meant to each other? Would he remember that she had loved him?

She had to keep focusing on the fact that what had been before, or what she imagined had been before, was no more; she had to be able to let go. James had died, but the death, the wake, the mourning had been prolonged; everything had happened in slow motion. The bullet had taken months to reach its target. It was shot from a rifle somewhere on the heights above that beach, and it had then moved through the half-light, seeking its target among many possible targets. Its target was her husband, and it had pierced his soft skin and his skull, sending vibrations and warning tremors through the brain. Death and mourning had already begun in that instant. Months later the last handful of earth landed on the lid of the coffin and the mourners left the graveyard.

Bridget understood that it was now time for her to say goodbye and leave the graveyard, no matter how difficult it was for her to take such a step.

Dave returned with the information that James was nowhere to be found and that his horse was gone. Bridget simply nodded, unable to put into words the thoughts that had been rushing through her head: the fact that the horse was gone did not surprise her. It would have surprised her had it still been in the paddock.

The man placed a gnarled hand on Bridget's shoulder: it was probably the closest he could come to expressing the emotion that he felt the situation demanded. Words rubbed against each other uncomfortably as he suggested that James was probably off on his own for a while, getting himself back together again, and that he would soon be back. Bridget shook her head: without knowing why, she knew that James would not be back; he was not just trying to get hold of himself. He had left.

The old man changed tack, possibly thinking of James' outburst in the shed and the state of Bridget's face, and he told Bridget that it was probably for the best. Then he left her at the house, promising to call by the following day.

She had no idea of what would, or should, happen next; she was confused, shocked, relieved, upset. As the day became older, the one thing that became clear was that she could not stay in Gilgandra. Nevertheless, although she trusted her intuition, she still felt she should remain at the house for a few days; there was always a very slight chance that Dave was right, and James was simply trying to sort out his anger. While she waited to see which of the two possibilities was correct, there were things that she needed to do, and more importantly she needed to be on her own.

Whether she had wanted to or not she had been removed from both the bridge and the train. She had probably known all along that they could not keep standing on the bridge, and that she and James would eventually have to move, going different ways.

After a week, and no sign of James, Bridget considered writing to James' father to let him know. She was not sure what it was that she needed to let him know: that James had left her? That the house was now empty? That James had been violent? In the end, she decided that James' father was not her responsibility. Instead, she packed together the few items that she owned, helped Dave relocate the animals to his farm, and a week later Dave took her to the train station in Gilgandra. He waited with her on the station until the train arrived and then helped her on board with her battered suitcase and a box tied with string.

He had been kind to her, and she was aware that she would probably never see him again. She gave him a quick parting hug, thanking him for all he had done for her. As the train pulled out of the station, she watched him until the train gathered speed and she could see him no more.

Then she closed her eyes, knowing that this was definitely the point when her imaginary train was about to crash. She listened for a while, almost expecting to hear the crash that was bound to follow the train's terrifying rush down the hill.

Bridget never saw or heard from James again, but over the years there were many rumours: he had moved south; he had moved west; he was up north, somewhere in the Gulf; he was in gaol; he was working for one of his brothers; he was droving; he had died of influenza; he had remarried.

No one knew for sure where James was or even if he was still alive. As far as Bridget was concerned the man she had married, and whom she believed she had once loved, had died. Whether he fell from that bridge or whether his body was later lifted from the wreckage of the runaway train made little difference: he was dead. She had put the past behind her. Her feelings for him had been twisted around all the things that had happened after he came back home. She did not want to spend her life trying to explain to herself how one person could actually be two: she could have also died in the wreckage; she was thankful that she did not.

Chapter Twenty-Nine

ack in Molong, Bridget tried to explain things that she could not even explain to herself: James had left, and she knew that she should be thankful and relieved. Even so she still believed that some small part of her had not stopped loving him, in spite of everything. That same part of her wanted to believe that he still loved her, at least a little. At first glance nothing made much sense, and yet it all made perfect sense: the James who had returned home to her was not the man she had married. He had become someone else, and now he had left her.

Patrick insisted that there was nothing sensible about James leaving his daughter. Marriage vows were important: men were not supposed to leave their wives. Nevertheless, when he saw the bruises, in varying shades of blue, green and yellow, he decided that it probably was sensible after all. He was angry that Bridget had been treated in such a way: angry with James but also angry with himself for not having been more aware of what was going on. Although he felt a tinge of dishonesty in feeling vindicated — he had never really liked James — he was convinced that the man who would mistreat a woman as James had mistreated Bridget had gone too far, no matter whether chastisement was a God-given right or not. On occasions when he was feeling more magnanimous he could almost accept that James' war injury could have been the catalyst, but he still had no intention of excusing him.

Mary, on the other hand, was not as certain that the hierarchy within the family had been God-given, but she was prepared to accept its existence in the same way as she accepted most things. Like many women, she had discovered that there was a strength in quiet, superficial acceptance, even when it came to things like male dominance. She was thankful that Patrick almost never hit her, although he could often raise his voice and become belligerent. While feeling very sorry for Bridget, she was thankful for both of them that James had moved on. Unlike her husband, she had no problem accepting that her son-in-law's injury would have changed him: like her daughter she disliked everything to do with the War, and like her she could see that it spawned far more negatives than positives.

Bridget had not thought to construct a story that would exonerate James or even herself, though secretly she held to the belief that neither of them was to blame. She wanted to blame everything on the War, and she certainly had no interest in exonerating the War.

She felt that she did not have to absolve anyone. She did not have to explain herself, or James, to anyone. What had happened was unfortunate. It should not have happened, but it did, and life would go on. It was as simple as that. People could assume and speculate and imagine and believe as much as they liked, but her life, and James' life, had nothing to do with other people's assumptions and beliefs. She needed to be alone to gather all the pieces together and make some sense of them. She did not feel she was being difficult: she was in mourning.

The person who understood her the most was Thomas. While Patrick thumped the counter and shook his head and told everyone who was listening or not listening what he thought of James and men like him, and Mary simply felt sorry for everyone involved, Thomas appreciated his sister's need to be on her own and to mourn what might have been. Privately, he was relieved that James had moved on. He had suspected what Bridget had not wanted anyone to know, and was thankful that James was now no longer part of her life. He trusted that Bridget's life would keep going in a forward direction whether James was part of it or not. Its overall shape might be different, and James would simply be a memory, relegated to the sidelines, but there was no way of stopping its movement forwards.

Bridget might have felt lost, but she also felt safe. For the first time in many months, she could relax. The feeling was exhilarating, and if it were not for the strange, unexplainable sense of loss, she might have felt that she was on the cusp of something brighter and happier. Her thoughts, however, refused to take that step forwards, and instead she found herself often wondering whether, without the War, James would still have been the old James. He would not have needed to go anywhere, and they would still have been together.

Whether there had ever been both an old James and a new James was something Bridget did not question; for her it made sense that James, her James, had been changed by the War. She did not want to spend too much time considering the possibility that he might not have been changed at all, that he might have always been the person she had learnt to fear. She did not want to think that the man she fell in love with and married was the same man who swore at her and beat her. In her imagination she clung to the image of him when they first met, refusing to deliberate on any uncomfortable, darker images of him.

Despite life moving in a less frightening new direction, the future for Bridget looked particularly bleak. She was a married woman: her husband was still alive even if she did not where he was. Divorce was not a possibility: it was not even a word that she could comfortably take in her mouth. She was beginning to understand that the years stretching out before her would be the lonely life of an unmarried woman, or of a widow without any possibility of remarriage. The more she thought about it, the more she understood the position James had placed her in. She might be safer, but that was all. If James had not left her, there was a good chance that he would have eventually killed her, but she would at least have had a life with him, even if it would have been short. There would surely have been good days amid all the bad ones.

She knew that what she was thinking was without any kind of common sense. She was lonely and confused, and she was no longer sure that she was completely grateful that James had gone.

In spite of Bridget's indecision and confusion, life began to fall into a routine of sorts. She helped her parents at the pub while looking forward to being reunited with Joseph in August. She thanked God that she had Joseph: he was a reminder of happier moments; he was both her present and her future.

She began several letters to Seamus, where she attempted to explain that James had left her and why, but none of them managed to say what she really wanted to say in the way she wanted to say it, and she tore them all up. Nevertheless, for some vague reason, she felt that he needed to know, and after deliberating for several days she took a new piece of paper and, in a few short sentences, explained that James had walked out on her. She had never before told Seamus about the violence; she had not told him much about James at all.

Her problem with the letter had been what to include and what to leave out. Was it necessary for Seamus to know that James had been violent towards her? Did Seamus need to know that James had changed from the man he had been when she married him? Should she now explain why she had been in Sydney at the beginning of the year? Was it necessary that he knew that she had spent those weeks expecting to be arrested and tried and executed?

In the end she avoided everything that could be deemed awkward, and she wrote that James had suffered greatly as a result of his injury. It had changed him in ways that neither of them had anticipated. At times he could be aggressive, she wrote, hastening to add that it was not his fault: it was something completely beyond his control.

She did not write that she had almost killed him.

Seamus wrote back to her, regretting what had happened. If the news about James' brutality had disturbed him, he did not give any indication of it in his letter. He merely wrote that he was relieved that she was safe, and he hoped that she would continue being so. He had known that James had been injured, his mother had told him, but he had no idea that the consequences of his injury had been so great. Even though it was very sad that James was a casualty of war, it would make no sense if there should be two casualties instead of one.

After this letter, there was a regular stream of letters in which he wrote about ordinary, everyday things without very much emotional input. He wrote about Joseph, and Bridget felt some satisfaction when she gathered that her son was missing her, even though Seamus refrained from saying as much directly.

She found herself eagerly anticipating his letters. Despite their ordinariness, or perhaps because of it, they became the one bright spot in a life that was galloping towards despondency and a sense of futility.

In August, Catherine arrived home with Joseph. For a few weeks life took a small upswing, as Catherine and Joseph talked about things related to Penrith and Sydney, things far removed from Molong and Gilgandra and James. While Catherine had been with Mrs Byrne in

Penrith, she had met Fynn, ten years her senior, and from what Catherine related Bridget suspected that the meeting had already blossomed into romance. Fynn was widowed with two small children, and from Catherine's glowing report he seemed kind and respectful. He had asked her to return to Penrith as housemaid, though Bridget was quite certain that the role of housemaid would soon be replaced by the role of wife and stepmother.

Once Catherine had returned east, life settled back into its regular pattern. Mary was happy to have her grandson in Molong, and Bridget continued to look forward to Seamus' letters.

Chapter Thirty

It was a Tuesday in March 1918, and Thomas had left that same morning to stay with Martin for a few days, taking Joseph with him. While Martin needed Thomas' help digging a new dam, Thomas decided that Joseph could spend time with his cousins. But without Thomas, and without Joseph running in and out of the kitchen, everything felt empty, almost deserted, a feeling underlined by an unexpected lack of customers in the pub itself. A sleepy afternoon heaviness that was rapidly developing into some kind of hypnotic coma had wrapped around everything, and Bridget knew she needed to get outside and breathe some fresh air.

When she said that she was taking a short break, Patrick, sitting on his stool behind the bar reading the paper, nodded at her without moving his eyes from the page. She would not be long, a couple of hours at the most, and she would be back before the late-afternoon customers arrived.

She pulled on her gloves, fetched her hat and walked out the back door of the pub. From the back door, which connected to the kitchen and the stairs to their private rooms, Bridget was able to look out over a small half-fenced-in paddock with two red-brown cows, a couple of sheds, one in a sad state of disrepair, and the outhouse. From the stone steps beyond the door, a track circled off to the left, around the side of the building, eventually joining with the wide, and usually dusty, road at the front.

Although it was still summer-warm, there was the slightest hint of autumn, a brilliant blue sky and an air devoid of biting, irritating insects. On some level, Bridget appreciated the warmth and the sky, but all she really wanted was to be able to remove her thoughts not only from what had happened in Gilgandra but also from what the future might be lining up for her, against her will.

When she reached the front of the pub, she hesitated for a moment, wondering just what she should do with her small, precious window of freedom. She spent a couple of minutes looking up and down the wide street, before deciding to walk down to the creek.

She was not used to having time to herself: time when she could think through things without anything or anyone trespassing on her thoughts. In the pub there were always other people filling the space between her and her thoughts, sometimes even pushing their way into them. It was so difficult to focus on the things that were important to her when there were other things and people always clamouring for her time. Her mind went off at a tangent, and she wondered about existence being completely dependent on such connections, desired or otherwise. In her mind, she could see a spiderweb of complicated lines joining a multitude of people, the image repeating itself in all directions beyond what her mind could manage. Perhaps being on one's own was an illusion; perhaps the very structure of existence was all the connecting lines. She was not sure if the awareness was comforting or not.

As a child, she had usually been referred to as 'that O'Connor kid' or 'Patrick's lass', descriptions that firmly established her position as a part of a larger whole, not as Bridget, the individual she believed herself to be. Once she married James, the descriptions changed only slightly, putting James in her father's place. She wondered whether her worth as an individual could only ever be measured in relation to another person. Now that there was no James she was in a no-man's land.

Even though the thought of being Bridget without any subtext was new and exciting, if somewhat daunting, and even though she had a feeling that it could mark a new beginning for her, she could not get away from the image of the spiderweb. The idea of establishing an own identity, completely detached from other people, suddenly seemed impossible. If she remained where she was she would simply become an appendage to the O'Connor pub, but moving away from Molong was a terrifying thought: she had a small child, she would have to find work and somewhere to live. Her abilities were rudimentary: she had never known anything more than basic, if somewhat impoverished, endurance. Perhaps escaping from the spiderweb was something that was well beyond her capabilities.

Her mind returned to the present, to the small, precious wedge of time that was now completely hers. Time when she did not have to think about anyone else, when the sounds and images around her were not demanding that she should listen, reply, act or even think. Minutes and moments that gave her a chance to work out what she was going to do next. A time when she might actually be able to decide how she should extricate herself from that spiderweb and whether or not it was even worth the energy.

Since she and James had gone their separate ways, she had let herself be swept along by all the daily, mundane tasks, hoping to be able to remove herself from what had happened. She no longer believed that James should still be part of her life: she knew now that it could never work. Even so, she still occasionally missed *her* James and everything they had had and might have had. She missed the future that she had imagined she would have had and that had now completely fallen apart. Dwelling on what was no longer possible could not change the past: she needed to be able to move on. While she knew that she had to move on and that she had to establish an own identity, she was not sure of the direction in which she should be moving.

The creek ran behind the railway station, and in order to reach it Bridget had to pass the main building. As she came closer, she noticed that a train must have recently arrived. Although her mind was caught up with other things and problems, she was aware of the few people in travelling clothes standing in front of the low-slung timber building with their luggage; she also noticed several horses and carts in the yard. The station porter was helping a man, one of the passengers, load some wooden boxes on to one of the carts.

As she ran her eyes over the people loitering near the entrance to the station, talking to each other or waiting for a ride into the town, Bridget guessed that there had not been many people alighting at Molong. Her mind stopped trying to solve her problems and, with some relief for the small reprieve, she concentrated on the scene before her.

She saw an elderly couple that she knew, the man smiling politely in her direction while touching his hat. She thanked him with an almost imperceptible nod of her head and was about to round the station building and head further along towards the creek, when a person standing at the far end of the station caught her eye. It was a man, and there was something about his appearance or the way he stood, or both, that put her in mind of someone she knew.

While she was trying to work out who it was and if it was the person she thought it was, he began walking in her direction. Either he had also noticed her or else he was simply a person who needed directions. Or perhaps he was on his way towards the station exit. She chided herself mentally for assuming something that was well-nigh impossible.

Until she understood that it was not impossible.

Seamus dropped his travelling case to the ground and ran the last few yards. Wrapping her tightly in his arms he laughed. At first he said nothing, then he began talking about destiny and signs, good ones. Finally, he talked about things that happen simply because they are meant to happen. After a minute or so, it was as though pieces of a puzzle suddenly locked tightly together, and he took a step back and asked, 'But how could you possibly have known? I had expected to take you completely by surprise.'

Bridget was totally overcome. He *had* surprised her: not for a moment had she been expecting to meet anyone outside Molong station, and definitely not Seamus. She needed time to come to terms with what was happening, to assure herself that what seemed to be happening actually was happening and that she was not dreaming. While she had been walking towards the station, her thoughts had been directed at trying to solve her present predicament; she needed now to redirect them to the man standing in front of her.

While grappling with her thoughts, she smiled, partly because she was overwhelmed, and smiling was her default expression, but mainly because she was so delighted to see Seamus. She found it difficult to believe that he was actually standing there with his arms around her, and because it all seemed so impossible, the thought that she may have been simply imagining things pushed its way to the forefront. Perhaps there was actually no one there, saying how happy he was to see her. Perhaps the other people from the train, most of them now leaving the station, were silently wondering what she could be doing, standing in the station yard, staring into an empty space.

She closed her eyes. If she was only dreaming, then it made sense that Seamus would be gone when she opened her eyes again. But when she did open them, he was still standing there, and his arms were still around her.

Wanting to believe that it really was Seamus, she let her hand move over the coarse material of his jacket sleeve, feeling his warmth beneath all the blue-grey. The touch of his clothing, the sensation of his body next to hers, the sound of his voice telling her how happy he was — surely all these things had to be real? More than anything she knew that she wanted them to be real: she did not want him to suddenly disappear.

At some point she had to stop disbelieving and accept that lines between dreams and reality sometimes actually do merge.

Seamus let go of Bridget, walked back to where he had left his case, picked it up and then rejoined her, taking her gently by the arm. 'It's not a dream, it really *is* me, Seamus,' he said, a smile flickering at the corners of his mouth. He could understand that she was amazed, even confused, but he had travelled on a train to a place without buildings or traffic or noise or even people, just to tell her how much he had been missing her. He needed her to understand that he was not just some incredible hallucination.

She looked at him, no longer believing that he was a figment of her imagination. She knew that she had missed him as well, but it had not been something she had dared admit to herself. Not before now. The longing had been there in the background, hidden behind everything else: she had simply not permitted herself to acknowledge it. She had not allowed herself to dwell on how she had felt when he had been near her, or on how his voice had sounded when he was serious or happy or even sad. She had made sure that all her memories of him had been given a layer of respectable anonymity that had, in turn, often rendered the experience ordinary and unremarkable.

Now she could accept that she had lived for his letters, squeezing out a small amount of sustenance from the one while waiting for the next. The letters had divided the months into weeks and the weeks into days, giving her something to which she could look forward. If, during this time, her thoughts had ever wandered further afield, cautiously examining possible futures, she had reminded herself that Seamus could never be anything more than a brother-like friend. To cross that line, even in her imagination, was taboo.

With him now standing in front of her, his smile reaching out to her and pulling her into something that she suspected was both unacceptable and prohibited, she was unable to look upon him as a brother. She instinctively knew that he was more than that, ever so much more.

While she was being pulled into this imaginary, perfect world, she wondered briefly how this awareness of his importance to her was going to work out. As far as she could see, wanting it to happen was simply adding more pain and frustration to her life. Had things been different, had she not been a married woman with an absent husband, she would have gladly agreed to share her life with Seamus. It was, after all, something she had hesitantly dreamt about since she first met him all those months ago. Now, when she was faced with what she wanted, and what he obviously wanted, she knew that it was not possible. There was one insurmountable fact in the way.

They took the detour by the creek, not wanting to let the spell that had been cast over them be broken by chance meetings with other people. They had been pulled together into something of which both of them were aware but which neither of them would have been able to explain. At a bend in the creek where weeping willows were attempting to join the water with the sky, Seamus removed his jacket, spreading it out on the grass, and they sat for a while, still caught up in whatever it was that they could not begin to express in words.

Seamus told Bridget more about the train trip, still somewhat astounded by all the open space. He had never understood that the horizon stretched so far; the horizon he was used to usually disappeared quickly behind the irregular shapes of buildings. He had never actually seen a horizon that curved so perfectly.

After exhausting most of the details about the train trip and the landscape — Seamus kept returning to his disbelief that there could be so much space — they talked a little about James, both the James from before and the James from after. While they were talking, Bridget's attention kept wandering to the willow branches touching the water's surface, and she was fascinated by the small patterns they made; patterns that were constantly changing. She felt that life was very like the patterns, nothing was fixed. Everything was in a state of flux. Some patterns were positive, others were not.

A fish jumped out of the water, breaking the surface with a soft sound, scattering droplets of water. Bridget started, then laughed as she saw what it was. Another fish jumped as though in competition with the first.

When Seamus finally pulled her to her feet, they continued following the creek until Bridget feared that they were probably getting too far from town. They turned and began to walk slowly back towards the pub.

He had asked where the closest hotel was, and she had replied, saying that he could stay at the pub: there was a small room beyond the storeroom out the back. Someone had stayed there once, years ago. It was not luxurious, she told him, but once they cleared out some of the clutter, there would be a bed, and he would have a space of his own.

He had then looked at her, questioning the bit about being on his own. It was not what he wanted, he said, and then hurriedly added that the room next to the storeroom would be wonderful for the moment, that was not what he was referring to. He was thinking further ahead; he was talking about the future. Their future. If she would have him, he wanted to marry her.

Her thoughts could not get past the hurdle that, for her, had suddenly taken on immense proportions: she was married; her husband was still alive. Somewhere. She knew that she wanted to marry Seamus, but she also knew it was impossible.

She gently reminded him that she was still married and that there was nothing she could do to change the fact. The dreams were still there but so was the reality, and she understood that there was no solution. Searching for one was doomed even before she started looking.

Putting the fact that Bridget would most probably never see her husband again to one side, Seamus was well aware that she would not be able to divorce James. Like Bridget, he understood that there was no obvious solution. James might no longer be part of her life, but he was still impacting on it, and he would continue to do so.

Seamus was silent for a moment, before suggesting that there could be a solution after all. Whatever they had together was something between the two of them; it should never have anything to do with other people. If she were to move to Sydney with him, it would be their secret. As far as others were concerned, James had died; she had become a widow; and she had remarried. He smiled reassuringly, obviously waiting for her consent.

Bridget stopped walking and the two of them stood in the middle of the path, facing each other. She looked at him, a surge of conflicting emotions rushing through her. She was completely aghast, but at the same time she was overwhelmed by what he was suggesting.

'It would be bigamy, Seamus!' She felt as though she had finally come up against the brick wall that she had known about all the time but had hoped would somehow disintegrate.

Seamus smiled and shook his head. He argued that if they were not officially married then it could hardly be called bigamy, because as far as the law was concerned they would not be married. If there was no bigamy, then there could be no gaol. Continuing with this line of thought, he was also quite sure that God would be understanding, especially after taking a good look at all the details. As Seamus pointed out, James was not even a true believer — he had never really been one of them — and it was more possible that God was grateful that James had moved on. He would know what the situation had been like with James; after all, it was He who created everything. In a way, He had probably created the very situation that they now faced.

Bridget looked at him, trying unsuccessfully to grasp everything that he had said. She was speechless that he would suggest such a thing: she found it incomprehensible that he was prepared to enter into a relationship unsanctioned by either State or Church. Just for her. No one had ever done anything even remotely similar for her before. She could not believe that she was worth it.

'But... ' she finally managed to say, before her voice disappeared yet again. Although there was so much she needed to say, she could not get the words to line up in the right way.

Seamus was still standing there, looking at her. Perhaps he understood about all the words that refused to come together in the right order, or perhaps he was simply thinking through all the things that had been said and all the things that still remained unsaid. 'There is no "but",' he said. 'This is what I want, and I'm hoping that it is what you want as well.'

For a moment, Bridget continued to look at him, then deciding that something needed to be said, despite the content or the order of the words, she breathed in deeply and said, 'I'd be honoured, Seamus. I just can't understand why, how, you could… '

He had already dropped his case to the ground, and now he wrapped his arms around her. The words she might have uttered, and the questions that were never asked, withdrew, and all that was left was the certainty that this is what she wanted to do. She may have found it difficult to follow Seamus' line of thought completely, but she admitted to herself that there could well be a sliver of truth in what he was saying. If she could hang on to the belief that this was a good thing he was proposing, then perhaps everything would work out all right.

Chapter Thirty-One

For Bridget, it felt as though her life had suddenly fallen off a cliff, taking her with it, and there was now no returning to what had been. There was no way of scrambling back up the side of the cliff, grabbing hold of the puny vegetation, searching for non-existent footholds. Similar to when her grandparents were forced to turn their back on Tipperary and Ireland, life had forced her beyond what she knew, into something that was both unknown and frightening.

She remembered how, all those months ago, she had thought about her grandmother surrounded by hunger, devastation and death, and she had wondered about Catherine's relationship with God. Had it been strong enough to survive the awfulness of her life, or was it the other way around? Was it her grandmother's belief in God that helped her persevere?

She had no way of knowing what her grandmother thought or believed at any stage of her life. Although she could speculate and give free rein to her somewhat wild imagination, she could not know anything about Catherine's relationship with God.

She could only imagine what it might have been like, while admitting that many of the thoughts and reactions she had given her grandmother were nothing more than reflections of her own way of thinking and, in many cases, her own way of relating to God.

No matter what her grandmother thought or did not think, Bridget knew that God was not responsible for Catherine and her family having to leave Ireland. God had nothing to do with famine and political injustice, in the same way that He had nothing to do with the War that they hoped would soon be behind them. Thinking about God's mantle of impartiality, she doubted that He would be particularly interested in checking who was legally married to whom and whether or not a union had been blessed by His Church.

There were times when she wondered why God did not involve Himself in stopping wars or averting floods or even preventing evil people from doing ill to others. But now she wondered if perhaps He saw Himself as a neutral balance in a world that did not want to be balanced. A world where the bad more than often greatly outweighed the good.

Pushing a chunk of wood into the stove in the kitchen at the back of the pub, she pursed her lips and picked up a second piece. No matter where God was or what He thought or did not think, Bridget was certain that suffering was caused by people: people who saw right and wrong as constructs to be manipulated and pushed in directions that suited themselves. Thinking of atrocities carried out in God's name, she doubted that anyone had ever asked God what He thought, what He wanted. As her thoughts spontaneously moved to the War, she could not imagine that He had a preference for any one side, group, opinion or religion, in much the same way as she had no particular feelings for the rights or opinions of the ants that frequented the wood pile.

It was becoming obvious to Bridget that God cared little whether marriages were official or non-official. Surely the important thing, the only thing, was that balance between good and bad? She slammed the iron door shut and stood up.

It was possible that her life with James would have continued along a more normal path had he not gone to war. It was even possible that he would have remained the same 'interestingly different' person she had met in Molong all those years ago; she had no way of knowing. Perhaps the anger and violence had been simmering there all the time, waiting to be ignited by something like a war, or perhaps he did not even need a war to bring such cruelty to the surface. Whatever the case, he *did* go war, and for Bridget the real James, the man she had once loved, remained there, buried somewhere on a peninsula where so many others had lost their lives and were given a common grave.

Her old life, with all its hopes and promises, was being pushed into the past; in front of her loomed a new life filled with new, different possibilities.

Chapter Thirty-Two

March was already toppling over into its second half, while summer was deciding whether or not to let go of her grasp. But, even if the days were still warm, the nights were becoming cooler and darker, whispering of the approaching autumn and the winter that, though hidden, was impatiently waiting in the wings.

Bridget had become aware of how much her father had changed since receiving the news of Daniel's death. She had not noticed it at first, but now, when she was about to leave, she could see that he seemed older, less talkative, more introspective. It was as though, faced with the reality that his son would not be coming home, he had begun to look closer at his own mortality. She could see how, bit by bit, he had retreated into himself, drinking more while losing interest in the pub and even in its customers, many of whom had been frequenting the O'Connor pub for years.

Thomas was not interested in taking over the pub, and Martin, fully aware of what Bridget was only beginning to understand, had finally persuaded Patrick to hand back the lease and move to Cudal: 'We could do with some help around the farm,' he had pointed out, trying to make the move his father's decision and not his. Mary, concerned about her husband's decline and worried about his drinking but unsure of what she should or could do, agreed that it was a sensible idea. She embraced her eldest son's suggestion, while saying nothing and waiting for Patrick to accept Martin's offer.

She breathed a sigh of relief when the pub at long last changed hands, and the O'Connors were able to load Martin's cart with the few things that still meant something to them. A life lived on the sharp edge between having and not having could never yield a wealth of possessions, but among the assorted paraphernalia attempting to hang on to memories, many of them now blurred, were Fergus' four paintings carefully wrapped in one of Mary's crocheted rugs.

Mary had finally accepted that Daniel would probably not be coming home, but a small piece of her still prayed and hoped, unwilling to give up entirely. Even so, she was relieved to be moving away from Molong and the many shadows that taunted her, raising her hopes only to just as quickly dash them. She would always mourn the son who was no longer, but she was hoping to be able to find peace in Cudal, a peace that no longer existed for her in Molong.

Before the O'Connors packed up and left Molong, and a week or so before March began its downward run towards April, Bridget and Joseph took the night train to Sydney with Seamus. By the time they left, Seamus had spent more than ten days in Molong, sleeping in the small storeroom, helping Patrick in the pub, enchanting Mary with his many stories and talking with Bridget. Although initially dubious, Bridget's parents had eventually accepted that their daughter would be moving to Sydney with the man who, suddenly and unexpectedly, had pushed himself into their lives. Patrick, who had always felt uneasy with James, was able to accept Seamus as a fellow Irishman, disregarding the complexities of the proposed relationship; Mary was simply thankful that her daughter had possibly found someone who would treat her kindly.

When Thomas and Joseph returned from Cudal several days into Seamus' stay, friendships were affirmed or reasserted, and stories already circulated around the pub many times previously were pulled out and given a new life. Without exerting himself, Seamus had managed to slide into the O'Connor family in much the same way as a hand slides into a well-worn glove. After only a few days, Patrick was convinced that the Murphys and the O'Connors had been neighbours back in the old country. As far as he was concerned, it was God's will that they should now all be reunited.

On the day Bridget left Molong with Seamus and Joseph by her side, Thomas walked with them to the station, carrying his sister's bag and promising to visit soon. He would stay in Molong for a few more days and help his parents move, then he intended to head east. Perhaps he would eventually travel south, he had not decided yet. He had heard that it was easy to pick up farm work in Victoria, and from Victoria it was not that far to Devonport and Tasmania.

Bridget was very aware that her life was changing, but life was changing for everyone, and soon there would be no O'Connors left in Molong. Like tumbleweed they were spreading out over a wide area. Her mind swept over the list of change-causing situations: death, illness, family breakups. She paused in her thinking, wondering just how her life would have looked had it not changed, had there not been a war, had James simply remained 'interestingly different'. She would still have been with James, and she would never have had cause to meet Seamus. There was no point in looking backwards: no one could possibly have any idea how the present might have looked had the past taken another path. There was no way of knowing whether life in the present would then have been better or worse. She had to forget about the past, both real and imaginary, and concentrate on the present and the new life that was ahead of her. The old life, with all of its anxieties, panic and fear, was best left well ensconced in a past that was no longer her concern.

The train from Molong arrived at Orange an hour before the connecting train to Sydney. Seamus suggested that they would have time for a cup of tea, and as the three of them walked to the small cafeteria at the end of the platform, Bridget thought back to the time, more than a year ago, when she had sat on the platform at Dubbo railway station, thinking about a cup of tea and knowing that it was something well and truly beyond her means.

There were very few people boarding the Sydney train, and the three travellers from Molong were the only passengers in their compartment. Bridget let Joseph lie on one of the two hard benches, covering him with a shawl, and then sat next to Seamus on the opposite bench.

It was quiet, except for the repetitive, comforting sounds of the train. The half-dark was both soothing and peaceful. Her hand slipped into Seamus' and they sat together, silently united with each other and everything immediately around them. Bridget could feel herself slowly drifting off to a place that resembled sleep but where she was still aware of the train and the sounds and the fact that Seamus was sitting next to her, holding her hand.

She remembered the train trip all those months ago, when she was expecting to be executed for a crime she did not then know she had not committed. For a few moments her thoughts considered the word *crime* and what actually constituted such an offence. Then she quickly erased the jumble of thoughts and images, not wanting to relive the terror and the worry that had haunted and tormented her for so long.

Her thoughts scattered, like the waves and disturbances seen on water when a stone breaks the surface. Then they slowly merged with other images and dreams, lingering for a short moment before breaking up and reassembling into new, different thoughts or dreams. Without any warning, she found herself thinking about Sarah and Oswald.

There was a strange kind of sadness or emptiness interlaced with the thoughts, instigated, no doubt, by the fact that she was on the verge of certain happiness while her sister was facing an unsure and, possibly, miserable future. Perhaps Sarah would soon receive the telegram that no woman ever wanted to receive, and while refusing to see herself as a widow, believing that a refusal might perhaps negate the information in the telegram, she would then sort through all her memories of Oswald, picking out the ones that were dearest to her, placing them somewhere where they were obvious and easily accessible.

What neither Bridget nor Sarah could possibly know in March 1918 was that Oswald would survive the War, and that he would return to Sydney within twelve months. Admittedly, he would arrive home with a head filled with images that he would never be able to share with anyone and which would disturb his nights for years to come, but he would be alive and he would be home. He would thankfully return to the family carting business, deciding that he had had sufficient change and adventure to last him for the rest of his life, and he would be aware, possibly to his surprise, that he was finally content to be doing nothing else but carting all kinds of paraphernalia around Sydney and, most of all, to be back together with Sarah.

When, some time later, Seamus squeezed her hand, Bridget slowly began to pull herself awake. In the somewhat confused haze between sleep and wakefulness, she was aware that she felt both happy and grateful, and something was telling her that this feeling had everything to do with Seamus being next to her. This awareness became stronger as she pushed the last remnants of sleep away from herself. She ran her fingers through her hair and straightened her skirt, her eyes now fixed on Seamus. Her life had changed in ways that she would never have been able to imagine. She had not been hanged, instead she had been set free from a relationship that had transformed into something terrifying and violent. As she attempted to anticipate what the future could now hold for her, she was certain that her new life would be devoid of unnecessary fear and anxiety. She felt a lump rising in her throat, knowing just how much this new life of hers was thanks to the man sitting next to her.

Letting go of Bridget's hand, Seamus fumbled in his coat pocket for a moment, before pulling out a plain silver ring and slipping it on to her finger. At the same time, he was struggling to express his love for her, but there was no order in the words: Seamus, who was always able to manage words, grouping them together to explain, describe and even amuse, suddenly found that he was no longer in charge. The words telling Bridget that she would always be his wife and his friend tumbled over each other, making little sense just when, more than anything, he wanted to tell her how much she meant to him.

Bridget was unaware of any ineptness. All she was conscious of were the words *friend* and *wife*. It did not matter to her that the words were caught up with other words not quite able to express what Seamus wanted to say. She knew what he wanted to say, and for her that was all that mattered.

The words spread themselves across the sounds of the train and the quiet breathing of the sleeping child. They moved around the small compartment, which smelt of polished timber and smoke and luggage. They grew in size, until there was nothing else, only the two of them and the words *friend* and *wife*.

Bridget reflected that life was nothing more than a long chain of situations and happenings. Some of the links were corroded before they were even linked to the chain; others continued to glow and shimmer long after they had been attached. In spite of the contrasts — the dullness, the brightness and even the rust — she decided that every link was necessary. If it were even remotely possible to remove links that failed to shine, a life would be different, and perhaps the bright, shiny links would lose their radiance and become, like the removed links, dull and uninteresting.

Life could never be anything but a mixture of the tarnished and the sparkling. Bridget thought for a moment how all the situations in her life so far had led to her sitting on a train with Seamus. She could not know what other links would be added to the chain. She suspected that not all of them would be radiant and shining, but she believed that she would be content and happy with Seamus by her side, and she hoped that she would be able to manage any difficulties that may be lying in wait.

She was still officially Bridget Jackson, she would always be Bridget O'Connor, and in her heart, and as far as everyone around her was concerned, she was now Bridget Murphy. But she was quite certain that she was, and always would be, simply Bridget.

ACKNOWLEDGEMENTS

For exceptional insight and attention to detail in reading the manuscript, as well as for meticulous editing, I thank Monica unreservedly. For the wonderful cover design and technical advice, my thanks and appreciation go to Annette. For reading and commenting on one of the first drafts, I am indebted to Jane.